THE CADUCEUS AND THE SWASTIKA

DISCARDED BY
ELK GROVE VILLAGE PUBLIC LIBRARY

A novel by Steven M. Hacker

This is a fictional story, with fictional characters but inspired by true historical events. The book does, however, refer to many actual names, places, historical figures, and events. These figures, events, and places are solely for historical reference and authenticity. All the words, actions, attitudes, and behaviors are pure fiction. When real-life historical or public figures appear, the situations, incidents, and dialogues concerning those persons are entirely fictional and not intended to depict actual events or to change the entirely fictional nature of the work. In other respects, any resemblance to persons living or dead is entirely coincidental.

The Caduceus and the Swastika

Published 2016-Nano Press, LLC.
ISBN: 0692623221
ISBN 13: 9780692623220

The Caduceus and the Swastika follows the harrowing flight of three medical students and their professor as the insulated world of academia crumbles under the onslaught of Nazism. Max, Rebecca, and Stats want only to learn medicine, but the Reich has its own plans for their chosen profession, and still darker plans for them.

ABOUT THE AUTHOR

Steven M. Hacker, MD, graduated from medical school in 1989. He is the author of *The Medical Entrepreneur,* one of the top-selling practice management books for doctors. He is also the originator of several patents in the fields of electrical engineering, chemical engineering, and electromagnetic theory. He has been published in several textbooks and over twenty peer-reviewed scientific medical journals. Hacker received postgraduate residency training at the University of Michigan and the University of Florida. He is a frequent public speaker and was the founder and course director of the Medical Entrepreneur Symposium.

This is his first novel.

To Jill, Simon, Elliot, Emily & Rosie.
To my parents.
To my teachers.

"Most people say that it is the intellect, which makes a great scientist. They are wrong: it is character."

Albert Einstein

Before the Nazi uprising, the University of Breslau was home to the finest medical school in the world. In the 1930's, the Nazi government was determined to take control of the medical profession. The doctor's function changed from that of teacher, caregiver and patient advocate to a champion of the state. Physicians were integral to providing a scientific legitimization of racial superiority and were prominently represented in Nazi leadership and membership. This Nazi strategy, the practice of politicized medicine, was embraced by a self-serving medical community given the benefits of acquiring prestigious university positions and funding for research.

CHAPTER ONE

Max sat in the front row, center seat, wondering whether he had what it took to make it through the class. The University of Breslau's Medical School was perhaps the finest in the world. Nobel laureates, philosophers, military heroes, and heads of state had sat right here in this very room.

His eyes wandered over to the student beside him. She had short blond hair, a short plaid skirt, and long legs.

"Hello," he said.

She didn't acknowledge the greeting.

"Got it," he murmured.

To his left sat a boy who looked Jewish but had the muscular build of a gymnast, or maybe a rugby player. He hadn't shaved in a couple of days.

The boy, gazing toward the lectern, proclaimed, "You've been warned."

Max looked away as the authoritative boy twirled his pencil deftly between his fingers.

"This guy Rosenthal," said the youth, pointing the pencil toward the teacher, "He'll make our lives miserable. He turned to Max, "Ever hear of Melkersson-Rosenthal syndrome?"

Max looked at the chalkboard, ignoring him.

The muscular boy persevered. "You know, when your tongue looks like your scrotum and your lips look like balloons?"

"*What?*" Max asked.

"Yeah, and your face doesn't—"

A loud *thwack!* Interrupted the boy.

"Shit!" Max said.

A large textbook lay on the floor, where the teacher had thrown it. Now he walked over and pressed his foot down on it.

"Forget textbooks," he said. "By the time they're published—certainly by the time you've read them—the information's obsolete. In short, the book is garbage. And I ought to know—I wrote it!" Rosenthal looked up from the mess he had created on the floor.

"Who here has read a journal?"

A few students raised their hands. Max didn't.

"Listen to me. You'll need to understand how to read a medical journal, how to critically evaluate it.

And please, don't be naive and believe the bullshit just because you read it in a peer-reviewed journal."

He paced back and forth behind his desk.

"Half of what you read is lies, and most of the rest is crap. Politics in academia has killed the scientist. If you don't approach the literature with a critical eye, you'll be practicing medicine in the Dark Ages."

He stopped pacing and seemed to look straight at Max. "You'll be a failure if you don't take issue with the written word. Question everything. Author bias will ruin every scientific treatise. So . . ." He walked around some more. "Challenge it, and then do what?"

He waited. No answer.

"Then ask, 'Why?'"

Max was spellbound.

Rosenthal collected himself, tucked his shirt back into his pants, adjusted his tie, and took a deep breath. "Unfortunately for you, as the unthinking twits you are, you'll still need to memorize most of what's inside this book on the floor." He pointed at it with his foot, as if pointing at a dead cat in the road. "So keep what I said in the proper context. You'll get graded both on your test scores and on your analytical skills"

Max turned to the irritating boy at his left. "That was interesting."

"What an asshole," the boy said.

CHAPTER TWO

Max took home his book and memorized every bit of anatomy minutiae. First, he decided, he would learn the nomenclature. That was the easy part. He created his own study technique. He would read the chapter first, underline the important facts, and then write them down on note cards. Then he would quiz himself on the note cards, over and over again, until he knew it cold.

He studied tirelessly in this manner every night, in the library.

Tonight, though, Max noticed another student, sitting alone at one of the tables at the end of the stacks. The same beauty he had seen the first day in class! She appeared just as unapproachable as before.

Feeling a lump of dread in his stomach, he got up from his cubicle and walked over.

"God is Dead," he proclaimed.

She didn't look up.

"Kant said 'God is Dead.' Was he right?"

"Nietzsche," she said, looking down.

"So you prefer him to Kant?"

"No, but Nietzsche said it. Not Kant." She still hadn't looked at him.

"Nietzsche, Kant—Germans, either way. Not much difference."

"Not really. There *is* a difference."

He paused and turned her answer over in his mind, then pressed on. "The more we accept science, the less we rely on religion. Eventually, religion dies."

"Very good. That *is* Nietzsche." She looked up with a smile. "And," she said, "science ultimately kills God."

Max smiled back at her. "There's no truth," he said.

"Again Nietzsche." They smiled at each other.

"Anything that's declared a natural law . . ."

"Is only relative to man's perception of reality," the girl said.

"Touché."

They both laughed again, and Max put out his hand.

"Hi, I'm Max."

She pushed her glasses up in a way that made him feel giddy.

"Hi, Max. Marta," she said, and shook his hand.

He was too smitten to think of anything else clever to say and just stared awkwardly at her for a moment. She, sighed, chuckled to herself, and went back to her book.

"Well, nice meeting you. I'm going back . . ." He pointed behind him. ". . . uh, over there and study now." She didn't look back up, and he walked away.

CHAPTER THREE

The next day in class, Max returned to his usual seat. Next to him sat the annoying Jewish-looking kid. The enchanting girl he had argued philosophy with in the library was absent. Max looked around, assessing his competition. Who was smarter? There were two other females in the class. Neither was as interesting to look at as Marta, but Rebecca, with her big dark eyes and gentle smile, came close. Both she and Max were from Stettin, the small neighboring town just west of Breslau. As young children, they had attended Hebrew school at the Grüne Schanze Synagogue. Though it was many years ago, Max still remembered Rebecca as a child, and that familiarity made it seem as if they were old friends, or perhaps distant cousins. The other girl in the class, Ida, was irritating. Her doting nature made her seem more like a grandmother than a schoolmate. In the row above them sat Karl, Alexander, and Christian. Max thought of them as cut from the same cloth, and they did indeed seem related, though they were not. They reminded him of clerks, maybe the sort who might work in a patent office or a bank. And while they all were smart, none of them looked *hungry*. Finally, sitting alone, was Hermann. Physically intimidating, he had a muscular build, small eyes, and a square jaw. At a glance, he looked more like a stevedore than a student. It didn't matter, though. Max knew, he had to beat them all.

The bell signaled the start of class. Professor Rosenthal was late.

The kid sitting beside Max muttered, "This guy was probably late to his own bris. "

Max said nothing.

Looking bored, the boy tapped Max on the shoulder. "Say, Curveball, you got a name?"

"Max," he said.

"That a Jewish name?"

"It's German."

"Sounds Jewish to me, Curveball, but whatever." He stuck out his hand. "My name's Jakob. Grandparents call me Jake; everyone else calls me Stats."

"Stats, then," Max said, and shook his hand.

Just then, Professor Rosenthal came in, breathing as if he had been running. Sitting in the front row, Max could see the beads of sweat on his brow. Rosenthal took off his sport coat and draped it on his chair, revealing two large patches of sweat in his armpits.

"Anatomy is the foundation on which your medical education rests. Anatomy is neither logical nor intuitive; it just is. Thus, it requires rote memorization. You will learn only through repetition and dissection. By dissecting cadavers, you'll see and touch what you must memorize. Dissecting makes it real and, therefore, easier to remember. What you need . . ."

Max found the lecture uncharacteristically monotone and empty of emotion. Rosenthal stopped and, without finishing his sentence, wiped his brow with his forearm. He stood silent for a moment, as if distracted by an intruding thought.

Max waited.

The professor opened the textbook. "In this chapter, you will dismantle every bone in the skull. You'll dissect the brain, the cerebellum, brain stem, and cranial nerves. Then you'll move centrally down the body to the peripheral nerves."

He paused again. His hands were shaking.

"Dr. Rosenthal?" Max whispered, leaning forward in his seat. "Is something wrong?"

No response. The professor's eyes darted around, reminding Max of a trapped animal. Then the man seemed to get a grip on himself. As if awakened from a catatonic state, he whispered under his breath, "I'm fine," and resumed the lecture.

Now his tone was engaging and energized. Max found the shift disturbing and felt embarrassed for the man, who seemed incapable of internalizing his dramatic swings between mania and catatonia.

When he finished his lecture, the students, seemingly oblivious, closed their notebooks, got up from their desks, and left the lecture hall.

"Max, may I speak to you?" Dr. Rosenthal asked from the lectern.

"Me?" he asked, surprised. He put his books into his canvas book bag and approached the professor's desk

Dr. Rosenthal didn't look up. He rearranged some papers on his desk.

"You did well on the first assignment—I just wanted you to know." He paused. "Keep up the good work." Again he wiped his brow on his shirtsleeve. "Just keep everything in perspective; that's all."

"Thank you but —"

"You know that over seventy percent of German physicians earn less than what they need to support their families?" He still didn't look up, just moved the books around on his desk. "You know what that means?"

Intrigued by the question, Max replied, "What?"

"A tenth of German physicians are starving, and too many medical students are graduating. There's no room for more doctors. You'll be working for starvation wages."

"And?" Max answered, unsure why his professor should bring this issue up with a student he had only just met.

"Graduating doctors will be unemployed doctors, wherever they go." He looked up from his desk, searchingly into Max's eyes. "Your dismissed; that's all," he said, and walked away.

CHAPTER FOUR

Leaving the classroom, Max walked outside and through the arcade, to the courtyard of the university's main academic building. He pulled his jacket from his book bag. The day was cooler than usual, and the few remaining leaves on the sycamores were bright yellow. He buttoned his jacket and walked up to Stats.

Stats stopped in the middle of the quadrangle, but turned his head away from Max. "Just before our lecture, a few of the teachers were gathered around the radio, listening to today's public rally."

"I was unaware," Max said.

"Where have you been? The National Socialists announced their solution to the rising number of unemployed doctors."

Stats turned to Max. Holding his fist up to his mouth as if it were a microphone, he imitated the man's voice on the radio. "The misery of the rising generation of German physicians will immediately be solved when, in the future Third Reich, fellow Germans are treated only by physicians of German descent." Stats chuckled nervously. "So basically, Jewish docs can only see Jewish patients."

"After class, Rosenthal called me over to his podium and lectured me about the future of medicine. It seemed very odd."

"You've been warned," Stats said, kicking a sycamore ball before him as he started away across the courtyard, "Again."

CHAPTER FIVE

Max loved everything about the anatomy lab: the smell of the formaldehyde, the shine of the metal tables, the clank of instruments dropped on tabletops—all of it. It was an orchestra of strange smells and beautiful sounds, and he looked forward to it.

Today, however, was different. He had searched for the past hour, unable to locate the ulnar nerve. His patience turned to impatience, his impatience to frustration. He threw down his retractor with a clatter. If he couldn't identify the ulnar nerve, then he couldn't locate the radial nerve, which ran beside it. And as part of his grade, he must find them to dissect the sheath that surrounded the radial nerve.

He felt a hand on his shoulder.

"Curveball, you're sweating it," said Stats. "Can I help?"

"I can't find the damned ulnar nerve," Max said.

"Here."

Stats pulled a stool up next to Max, he picked up the scalpel and retractor, and dissected beautifully to the desired plane. In a moment, he exposed the glistening fibrous threads of the radial nerve's sheath. Max looked on, amazed at such effortless dexterity.

The task completed, Stats laid the instruments back down on the table.

"You don't have to help me."

"What, and watch you fail the next exam?"

"And if I score better than you?"

"You care too much, Curveball." Stats smiled. "I, on the other hand, couldn't really give a shit."

"If you don't give a damn, why be here?" Max said as he probed the skin of the cadaver with his fingers.

Stats himself seemed not to know. There was an uncomfortable silence. Finally, he said, "Look, I'm doing this for my family. They want me to be a doctor."

Max looked at him but said nothing.

"You know why they call me Stats?"

Again Max didn't answer.

"Since I was twelve, I worked in my dad's shop. Numbers came easy. It didn't take me long to figure out a way to make his accounting more accurate—you know, tabulating numbers, simple math and stuff, inventory, stock management. Stuff you'd find boring as hell. I liked it because it came easy." He picked up the retractor and twirled it between his fingers.

Annoyed, Max grabbed the retractor and laid it on the table.

"My family did everything to get me here and put me through this damn medical school," Stats said. "I'm not about to disappoint them. But you know what I *really* wanna do?"

Max didn't answer. The lab proctor, a young anatomy instructor in a white lab coat, was looking over at them.

"Okay, who starts at first base for the Tigers?"

"You're asking me about American baseball?" Max asked as he glanced around at the other students, absorbed in dissecting their cadavers.

Just behind them, the proctor said, "Gentlemen, others are trying to work. Please be considerate." He picked the retractor up off the table, handed it back to Max, and turned and walked away.

When the proctor was gone, Stats whispered back to him, "No, I'm talking about *Greenberg.*"

Max gave him a blank look.

"Does fifty-four home runs and a three seventy-six average mean anything to you?

"Not really."

"Greenberg's six four. How many Jews do you know that can hit home runs and stand six foot four?" When

Max shook his head, he said, "Look, if I could do anything, it'd be this."

Stats cupped each hand over his ears as if wearing a radio headset. After checking to make sure the proctor was occupied with another student, he said in a low murmur, "Greenberg steps to the plate, ignores the anti-Semitic rants of the country yokels in the stands, cleans the dirt off the home plate, just like he's wiping his feet on a floor mat. He straddles home plate. Like a dinosaur after killing its prey, he balances himself, props his bat above his shoulders, stares down the pitcher, and then, the towering figure, with power bestowed only by the gods, readies himself, takes the first pitch. Ball one."

The proctor walked back over to the boys. "I suppose I wasn't clear. Get back to work, or excuse yourself."

Stats stood up. "Given the choice, I'll excuse myself," he said. "Good day." Then he turned to the cadaver. "And a good day to you, too."

CHAPTER SIX

Behind the counter in the cafeteria, the tired-looking elderly woman in a surgical cap greeted Max with a smile.

"You know her?" Herman asked as they approached the food line.

"Work study," Max said. "It's how I can afford to be a student here." He reached into the refrigerated section and picked up a glass of milk.

The three boys passed through the line, inspecting the dessert plates. There were small squares of chocolate cake with fudge frosting, cookies covered with colored fruit, and a few small silver bowls with noodle pudding. The pudding had raisins.

"Is this *kugel*? Hey, excuse me," Stats said, trying to get the cafeteria worker's attention.

"It's noodle pudding," Max said. "Just take it."

Hermann grabbed a plate with a small slice of chocolate cake, then a glass of milk. "You boys ever wonder why they'd let those women into our class?"

"'Those women'?" Max asked.

"Breslau *is* the only university where women are allowed to attend medical school," said Stats.

"It's pointless," Hermann said. "Aren't they going to be having babies soon?"

They paid for their desserts and sat down at a table.

Stats looked at Hermann. "That's kind of jaded."

"Maybe so," Hermann said, "but why bother going through all this bullshit?"

"I don't think it's that simple," Max said.

"Just wait. By the time we graduate . . . " he paused and took a bite of chocolate cake. "Their maternal instincts start to rear their ugly head, and then . . ."

"And then *what*?" Stats asked, stacking the pepper shaker on top of the salt shaker.

"And then they'll all be irritable bitches," Hermann said. "You can see it in the senior students. They're miserable."

Seeing Stats's growing annoyance over Hermann's comments, Max said, "Weintraub's Syncopators are playing at the Hot Club tomorrow night."

"I can always find time for good jazz," Stats said. "Count me in."

"He was born in Breslau," Max said while using his fork to surgically remove the raisins from his noodle pudding.

"Who?" Hermann asked.

"Stefan Weintraub."

Hermann frowned. "Who's that?"

"You never heard of Eddie Rozner? Addy Fisher? Leo Weiss?"

From Hermann's look, it was clear he hadn't.

Ignoring the sharp look from Max, Stats said, "You know, the Syncopators." He mimicked a drummer, forefingers doing a paradiddle on the tabletop. "Breslau's their hometown. They're coming back for a concert. Tomorrow night. Music!" He flicked his hand in the air like a drummer hitting the hi-hat.

"That's Negro music," Hermann said after gulping down the last of his cake. "It's inferior to German culture."

Max frowned at Hermann, pushed his bowl aside, and turned to Stats. "Jazz is . . . well, like Rosenthal says about anatomy: it just *is.*"

"Maybe so," Hermann said, "but I don't get it.

Max grinned. "You *don't get it*? Jazz is freedom. It's real. It's a sweet *fuck you* to the establishment." He flicked his hand outward from underneath his chin toward Stats.

"Not sure we're doing anything to any establishment," Stats said, "but I'll be there.

"Sorry, boys, but you won't see me," Hermann said as they got up and headed back to the library.

CHAPTER SEVEN

Max wished he had enjoyed last night's concert a bit less. Tired, queasy, and with a pounding headache, he took his seat in Rosenthal's class.

He read the notice on the chalkboard: "Tonight after classes, 5:00 pm, Hofbrau House. A celebration of the examination. Beer on Me."

The test started promptly at nine.

"Good luck," Rosenthal said, handing each student the exam.

"Once everyone has their tests, you may start. Bring me your completed exam when finished."

Max grabbed his exam, found his seat, and went to work.

Ten minutes into the exam, he looked behind him at the clock and noticed something he wished he could unsee.

Hermann sat behind Stats, one row higher and slightly to the left. Since Stats wrote with his right hand, his answer sheet lay exposed on the left side of his desk. And there was Hermann, straining, leaning, and readjusting so he could look over Stats's left shoulder and see his answers.

At first, Max dismissed it as Hermann just shifting his big body to get comfortable in his seat. But there it was again.

Max couldn't help himself. He looked over his shoulder again and then turned to the teacher. Rosenthal seemed oblivious. It couldn't be.

But Max had his own exam to concentrate on. The next question dealt with the function of each of the twelve cranial nerves. He remembered that the nerves exited from the brain stem, and as he recalled each one systematically and specifically, he whispered to himself the function of each, including the hypoglossal nerve. He looked up as he searched his memory for more answers. The room was quiet except for the soft scratch of pencils on paper.

Suddenly, the silence was interrupted by the sound of a pencil hitting the floor one row above him. No one else seemed to hear it, but to Max it sounded like a tree limb falling. Startled, he looked back to find the source. Hermann had apparently dropped his pencil close to the back of Stats's chair. Nothing odd in that—pencils got dropped sometimes.

Intrigued, Max watched through the corner of his eye as Hermann picked up his pencil, all the while stretching his neck like a cobra or better yet, a python periscoping.

Max couldn't believe it. The guy was reading Stat's test answers! And Rosenthal had stepped out of the classroom.

Fifty minutes passed, and the test period officially ended. Rosenthal came by and picked up each student's examination and answer sheet.

"How'd you do?" he asked Max, looking piercingly into his eyes.

Max handed him the paper. "All right, I think."

"We'll see."

Making his way through the room, Rosenthal asked the same question of each student and gave each the same reply: "We'll see."

With all the exams collected, he dropped them on his desk and said, "Well done! See you at Hofbrau tonight."

CHAPTER EIGHT

Max left school and went back to his apartment. He knew about the honor code and knew he had an obligation to report what he had seen.

Walking home, he half noticed the familiar surroundings, the wrought-iron fence between the sidewalk and the manicured city park. He looked through it and watched a child play with her young mother.

He enjoyed seeing the same people, at the same little park, around dusk each day. It was part of his routine, and somehow comforting. The weather was changing, and the dazzling blue autumn sky would soon give way to winter gray.

On a park bench sat an old man, always alone and always wearing the same long overcoat, the same tired hat and shoes. He and the young mother never seemed to notice each other. They were like islands, separated by the sea of their different lives.

The oldster's scarf had fallen off his neck and lay on the ground behind him. Walking over, Max picked up the scarf and handed it to him. The old man smiled and wrapped it around his neck.

As Max turned to walk away, the old man said, "How's school going?"

"It can be a challenge," Max replied, surprised at the old fellow's boldness. "But I'm handling it."

The man assessed Max, starting at his feet and moving upward to his eyes. Apparently satisfied, he said, "I'm Wilhelm," and reached out to shake Max's hand.

Max found the tone of his voice soothing.

"Max," he said, shaking hands. Max was quiet for a moment, then said, "I see you here every day but have never said hello. I'm embarrassed by that."

"I'm old; I look funny. I dress funny." He pointed to his clothes. "Don't feel bad," he said, brushing a speck of lint off his worn pants.

"I could just as well have said hi to you." He gave a sad smile. "But we're saying hello now, at least, and that remedies past incivilities."

Max sat beside him on the bench, put his book bag down, and looked out at the autumn sky. He turned to the man and asked, "If I may ask, what brings you here every day?"

The man laughed quietly to himself. "I worked at the medical school as a pharmacist for the past twenty years and I enjoyed teaching the students when they rotated through. I still go in a few nights a week and help out part-time."

"Right here at Breslau?"

"Yes, the university." He tilted his head in that direction. "I'm a lot cheaper than the newer pharmacists. And no benefits." He smiled.

"But why the routine of coming here, to this little park? I see you here every day."

The old man looked up and away as if reaching for a memory. "Three years ago, on what would have been our fiftieth anniversary, my wife passed." He paused for a moment. Max could see his lips tremble.

"This was our favorite park. We'd spend nights here, watching mothers play with their children. We never had our own children. This was where I came with her."

Max saw the tired old eyes grow moist.

"I used to visit her at St. Elizabeth's every day." He pointed past the park. "But that wasn't where we were happy. That was where we went when she was dying. Here . . ." He pointed emphatically at the ground. "This park is where we were happy."

Max listened. They both were quiet for a few moments.

"I'm sure life is a struggle without her."

"The days are fine. Really. I'm good during the day. It's the nights that are difficult. The nights are too quiet. That's why I keep working. I go to the pharmacy at night to get my mind off being alone."

Max sat for a few more minutes and then decided it was time to go.

As he left, he said, "It was really nice finally meeting you, Wilhelm."

"And to you, Max. Be safe."

"I'll see you tomorrow."

"Very well, then," the old man said, leaning his tired head back and closing his eyes.

CHAPTER NINE

Max waded into the sea of cheerful, exuberant patrons. The Hofbrau crowd was mostly young working-class Germans, with a sprinkling of frustrated poets and cynical intellectuals. The place smelled, though not unpleasantly, of spilled beer and sweat. Max gazed up at the stage, where the Mad Bavarian usually entertained, but the stage was dark tonight.

He found his fellow students' table, greeted Stats and Hermann, and squeezed in between them on the long wooden bench. Dr. Rosenthal was conspicuously absent.

"How are you?" he asked Rebecca, ignoring Marta.

She smiled. "I'm fine."

"And your parents?"

Marta rolled her eyes. "You two know each other?"

"Our parents were friends," Rebecca said.

"We went to the same synagogue," Max interjected.

"All right, we get it," Stats interrupted. "You're from the same neighborhood. Exciting stuff."

"I don't really want to talk about them," Rebecca said to Max.

"We all have our problems at home," Marta said, flicking her hair back. "I won't go into mine."

Max announced to the others, "Hey, this guy doesn't want to be a doctor." Nudging Stats on the shoulder, he said, "He wants to be a baseball radio announcer."

Rebecca asked, "Why would you waste your time learning all this tedious crap if you want do *that*?"

Stats didn't answer, so Max did it for him. "He was told the only way to become an announcer was to attend medical school first. Isn't that what everyone does?"

Everyone laughed, and Stats and Max lifted up their mugs and clicked them together.

Stats said to Rebecca, "What about you? What specialty?"

"Do I have a choice?"

"You always have a choice," Max said.

"Oh, right. Well, let's see, what are my options in medicine? I could be a syphilologist or . . . say, a dermatologist that treats venereal disease."

"It's one and the same," Stats said.

Marta said, "Come on, it's not *that* bad.

Max saw the cynical glance that Rebecca gave Marta.

Marta said, "Look, there are options out there. You just have to do well; then you'll be picked for the specialty you want. Take Max—if he keeps getting the best scores, he'll do whatever he wants."

Rebecca said, "Jews don't get whatever they want. They get whatever's left. Dermatology and syphilis—it's the bottom of the barrel, and that's usually what's left."

Marta turned to Max and whispered just loud enough for Rebecca to hear, "Will you study with me for next week's biology exam?"

Rebecca turned away, irritated.

Rosenthal finally arrived at the table. He looked out of sorts.

"Sorry I'm late. Unexpected conference with Jessner." He looked around for a beer.

"All is forgiven, Professor," Max said on everyone's behalf, and slid the pitcher in front of him.

Marta stood up. "Excuse me," she said, "but I do have to go now. See you tomorrow. Max, I'll talk to you later." Wrapping a silk scarf around her neck, she said, "I have to help my parents with some chores at their house."

The other boys, Karl, Alexander, and Christian, who had sat crowded together at the end of the bench, quickly spread out to fill the space created by Marta's departure. Hermann poured everyone another round and set the pitcher down in front of Rosenthal.

Rosenthal brushed his sweaty hair off his forehead and lifted the pitcher. "Thanks, I could use one."

He cleared his throat, and the students, seeing he was ready to speak, huddled closer. "I'm glad everyone could make it," he said. "We all need a bit of relaxation, especially after working so hard. The intensity can be overwhelming. But enough of that. Let's drink to medicine, Germany, and friendship!"

He raised his mug, and they all banged it with theirs, sloshing beer onto the table.

"Max, you did it again. Congratulations. Stats, Hermann, well done. You both scored well." The boys smiled at each other and clanked their mugs together again.

"As I said, I was late because I was called in abruptly for a meeting with Dr. Jessner."

Max could see his irritation and then watched as he momentarily mumbled to himself, shook his head in disbelief, and then drank down the entire mug in one pull. He put it down on the table, picked up the pitcher, and poured himself another.

"What do you think he means by saying, 'People are watching me'?" making quotation marks with his fingers.

"How am I supposed to respond to that? I'm a professor." He slammed his mug down on the table.

"Anyways, Jessner told me today about the circumstances surrounding Jadassohn's resignation." The students looked at each other, confused by his disclosure. "It's Bormann again," he mumbled to himself, shaking his head. He raised his voice. "Bormann said, and I quote, 'Hitler holds the cleansing of the medical profession far more important than, for example, that of the bureaucracy, since, in his opinion, the duty of the physician is, or should be, one of racial leadership.'" He paused, sipped his beer, and repeated, 'The cleansing of the medical profession.'

Max watched him laugh nervously.

"Can you believe this horseshit?" he asked.

Max noticed Hermann looking uncomfortable with the conversation. "Excuse me for a moment. The restroom," Hermann said.

Rosenthal continued without looking up. "How much of this do you know?" He was asking all the students.

Max watched as no one answered. But Rosenthal appeared not to care or wait for any response. "Well, you need to know, last month the National Socialists assigned Wagner the responsibility of controlling us—and that's now you, too—the doctors." He picked up the pitcher and started to pour himself another beer, then stopped when he realized that his glass was still full.

"Everyone knows Wagner had it in for Jadassohn. They've been at odds for years. Wagner wanted control over personal health information, and Jadassohn felt strongly about confidentiality. Obviously, Wagner won." This time, he downed all the beer in his mug before pouring himself another.

"So, what do you think happens? Of course: Jadassohn puts in his resignation. Jessner assumed the chairmanship. And now I'm dealing with Jessner. He's putting heat on me because he's getting heat from somewhere above him."

He stopped and looked at the students, expecting some comments. They were silent.

"Jessner, spineless weasel that he is, tows the party line. Anything to advance his own career. He's a myopic ass," Rosenthal said in disgust.

"Today it's Jadassohn; tomorrow it's me. But he'll get his, too; just watch."

Rosenthal wiped his mouth with his forearm and poured himself another glass.

CHAPTER TEN

Rosenthal weaved and bumped his way toward the restroom. Wobbling as he walked, he could hear the swell and ebb of the crowd noise. "Excuse me, damn it," he said, bumping into someone. "Excuse me." The more the beer took effect, the more estranged he felt.

Entering the bathroom, he noticed Hermann coming out. As they passed, Rosenthal grabbed Hermann by the arm and pulled him aside. He moved in close and placed his mouth next to Hermann's ear, still holding firmly to his arm so he could not move away.

"Your test was remarkably similar to Jakob's," he said.

Hermann looked down at the hand on his arm and pulled away, disgust written on his face.

"Hermann, you have a promising career. Don't squander it. I have an obligation to turn you in to

Jessner. You'll be expelled." Rosenthal belched and took a breath. Hermann looked skeptically at him. "I don't want to see that happen. You're a good boy, and I'm sure your father is very proud of you."

"You know nothing of my father," Hermann said.

Rosenthal continued, "I know of his service. Your dad's a hero. I'm sure he has high expectations for you."

Hermann shoved both hands in his trouser pockets and rocked back and forth, like a child waiting to receive his punishment. He stared down at the weathered wooden floor.

"I want to give you a second chance."

Hermann sighed, and Rosenthal could see the loathing in his face.

"Under two conditions."

Again Hermann avoided eye contact, watching people as they moved in and out of the bathroom.

"I want you to take back the exam and scratch through the answers you copied. I'll give you the grade you deserve, but I won't punish you for cheating."

Rosenthal could see tears gather in the youth's eyes.

"You think you're better than me?" Hermann said, at last looking him in the eye.

"Look, I'm trying to help you."

"You're no better than me," Hermann said.

"Just bring me back the exam by the end of the week. I'll regrade it. And one more thing: before you bring it in, have your father initial it."

Hermann acknowledged Rosenthal with a nod, but the hate showed through his face as he turned to walk away.

CHAPTER ELEVEN

Rosenthal always felt a little uneasy at a public urinal. If his face didn't give away his ethnicity, his circumcision might. It was always a concern. He stood close.

A tall, muscular German, loud and drunk, lurched up to the urinal at his left. Unbuttoning his trousers, he glanced over.

"*Juden,*" he snarled, and batted Rosenthal on the shoulder.

Rosenthal staggered forward, spritzing the floor and his own shoe. He buttoned up and hurried out of the bathroom.

The students were still huddled around the table when Rosenthal returned. His next mug of beer was poured and waiting. He sat back down and muttered, "Christians and Romans."

He paused before launching into what he knew was an inappropriate discussion with his students, but he was on a path of self-destruction. He threw discretion to the winds. He was like a marionette, with some vicious puppeteer pulling the strings and forcing him to say things he shouldn't.

"First the Romans," he said. Looking around at the puzzled faces, he could see they had no idea what he was saying.

"Under Constantine the Great in the fourth century, Christianity was the state religion of the Roman Empire. That's when it started, and it hasn't stopped since."

"What started?" Max asked.

"The Jew became the devil. The church's canonical laws forbade Jews to marry Christians. They forbade Jews to fill public offices. They forbade Christians to see Jewish physicians and forbade Jews from acquiring academic rank."

The noise of the crowded tavern seemed to swell and diminish in waves. "So here's the real question," he said, hearing his own words slur. "Where do you think the Nazis are getting this bullshit?"

Rosenthal felt the sting of disapproval from the students around him, but he didn't care. The room began to tilt, as if he were on a carnival ride. He closed his eyes momentarily to regain his equilibrium, but the shifting and tilting worsened.

"Well, I'll tell you." He took another gulp of beer. "And then, of course, the Crusades massacred Jews in Europe—first France and Germany. By the thirteenth century, Jews were expelled from England. In 1492, the year Columbus sailed, they were kicked out of Spain. You think I'm imagining things?" He looked around the table at the students. They were silent. "Paranoid, perhaps?"

He raised his mug and pointed it at Max. "Have you read Martin Luther's stuff? There's precedent, damn it. Wake up. Can't you feel it happening again?" But he could see that no one was getting it.

"Who do you think wrote this? And I quote." He closed his eyes. "'The Jews were the bloodhounds and murderers of entire Christianity, fully intentionally, for more than fourteen hundred years . . . They detain us Christians in our own country, let us work in our sweat, get money and possessions, while they sit behind the stove, lazy and pompous, bake pears, devour, booze, live sweetly and well from what we worked for. They've captured us and our goods with their damned usury.'"

He opened his eyes and looked back at them, waiting for a response. Seeing nothing but their disbelief, he raised his voice and tried again. "That was fucking Martin Luther. Damn it! Do you see what I'm saying?"

Max finally spoke up. "Yeah, but it ended three hundred years ago. The Enlightenment, remember? That's why it's different today. Look at the Americans, their Bill of Rights. The First Amendment guaranteed freedom of religion, and Europe followed. That's why we're here now, talking about this freely in a beer hall. I think you're overreacting, Dr. Rosenthal."

Rosenthal looked at Max and laughed. "You're not that naive, are you, Max?"

"Maybe I am. What about William the Third? He proclaimed all rights for Jews, after Jews fought and died for the fatherland, he made sure we should have the same privileges as everyone else."

"Then, I suppose you *are* that naive. The Congress of Vienna rescinded those rights."

Rosenthal could see the students getting more and more uncomfortable with the line of conversation. Still dizzy from all the beer, he took a deep breath with a sigh, said, "All right, who here remembers the role of acetylcholine, epinephrine, and the 'fight or flight response?"

CHAPTER TWELVE

The next day at the library was quiet. Students sat studying, taking books from the stacks, exchanging whispers. Marta sat at a table, with her books open.

Max walked over to her. "Mind if I join you?"

"Please."

Her skin looked smooth as cream. Her hair was piled up on her head, and her glasses rested down on her nose. One hand held a pencil over an open book. She looked up over her glasses, and Max could see her bright blue-green eyes under those long lashes. The top button of her blouse was undone, revealing the hypnotic swell of her breasts, rising and falling with her breath.

"So, you've been studying the extremities and nervous system?"

"Yes, of course, but I can't get it in *here*." She hit her head with the heel of her hand.

Max glanced up at the clock on the wall. "Hey, I have an idea," he said. "Let's finish studying at your apartment. The library closes in fifteen minutes anyway, and we could quiz each other and make sure we know this chapter cold."

"I don't think so," she replied. "Probably better if I just keep reviewing alone."

"If we each go home alone, you won't study. Neither of us will."

She hesitated. "I don't think I should . . ."

"Look at me," he said, giving her his most disarming grin. "I don't bite. And we'll both do better on the next exam."

She looked up at the clock on the wall, then down at her books, and scanned the library for familiar faces.

"All right, but I don't want to waste time talking. We study."

"Of course," he said, and they gathered their books. "That's the whole idea."

CHAPTER THIRTEEN

On the walk to Marta's apartment, the street was quiet except for their footsteps on the sidewalk.

They reached her apartment and went inside. Watching her pull books out of her bag, he tried to focus on something besides her beauty.

"Okay, show me how you're learning the metacarpals," Max said.

She took out the small set of study cards that she had written the mnemonics on. Max cut the deck, took half the cards, and gave her half. "I'll quiz you; then you quiz me."

As she spoke, Max vaguely heard her questions, though he was too mesmerized to pay attention to the names of the metacarpal bones.

"These your parents?" he said, pointing to a picture of a military man bedecked with ribbons and medals.

She turned away. "Yes, but I don't like talking about them."

"Why?"

"We're studying, remember? Anyway, my dad's an ass. He's career military but now involved in politics."

"What's wrong with that?"

"My parents are nothing I'm proud of, trust me. Look," she said, "I knew this would happen. We're not studying. It's late. You'd better go home. I'm as ready for the test as I'm going to get."

"You sure?"

"Yeah, I'm tired," she repeated.

"Okay," Max said. "I understand."

He picked up his books, grabbed his jacket, and headed home.

CHAPTER FOURTEEN

The solitude and the cool night air were invigorating. Walking passed Rynek, Max glanced up at the tower of St. Elizabeth's Church and smiled. He loved the city's traditional beauty.

Leaving the market square, he noticed three young men running into an alley. They laughed as they ran, and he pretended not to notice them. He passed the jewelry store, crossed the street, and stared in idle curiosity.

A long black coat flapped as if in slow motion, and he realized that the young men were chasing an elderly man. His brimmed black hat flew off and rolled to the gutter, and a few steps later, he stumbled and fell. The two assailants were laughing as they approached him. One held a bat.

To keep out of sight, Max darted to the other side of the alley. He peeked around the corner to see the old man scrabble backward on the cobblestones.

Too late, Max thought.

One of the assailants swung the bat into an empty garbage can. Max didn't know what to do. He watched as, somehow, the old man got to his feet again and began to run. He tried to get past them, but one of the young men stuck out his foot and tripped him, and he fell to his knees. Somehow, he was up again and started to run in circles, but he seemed to know he was trapped.

The old man turned around and faced his attackers. He was out of breath, eyes wide. Again Max heard the two young men laugh, this time louder. Then silence, until one of them yelled something Max couldn't understand. The one with the bat lifted it up above his shoulder and swung it into the old man's head with a sickening wet crunch.

Max turned away, unable to watch any more. Trembling, he walked away fast. He peered back around the corner, hoping to identify the attackers, but they had already slipped away into the darkness.

CHAPTER FIFTEEN

Stats had finished his studies and tried to fall asleep, but anxiety over tomorrow's exam got in the way. In between the names of metacarpals, he thought of the names of the starting lineup for the Yankees. His mnemonic for the hand incorporated Babe Ruth's last name. "R" was for "radial nerve," "U" was for "ulnar nerve," "T" was for "thenar eminence," and "H" was for "hypothenar eminence." He felt confident but not altogether certain. Turning on his Grunzig shortwave radio, he got only static, but then he turned the dial some more, slowly, with the precision of a master safe-cracker, back and forth until the American station came in. A baseball game was on. He closed his eyes, smiled, and finally relaxed and, with his head on the pillow, listened to the game.

The Tigers were playing the Yankees. The announcer introduced Hammering Hank Greenberg, in between pitches recounting the two home runs that had immortalized the man.

"He takes ball two, count two and two . . ." Stats listened as the announcer paused his story for the pitch.

"Pitcher winds up, releases. Greenberg hits foul over third base, count remains two and two . . ."

While the pitcher took a pause, the announcer recounted the batter's story. *"Everyone knows how Greenberg refused to play on that Jewish holiday. The Tigers were in the pennant race and needed him more than ever. In fact . . ."* He stopped his story as the pitch was thrown. *"High and outside. Full count . . ."* The announcer paused again, then resumed. *"The headlines read something like "the Jewish holidays come once a year, but the Tigers haven't been in a pennant race in decades. He swings and misses—sinker inside. Strike three; the inning's over."* Between innings, the announcer said, *"Of course, the rest of the story is what legends are made of. Greenberg apparently discusses it with his rabbi and decides to play on Rosh Hashanah—and, inevitably, hits the two winning runs. The* Detroit Free Press *actually ran "Happy New Year" headlines in Hebrew on its front page."*

The announcer's voice, and the images it conjured, relieved Stats of his angst over the anatomy exam, and he finally closed his eyes and drifted off.

CHAPTER SIXTEEN

Waiting for the doors to open, Stats bounced a small rubber ball in the hallway.

"I didn't see you last night," he said to Max.

"Couldn't sleep," Max said, trying to shake the image of the old man's murder out of his head.

"That's called guilt. Next time you say you're going to study with me, and you change your mind and go to Marta's instead, maybe you'll think twice." Stats caught the ball and dropped it in his pocket.

They both walked into the classroom and sat down. Hermann, sitting next to Max, seemed preoccupied with something he was writing in his notebook.

Marta breezed by them and took her seat.

Stats whispered under his breath to Max, "I hope it was worth it."

Rosenthal arrived. "Hello, class," he said. And without waiting for a response, he started the lecture. As tedious as the subject matter was, he managed to make it even worse with his emotionless monotone.

After class, Max caught up with Marta in the hallway. "May I walk you home?"

"Sure," she said.

Leaving the campus, they walked past the shops and cinemas on Mathias Strasse.

Max said, "You notice anything different about Rosenthal?"

"Not really," she replied.

They stopped in front of the Nord Hotel on Grunderzeit Circle. A police siren grew louder, and they were silent until the car sped past them. She turned down Schweidnitzer Strasse and led him past two new modern department stores that had sprung up on the same block.

"I still favor the old architecture," Max said, nodding toward the stately Gestelhaus Hotel and then over to the Stadt Theater. "William Knittel's design is obnoxious."

She appeared uninterested in the architecture. "Why do you always seem to be psychoanalyzing everything he says."

"I'm not psychoanalyzing anything. It's just . . ."

"He's an anatomy professor, nothing more. He's a means for us to get through medical school. He doesn't affect our clinical rotations or residency selections, so . . ."

"So?" He stopped walking.

She stopped and looked back at him. "So who cares?" She resumed walking at a brisk pace.

Max didn't comment. He just walked beside her, admiring the way she moved.

"How well do you know Hermann?" he asked, changing the subject.

"I know him," she said.

They continued walking. He was quiet for a few minutes.

"Well, I saw him cheat on the last anatomy exam."

"You *what*?" She stopped walking and turned to Max.

"I saw him do it a few times. He dropped his pencil just so he could look over Stats's shoulder and see his answers."

"You're imagining that," she said, and walked on. "You should be careful with what you say, though."

"I know what I saw."

"Then why don't you turn him in? It's required. If anyone found out, you'd get thrown out right along with him."

He stopped in front of the Bresauer Kaffee-Rosterei. Cherry strudels were arranged in displays behind a large glass storefront. He read the sign above the roaster: LA Gottstein and Sohn. In the apartment above the store, a young girl stood at the open window, staring solemnly down to the street. On the window beside her, "Georg Friedlander Fabrik" was painted in white and black.

"I wish I hadn't seen it," Max said. "I can't stop thinking about it."

"It's your responsibility to turn him in."

"It's not that easy," he said. They walked on past a delicatessen, where a man in a bloody white apron smoked a cigarette in the door alcove. "Well, nobody knows what I saw, so until I figure out what to do, I'm not going to say anything."

Finally, they reached the stoop of Marta's apartment.

Want to come in?" she asked.

"Sure."

Inside, she took off her coat, put her books down on the entry table, and walked over to the kitchen area. Max sat down on the couch and watched her. She lit a candle and carried it over to the coffee table. Without saying anything, she sat down next to him on the couch.

She just watched him without speaking. Unsure what to do next, he put his hand on her leg. She pulled away from him. Then she moved closer and put his hand back, higher on her thigh. She closed her eyes and leaned her head back, and he leaned in and kissed her. Her mouth opened, and he could taste her tongue. Feeling as if an electric current were running through him, he put his hand on her breast.

She looked into his eyes, then closed them and kissed him some more. And, then, just like that, she pulled away.

"I don't think we should do this," she said. "You'd better go."

Max looked at her, confused. She stood up abruptly from the couch.

"I forgot, I have to leave anyway." She blew out the candle, picked it up, and carried it back to the kitchen. "I'm supposed to meet at my parents for dinner."

She smoothed her skirt, tucked her blouse back in, and went to the front door and opened it. He left in awkward silence.

CHAPTER SEVENTEEN

The Assistant to the Deputy Gauleiter, Wilhelm Friedrich Loeper, raised his fork and shook the bite of schnitzel at her. She could see that he was trying to make a point.

"It's fine, Father," she said. "But why do you have to talk to me as if I were one of your constituents?"

"And you're doing well in class?"

She sighed. "Yes, Father."

Marta's mother didn't look up. She finished her third glass of wine and held it up, and a waiter obligingly poured her a fourth.

"So I hear there are many Jews at Breslau, is that true?" her father asked.

"I wouldn't know, Father. I haven't asked."

"What do you mean, you 'wouldn't know'? Are you blind?"

He bit the piece of meat off his fork. When Marta didn't look up, he pointed the fork at her as if brandishing a weapon. "Marta," he said, "if any Jew gets a higher grade than you, I want to know about it. You're German royalty, and I won't have any *Juden* scoring better than you. Do you understand?"

"German royalty? Ha!" She chuckled, then thought better of pointing out how delusional he was. No sense engaging him. He would stop soon; he always did. She looked at him, smiling through her disgust.

He began again. "What do you think of the Jewish doctors? Are they really as bad as everyone says?"

"Father, I'm not sure what you mean by 'as bad.'" She could kick herself for taking the bait. She should have let it go by.

"Well, you know: interested in profits, not really helping people." As he said this, he caught a waiter's eye and nodded at his wineglass.

"Father, how would I know a thing like that?"

Again she chided herself for engaging him.

"'How would I know?' he mimicked. "How many years will it take until you know anything? I've spent a fortune raising you, teaching you poise and etiquette. But look at you." He waved his laden fork at her. "I don't think it matters. You're like your mother. Look at her." He pointed the fork at his wife. "You'll always be like her. Common. Ignorant. You're an embarrassment to me."

Marta's mother didn't look up.

"Are we done?" Marta asked defiantly.

"No, we are *not* done!"

He took the napkin, smudged with Burgundy and schnitzel, from his shirtfront and placed it on the table. "Do you know what I see every time I look at you? I see the same wretched tramp your mother was when I first met her. I felt sorry for her then, but I don't feel sorry for you."

Marta got up from the table without saying a word, got her coat, and left the house. "Asshole," she muttered under her breath.

CHAPTER EIGHTEEN

Approaching Kuźnicza Street, Marta noticed a familiar face among those huddled around a fire burning in a steel barrel. She walked fast, not wanting to attract their attention.

It wasn't long before she heard rapid footsteps behind her. She walked faster and faster, but the footsteps grew louder, so she turned.

Their eyes met, and both smiled. Then they kissed. She took Hermann's hand and whispered in his ear, "Don't you know it's past curfew?"

They laughed.

"Stay over" she said as they walked toward her apartment.

"I can't. We're busy again tonight."

"Please?" She looked into his eyes with a playful grin.

"Can't. I'm working."

"I had dinner with my father tonight. What a dreadful bore."

Hermann appeared uninterested.

"It's happening now, tonight, not tomorrow. Right now." He gazed meaningfully down the street. "And you and I will be a part of it."

She pulled his arm, and he followed her to her apartment. They went in, and he slammed the door behind them. The moment the door closed, she lifted his shirt off over his head and unbuckled his pants.

CHAPTER NINETEEN

Marta picked up Hermann's shirt from the floor and pulled it over her head, then lay down beside him on her bed.

"Marta . . ."She felt the touch of his warm hand on the inside of her thigh. "Once we start, there's no turning back."

"Please, I'm aware of the implications," she said. "When will it start?"

"Tomorrow, we enforce the Reichsführer's Physicians' Ordinance. If any German doctors work with Jewish doctors—or treat Jewish patients, for that matter—they'll lose their license."

Hermann rolled over to her and began kissing her fervently, but Marta broke away and stared out the window.

"Wagner has asked me to help 'disassemble' Breslau."

"What do you mean?" she asked, still looking out the window.

"The Reichstag considers Breslau '*too* Jewish' for a medical school. The students, the doctors, the hospital—mostly Jewish. There's a Star of David on the front of the main admin building, for Christ's sake! The school's contaminated—populated by swine."

He rolled back off her and sat up in bed. "The Reich has made it their mission to purge Breslau. You know, decontamination." He stood up from the bed. He was wearing only his boxer shorts. She looked at his muscular body.

"*Purge?* What does that mean?"

"The medical school stays; the Jewish element goes. People like us, we stay." He went over to the chair, bent down, and pulled on his trousers.

"We're the activists, the founders, the entrepreneurs of social change," he said proudly.

"We'll be the beneficiaries. Our action will earn you a fast track to promotion. Your career will accelerate. From students to doctors to professors, then to department heads." He picked his shirt up off the floor.

"And best of all, we won't be taking directions from any Jew faculty."

Marta listened, and for the first time, she began to understand. It seemed crazy, but times were different now. Hitler had changed the rules.

Her thoughts turned to her father. Soon enough, he would learn what she already knew. Hitler understood today's youth. Her father was old Germany—anachronistic, inflexible, traditional. Old Germany was under the heel of the West, impoverished by the Treaty of Versailles.

"Marta, the first target is Rosenthal. He must go, and quickly. He's a loudmouthed, pathetic Jew. Useless. Did you know he tried to threaten me with his 'honor code'? He accused me of cheating—*off a Jew*!"

Marta watched as Hermann laughed nervously.

"Will we take orders from a Jew? No, especially not from a whining old bag of bones like Rosenthal. He'll be the first to go. Wagner has agreed with me."

"What do you mean, 'first to go'?" she asked.

"There's a list: Jessner, Jadassohn, and students, too . . . Max, Rebecca, Stats."

"Go where?"

"I don't know. Just off campus, removed from Breslau. That's not our problem. What's important is . . ." He put his shirt on and started buttoning. Marta get out of bed, walked over to him, pushed his hands away, and finished buttoning his shirt. He looked down at her.

"You'll be recognized as a great surgeon or a great teacher. You'll be a professor. All this is yours for the taking. No one will keep you from reaching your goals."

Marta buttoned the collar on his shirt, then brushed his hair to the side with her fingers.

"The point is, Rosenthal's life is about to get very complicated."

She started to help him cuff his shirtsleeve, then stopped and stepped back.

"What is it?" he asked.

"Someone else told me you were cheating," she said, and finished the cuff.

CHAPTER TWENTY

Max squeezed past the other doctors who lined the aisles, and bumped and wormed his way to the front row.

"Excuse me," he said, edging his way through the sea of older men in white lab coats. "Pardon me. Is this taken?" he asked.

The doctor scowled at him as he settled in the one remaining seat in the front row.

Dr. Jessner came to the podium. Max and the physicians in the audience applauded.

"Thank you. Good afternoon. Many of you came today, in the great tradition of William Osler, to participate in the University of Breslau's Grand Rounds. In this great academic tradition, we exchange ideas and thoughts in a Socratic theater, all in the effort to advance medicine. So thank you all for coming. And thank you for your enthusiasm."

He looked around the room.

"I apologize if there is not an empty seat in the house. And for those standing in the aisle, thank you," He nodded to the doctors standing in back of the theater and in the aisles.

"But we will make do." Clearing his throat, he said, "I have the distinct honor of introducing one of our own, a world-renowned faculty member. He is sure to enlighten, challenge, and engage us. So without further ado, I am pleased to introduce Dr. Curt Rosenthal." Jessner stepped away from the podium, shook Rosenthal's hand, and sat down.

Max joined the audience in loud applause.

Rosenthal walked slowly to the center of the theater. Max saw that his eyes darted back and forth and seemed not to make eye contact with the audience. His affect was odd, and he looked a little rumpled and disheveled.

Rosenthal didn't look up from the podium. The audience was silent. "Perineural invasion," he announced. He stopped, cleared his throat, and repeated, "Perineural invasion. This is the prognostic indicator heretofore never observed. Look at this histopathology."

Max looked at the projected image on the screen behind the podium.

"Notice the tumor. See the basophilia staining of the tumor cells." The professor raised a long wooden pointer.

"These malignant cells are everywhere, but most importantly, they're wrapping around this nerve." Again he pointed out the feature on the projected image.

"This is perineural invasion by a tumor. This is when the malignancy has taken the next step: invasion."

He stopped, still looking down, Max noted, his eyes darting over his shoulder, as if he expected someone to come and pull him off the stage. For a moment, an uncomfortable silence hung over the auditorium.

"Invasion . . . invasion. These cells, these basophilic intensely staining cells, are not just sitting in the dermis. They are not just routine basal cells. These tumor cells are *wrapped around* these fine neuronal structures. 'So what?' you might ask."

Max watched his sweating professor ramble, his eyes again darting back and forth.

"Well, these cells, when seen and when wrapped around these neuronal structures like this, it implies the malignancy is more aggressive . . . more aggressive." He paused and pushed his sweaty hair back from his forehead.

"So what? What does that mean? Look."

Max looked up and now the screen projected grotesque faces of patients deformed by cancer. The audience gasped at the parade of missing noses and ears and exposed jaws.

"It means it will do more harm. It will recur after treatment, and it needs more aggressive therapy. Perineural invasion—that's what it means . . . Now you know. Look for perinueral invasion on your biopsies."

Rosenthal closed his book and walked away from the podium. Max looked around, feeling embarrassed at Rosenthal's abrupt departure. As the audience murmured over this, then Max began to applaud, loudly and alone. After a few moments, the others reluctantly joined him.

CHAPTER TWENTY ONE

Rosenthal stayed late in his office that night. The rest of the faculty had gone for the evening, and the janitors had cleaned the halls and left. All the lights in the hallway were turned off. The only illumination in the building came from Rosenthal's solitary dimly lit office.

He felt physically and mentally exhausted. He knew he had failed miserably today. He turned off the lights in his office, walked out into the hallway, and locked his office door. He dropped his keys into his pocket and looked around. It was eerily quiet as he walked down the dimly lit corridor. He opened the stairwell door and made his way down two flights of stairs, the banister guided his left hand. His right hand held his briefcase.

He was startled to see three young men standing one flight below him. He stopped for a moment a few steps above them, briefly made eye contact, then quickly looked away. He continued down the steps and past the young men without acknowledging them.

The seconds felt like hours as he continued down the next flight. Jaw clenched, he kept his head down and his mind on his descent, on getting out and away. Past them now, he sighed to himself as he made it down three more steps. But when he turned the corner and started down the last flight, a fourth young man appeared. He tried to walk past, but the man stepped in front of him and blocked his descent.

Rosenthal quickly assessed the situation. These were not students. Their faces were unfamiliar. They all seemed to be dressed similarly, wearing white T-shirts, baggy khaki army pants, and thick black army boots. All of them were bigger than he, and muscular. He turned and looked back. The first three had moved down the stairs closer to him. He was now sandwiched between them. No one spoke.

With a cold lump in the pit of his stomach, Rosenthal tried to walk past the youth below him. Looking down and away, he mumbled, "Excuse me."

In response, the young man reached out, snatched Rosenthal's glasses, and playfully waved them about. His companions laughed as he put on Rosenthal's glasses and began to dance around with simian gestures.

"I'm a swine," he taunted. Isn't that true, Rosenthal? Isn't it?" His voice grew louder and more taunting.

Rosenthal didn't know how to respond, so he just stood there. Suddenly, one of the young men from above him reached down and yanked away his briefcase and tossed it past Rosenthal, to the man below him.

Rosenthal watched with blurred vision as the young man continued to mock him.

"I'm Jewish pig," he yelled. "I live amid the swill. Isn't that true? Isn't it?"

Rosenthal said nothing.

"You too good to answer us?" one young man asked from above him.

Before Rosenthal could answer, he felt a push from above. He gasped in pain as his knees crashed against the concrete floor of the stairwell. He winced but still didn't look up. Without his glasses, everything was blurry. The men were just moving shapes. He tried to squint, to focus better and prepare for an attack, but this was not possible.

He heard his briefcase tumble down the stairs, heard the papers flutter out, the pencils, books, and even his medications scatter throughout the stairwell. He closed his eyes and prayed for the nightmare to end. He remained silent.

The men crowded closer around him as he crouched on the floor. For a moment, they did nothing. They looked down at him.

One of the young men said, "He's not worth it. Let's go."

Another said, "You know the plan. We have a job to do."

"But I think we've done enough, don't you?" the other said.

The largest of the group said, "Not yet," and kicked Rosenthal in the gut. Rosenthal felt as if he might vomit from the pain. With no time to recover, he felt another painful blow in his left kidney area, and then immediately, another blow to his back, followed by a blinding pain in the back of his skull.

He could feel blow after blow, but now the pain was somehow less, as if the nerves were spent, the neurotransmitters depleted. He felt blood drip from his nostrils and the corners of his mouth.

When Rosenthal awoke, he hurt everywhere. His cracked glasses lay beneath him, and his belongings were strewn all about and down the next flight of stairs.

How long had he lain here? His hand trembled as he reached for his cracked glasses and put them gently on his nose. Suddenly, the blurriness resolved into clear shapes. Alarmed, he looked around for his assailants.

He was alone.

It was just before sunrise, so after gathering his scattered belongings, he scribbled on a crumpled paper, "Too sick to teach today. Find substitute or cancel class." He left the note at the department secretary's desk.

Then he made his way out of the school building and somehow got himself home. There, exhausted and battered, he collapsed onto the bed.

CHAPTER TWENTY TWO

The students gathered around the classroom door and read the sign. "Class Canceled. Dr. Rosenthal sick. Exam as scheduled Friday."

Stats sat against the wall, legs crossed, reading the overseas version of the *Sporting News*. Brooklyn's major league baseball team, formerly the Trolley Dodgers, had adopted just "Dodgers" as their official name. New Yorkers loved their baseball, and they loved their Dodgers. The Yankees had swept the Cubs 4-0 in the World Series. Ruth hit his famous "called shot" home run. Stats looked at the black and white picture of Ruth pointing to the bleachers and read the quote underneath—"That's one"—after he took his first strike. Stats smiled to himself and continued reading. Ruth took the second strike and held up two fingers: "That's two." And next, famously, he pointed to the outfield fence and took the next pitch deep for a home run. Stats smiled and murmured the line, "Thunder after lightning," as Lou Gehrig famously came up next and hit another home run.

Rebecca sat next to Stats. She had her notebook out, and like most of her classmates, she used the time to study. She glanced over at Stats and said, "You don't want to be a doctor."

"Look," Stats said, "I said I'd finish this, for my parents. So I'll finish. After that, I'll figure it out."

"Doubt it." Rebecca taunted him.

Max walked past them to the lecture hall door and read the sign posted there. Then he walked across the hallway to his school locker. As he opened the locker, a small folded piece of paper fell to the floor. It had been wedged between the locker door and its frame. He put his books back in the locker and looked around. No one noticed him. He bent down and picked up the piece of paper.

Unraveling it, he walked toward Rebecca and Stats. But when he noticed the dried blood on the paper, he stopped walking. He moved from the center of the hallway to a corner and leaned against it.

He immediately recognized the barely legible scrawl as the same handwriting he had seen day after day on the chalkboard. The note read, "Don't talk to anyone. I need your help. Rosenthal- Come to my house- 223 Kotlarska." Max placed the note in his pocket and walked back to Rebecca and Stats.

Marta approached, and suddenly Max became more attentive.

"Why the canceled class?" she asked.

"I don't know," said Max. "Does it matter? Just gives us more time to catch up on other stuff."

"See? He's a strange bird, that Rosenthal. And by the way, Grand Rounds was a mess."

"All right," Max announced to everyone without really acknowledging Marta's comment. "I'm leaving. Got to talk to my work-study supervisor."

And with the crumpled note in his pocket, he headed to the work-study program office.

CHAPTER TWENTY THREE

His work-study supervisor was unmoved by his situation.

"Listen, I'm not doing this for me," Max said, standing in front of the supervisor's desk. "I send the money to my mom. I need a raise."

No response.

"Look," he said, "what I mean is, my sister is on medications, and my mom's alone—she works at night. It's not enough. I send them most of what I make."

"I'm sorry," said the supervisor. "Everyone's struggling. We just don't have the budget for raises. You can always work more hours."

"*More hours?* I can barely manage now." He looked around. "C'mon, you gotta be kidding me. There's no budget for an increase?"

"Nope." The supervisor scribbled "Denied" on Max's request for a raise, then stuffed the request into his file and didn't look up again.

Max turned around and walked out.

CHAPTER TWENTY SIX

On Kotlarska Street, Max approached the building bearing the numbers "223." It appeared run-down and neglected—rather like Rosenthal himself. He walked up to the front stoop, looked around, and knocked on the door. No answer. He knocked again, waited, then walked around the back of the building.

At the back was a basement entrance—two horizontal storm doors that opened to the stairs below. The doors were old and weathered from years of exposure. The hasp between them was unlocked.

Max lifted one of the storm doors and swung it up and over. He peered down into the gloom. Straightening up, he started to close the door, but stopped, then muttered, "To hell with it," and stepped down into the darkness. The board steps, likely rotted, creaked under his weight, so he gripped the wooden banister and took it slowly.

Suddenly, the board below his left foot snapped, and he felt a pain as the ragged end bit into his leg. He stumbled down the last two steps, and sprawled onto the floor, where he lay quietly, checking himself for injuries.

"Who's there?" a quavering voice asked.

Max could see no one.

"I ask, who's there?"

"Dr. Rosenthal, is that you?" Max asked.

"Max!" A match flared, and a candle took flame.

To his right, maybe two feet away, sat Dr. Rosenthal, with his knees pulled up to his chest. His face was bloody, bruised, and swollen, and his shirt was dark with dried blood. His eyes darted back and forth.

"Max, thank you for coming here," he said. "I wasn't sure you'd get my note."

Max felt shaken by how his teacher, a professor and a brilliant physician, had been reduced to this condition. He wanted to help, but he also wanted to flee. He was confused. At last, he said, "What happened?"

"Max, did anyone see you come down here?"

"No."

"Are you sure? Did *anyone* see you?"

Max shook his head.

"They're watching my every move," Rosenthal said.

"Who is, Professor?" Had the man at last come unhinged? He was surely having a breakdown.

"*They* are," Rosenthal yelled back.

"Who are 'they'?"

"Max, Can't you see them? They hate us. They want to kill us. They're going to kill me. It's not safe to go anywhere. I'm not safe. Max, did they see you come down here?"

He didn't answer.

Rosenthal rubbed his eyes with dirty palms. "I'm sorry you're here, I really am. But I had nowhere to go, no one to turn to. Max, they know where I live. They know I'm here right now. And, Max, oh, God, I'm so sorry, but now they know you came down here with me."

Rosenthal put his head in his hands and wept.

Obviously, the man was suffering a psychotic break.

"They beat me, Max. Badly . . . at the school. I can't go back. I need your help."

Max stared, listening but not really comprehending. He glanced back at his once energetic, animated teacher, now looking defeated and oh, so frail. He clearly had taken a beating. He couldn't have made this up.

Max looked down at the flickering candle, and suddenly, his mind was clear. Rosenthal wanted his help. Whatever help a poor medical student could give a distinguished professor, he would give, however crazy it sounded.

"I'll help you."

CHAPTER TWENTY SEVEN

At the door of the Hofbrau, Max greeted Marta with a kiss. She turned and offered just her cheek.

"How are you?" he asked.

"I'm worried about the pharmacology exam. I still don't understand it."

Her worries about the test seemed trivial compared to Rosenthal's plight. But it did remind Max of the harsh realities of school. He still had to prepare himself. And he still needed to get more money to pay for Sasha's medications. Anxiety crept over him. He nodded at Marta, though most of him had quit listening as concern over his conversation with Rosenthal outweighed his other concerns.

"You'd think he'd have the courtesy to give us notice. Instead, we get a cancellation sign on the classroom door."

Max wasn't listening. He watched her speak, watched her lips, her eyes, captivated by her seductive beauty.

"I tried to get a raise at work study, but they said no. I'm not sure what to do about my sister."

He could see that Marta didn't care, although common courtesy demanded that she say something.

"Well, what are you going to do?"

"I don't know. Sasha needs medicine, and my mother can't afford it. I have to do something, and fast. She has only a few days of pills remaining. Her seizing is getting worse. I need more money."

Marta watched the table of inebriated patrons next to them sing "Hofbräuhaus! One, two, down the hatch!"

"Look," she said, "I have to go. I need to study—can't spend time drinking here right now. See you tomorrow."

He watched her get up and leave, took another sip of his ale, and felt the cool bubbles break against his palate. He paid the bill and walked home alone.

A welter of thoughts tumbled through his mind as he lay in bed. He had trouble sorting them out. Try as he might, he couldn't erase the day's beginning, the look on Rosenthal's face. It dawned on him that it was the second time he had ever seen real fear. The first was when the old man ran into the darkened alley. Max burrowed his head deeper into his pillow, but the memory penetrated with unrelenting clarity. He thought about school, his preoccupation with grades, and how his studies might suffer if he let himself get distracted by Rosenthal's crazy gibberish. Then, as if changing a radio station, he switched to his next concern: Sasha. He worried about her having another seizure without her medication, and thought of his mother, alone and unable to help her.

He folded the pillow over his head and tried to forget today for a few minutes. Unable to sleep, he got up out of bed, stretched, and went to the only window in his apartment. The few people out on the streets at this hour, silhouetted in the streetlamps, looked lonely. Perhaps, like him, they could find no refuge from their worries.

CHAPTER TWENTY EIGHT

The next morning, Max had to work at getting dressed. As he had discussed with Dr. Rosenthal yesterday, it was absolutely critical that he be the first student at class today.

Class started at nine a.m. sharp, although most of the students had become accustomed to Rosenthal's tardiness, so they had begun to drag in late as well. Max paced anxiously in front of the lecture hall door. He dare not look in.

At three minutes to nine, Rebecca, Stats, and Marta showed up, walking toward him. His heart pounded. He must, according to Rosenthal's explicit instructions, be the first to enter the room, but the class must be gathered behind him.

Max waited until most of his classmates were behind him at the door, waiting to go in. It was time. He pulled open the door. As he entered the classroom, a series of screams and shrieks erupted behind him. Hanging from the rafter, at the very back of the lecture hall, was Rosenthal. A noose was around his neck, and a chair had fallen on its side beneath his dangling feet. He looked bludgeoned and swollen. The bloodstained clothes from two days ago were tattered and worn. Clearly, he had been beaten. His pants were sagging off his waist. His tall, lean body hung motionless, indifferent to the students' horrified cries.

Max couldn't believe his eyes. He was awash in a confusion of thoughts and emotions. Then rational thought took over, and he pushed his classmates back out the door. No one should see a person, let alone an esteemed professor, in this humiliated, demeaned state. "Get out!" he yelled, and closed the door behind them.

The cries and screams from the students soon alerted the faculty, and several professors, along with the dean himself, came over to the lecture hall. Max stood in front of the door and made it clear that out of respect for his former teacher, no one should enter. He spoke with the dean, who agreed. No one should see Rosenthal, except to take the body down.

Out in the corridor, speculation was running wild. It was murder. It was suicide. No one knew, though. "I could've done more," someone said. "I should have reached out to help." Max heard it all. But like a loyal dog guarding his fallen master, he did not move from the door. No one was going in.

Finally, two men came from the morgue. They carried a black body bag and wheeled a stainless steel gurney along with them. Devoid of emotion and perhaps a little annoyed at the routine task, they went about their task. Both wore the gray cotton coverall uniforms that identified them as working in the morgue.

One of the workers was heavyset and balding, the other tall, with flaming red hair and what appeared to be a single brick-red eyebrow bridging the top of his nose.

Max opened the door quickly to let them in. The two men pushed their sterile metal gurney past him, and he quickly shut the door behind them. Max kept his post in front of the door but moved slightly to the side of the square window so that the crowd out in the hall might see the men as they took the body down and stuffed it in the canvas bag.

As the men pushed the rolling steel table out of the lecture hall, Max moved away, relieved. He had finished his task. The faculty and students were silent. They parted as the table rolled past, some touching it as if to pay their last respects.

Their concern for the dead seemed a marked change from their disdain for him when he was alive. Max bristled to see them acting so sad and solemn.

What a joke, he thought. *Tears and sobs when he's dead, but only judgment and ridicule when he lived.*

Now that the two men had loaded Rosenthal's body in the van and driven off to the morgue, the crowd seemed uncomfortable. Faculty members retreated back to their offices. Students picked up their books and wandered off. Max, however, couldn't go back to what he was doing. He looked for his friends. He needed to be with someone. He needed to talk, to grieve. He sought out Rebecca and Stats.

Marta and Hermann, meanwhile, decided to seize the opportunity and quickly left school. Standing in her apartment, Marta pushed Hermann against the wall, and his hands were all over her.

She pulled away for a moment. "So, did you kill him?" she asked between kisses.

"No. Lucky bastard killed himself. We were going to, though."

"Do you think he knew?"

"I'm not sure what he knew, but somehow, he beat us to it. Pathetic coward—he was first on our list. No Jew threatens me."

"So, do you think he knew?" Marta asked again.

"Who cares? I think he was just so damned scared and didn't see any way out of his miserable life. We were watching him. He was cooped up in his basement and didn't come out the whole damned day. There was one thing, though . . ."

"What?" she asked.

"I'm not sure what the importance of it was."

"What?"

"Well, we staked out his house and watched everything. Nothing notable . . . except for one thing." He held her shoulders and pushed her back a little. "Apparently, our mutual friend Max visited the professor, and he stayed with him most of the morning and later into the afternoon."

"What does that mean?" she asked.

"Who knows? Rosenthal was a quivering bundle of nerves. He was on the brink of suicide. Max was probably acting as his psychiatrist." He paused and then pushed her playfully down onto the bed.

"Well," she said, "obviously, he wasn't very good at it."

They laughed.

"There is something that still bothers me, though." He fell into bed with her.

"What's that?" she asked, pulling him to her.

"That little prick told you I cheated. He thinks he has something on me. I don't like being threatened by anyone, especially a *Juden*."

"And what's your point?" Marta asked.

"My point is . . ." He could see that she was waiting for him to complete his thought. "My point is, I don't trust Max, and he doesn't trust me, so I'll act first. Rather, *we'll* act first. The Reichstag expects it. If we, you and I, are ever going to get anywhere, we must demonstrate our commitment to Von Schirach"

"That pompous ass?"

Hermann smiled as he thought of Von Schirach. "He's responsible for the success of Hess's *Hitlerjugend.*"

"So?" Marta asked.

"So . . . Hitler Youth is now over one million strong, because of Schirach." Hermann quoted Schirach, chapter and verse: "'The future of the German nation depends on its youth, and the German youth shall have to be prepared for its future duties. The German youth shall be educated physically, intellectually, and morally in the spirit of National Socialism to serve the people and the community, through the Hitler Youth.'"

He hoped he had impressed Marta.

She said, "I don't think Max is anyone we need to worry about."

Hermann snapped, "When did I ask you what you think?"

She looked at him, hurt and confusion on her face.

"If I want your opinion, I'll ask for it. Meanwhile, let's just pretend you didn't say that, and let's pretend you have the intelligence to understand what I'm saying."

He got up out of the bed.

"So don't open your stupid mouth or interfere, and I'll be promoted to officer in Hitler Youth. And you . . ." He looked down at her with a tolerant smile. "You'll receive your coveted faculty appointment at Breslau." He held up his finger as if admonishing a disobedient child. "If—and *only* if—we can show Von Schirach our efforts."

CHAPTER TWENTY NINE

It was the middle of the night, and again sleep eluded Max. He had forgotten about Sasha, and now he couldn't blot out the image of Rosenthal, bruised and battered and hanging by a noose.

Still in his pajamas, weary but unable to sleep, he paced the floor of his apartment. He looked out his window and noticed a few dozen young men on the street. In the glow of the streetlamp, he could see their brown shirts and black combat boots, the swastikas on their upper arms moving in unison as they marched.

These were Hitler's *Sturm Abteilung,* his private army, and they were marching not fifty feet outside his window.

He thought of his mother and, of course, Sasha, and how he much he missed them. He had known, ever since he left them to attend medical school, how their delicate lives depended on each other. His mother had become Sasha's caregiver, and that role of being needed helped her past the depression of her widowhood.

The men continued marching, their boots clattering rhythmically against the bricks of the street. The left arm, with its swastika imprinted on a red band, was held flexed across the abdomen while the right arm swung back and forth, fingers rigid, as they followed each other like windup tin soldiers.

Even at this late hour, onlookers lined the streets, right arms angled upward in salute as they proudly watched the soldiers march past.

This was not his quiet university town anymore. Change was coming, and there was nothing he could do about it. Everything seemed beyond his control. Oh, for the carefree years of youth!

He thought fondly of summers with his grandfather. The ease of it all. Papa would take him sailing on Lake Constance in Meersburg, that sleepy cottage town on the north side of the lake between Friedrichshafen and Überlingen. The dreamy, languid days, the unforgettable emerald hue of the lake, digging night crawlers and catching fish and sleeping under the stars. There, it seemed, he was always barefoot and always happy. He smiled.

How he yearned for those simple, beautiful days. The fiery sunsets that melted into the lake, the smell of Grandmother's Shabbat dinners and baked challah.

Max closed his eyes, and for that one minute, he was there. Why couldn't he go back? Those days were gone. Time, like the men on the street below, had marched on by. He reached out, opened his hand, and grabbed at the air. A tear rolled down his cheek.

And again, just like that, he was back in dreary Breslau, with the fading sound of marching boots in his ears, while thoughts of Rosenthal, medical school, and Sasha consumed him.

He loved his sister's innocence. She never looked outside her small encapsulated world. She could live within the confines of a single day. That was her gift. It was a fragile, glass-encased existence, he knew, and it could shatter at any time. She was always a seizure away from chaos.

He wanted to sleep, just for a few minutes . . .

No, Sasha wouldn't see it coming. She wouldn't recognize the boots on the street and what they meant.

Rosenthal had been right. At first, Max hadn't believe it, and then suddenly, he couldn't help but see it everywhere. It was like a riddle: once you knew the answer, it was too obvious.

Max felt helpless. He had lost control. He needed more time to study, Sasha needed more phenobarbital, and he needed more money to buy it.

He forced himself back to bed. It was four am. Oh, for two hours of quality sleep! He stared at the ceiling and thought about medical school and how so much had changed in so few days.

Again his mind would not relent.

Was Rosenthal all that crazy? Was he really that paranoid? Or was it insight? Maybe he just recognized life's probabilities before everyone else. Maybe he was so rational, it was irrational to think him otherwise.

It didn't matter. Max had problems he had to fix. First, he had to find phenobarbital for Sasha, and, second, he had to finish medical school. He had to adapt to a changed environment. He had to live with a new set of rules in place. "Live" was perhaps too mild a word. "Survive" was closer.

CHAPTER THIRTY

Stats knew he had broken the law. He also knew who Ernst Roehm was.

If it could happen to the leader of the SA, then it could happen to anyone. So how could he take the Nazis seriously when, on the one hand, they preached their doctrine of racial "purity" and, on the other hand, they knowingly allowed a homosexual to rise through the ranks. It was generally assumed to be an exception, but this situation would no longer be tolerated. Roehm was proof, and Paragraph 175 of the criminal code, was the legal precedent.

It was an effective recruitment tool. More moderate Germans were swayed by Nazi lunatics broadcasting that the country's economic problems were some sort of divine punishment for the "wanton, immoral acts of a few."

Stats turned to his friend Herschel. "That kind of bullshit demagoguery is spreading like a virus."

"Can we stop it?" Herschel was a graduate doctoral student—only a few years older but many years wiser than Stats. Stats stared adoringly at him. He was tall and lean, prematurely gray at the temples.

"I don't know," Stats said. "Does it matter? They've found an effective message to stir up national pride." Herschel picked up the coffeepot and poured himself a cup. He then lifted the pot and offered it to Stats.

"I'm fine," he said. "But it's no coincidence, their linking homosexuality to Jews."

Herschel sipped his coffee, then said, "That's because they're the only ones defending their civil liberties."

"It's Himmler. He's a fucking backstabbing opportunist," Stats replied, watching for Herschel's reaction. He envied his control.

"If it weren't Himmler, it would have been someone else," Herschel said. "It starts with Hitler."

Stats hadn't anticipated his relationship with Herschel, and they certainly didn't advertise it. They were rarely seen together in public, and although the freedoms they enjoyed had vanished overnight, their relationship had always been private. Stats hoped it would stay that way. The last thing a medical student needed was "registration" and a Gestapo dossier. It would be grounds for expulsion from medical school.

Stats watched Herschel dress. Then he went to the bedroom, took off his bathrobe, and pulled his trousers on.

He felt the touch of Herschel's finger on his back. Stats closed his eyes and hoped to feel more, but he felt cheated when Herschel asked, "What's this?"

Stats glanced down at the red mark.

"Irritation. Probably from my pants," he said.

"You have it all over your back—it's not rubbing from your pants."

"I do?" Stats asked. "What is it, then?"

"I don't know, but it's everywhere. Get an appointment with Guildenwasser," Herschel said, and kissing Stats, he left for work.

CHAPTER THIRTY ONE

For Stats, the weekend was unbearably long. His rash persisted, and his anxiety grew. He worried about everything from syphilis to psoriasis.

"I'm here to make an appointment with Dr. Guildenwasser," he said to the clerk at the health clinic.

Moritz Guildenwasser, staff physician for the University of Breslau, had won the Teacher of the Year Award for the past ten years. More importantly, he was one of the best clinicians in Germany.

The clerk, scribbled in a schedule book and said, "Come back at nine thirty."

"But I . . ."

"Next."

The morning's anatomy lecture started at nine. He would miss half of it. It was the first day for Rosenthal's replacement to lecture.

The new instructor waited for the students to wander in. A copy of his syllabus lay on every student's desk.

Stats looked him over. He appeared too young to be an instructor, but that wasn't the oddest thing about him. He was dressed in a black suit, sharp and well fitted, and wore a red armband with a swastika on his left arm.

"I'm Professor Gerhart Warring." He seemed quite proud of himself and his title.

"I've been reassigned by the Reichstag to teach the remainder of this anatomy class. I expect military-style behavior and attendance. I have modified the syllabus. Please refer only to this one, as it will replace your prior one."

He held up the new syllabus for the students to see.

"I'll be teaching through the use of cadavers and will demonstrate, in doing so, where the Aryan race acquired its superiority." He stopped for a moment, paced around the podium, and gave the students an icy stare.

"I'll show you where other races, through genetic pooling, have derived their racial inferiorities. Genetic dilution." He shook his head as if at a poorly behaved child. "You'll be expected to know these facts for your examinations."

Stats glanced at the clock on the wall. Anxious to get to his appointment, he stood up from his desk, excused himself to the student next to him, and walked toward the door.

"Young man, where do you think you're going?" Warring asked.

"Not feeling well, sir," Stats replied. "I need to be excused."

"Get back to your seat. You've not been dismissed."

Stats looked around at the other students.

"Sir, with all due respect, I'm not feeling well. Typically, students who don't feel well go to the infirmary." He knew he might regret what he was about to say next, but he said it anyway. "Had you received proper medical school training like the rest of us, you would know that."

Some of the class chuckled at this retort.

"What's your name, boy?" Warring asked.

"Jakob, sir."

"You're a Jew, aren't you, Jakob?" he asked. The classroom was silent. Religion was never discussed in school. The unusually personal question caught Stats off guard.

"Why is that any of your concern, sir?"

"All *Juden* in this class are my concern." He waved his hand indifferently. "Be on your way, boy."

Stats could feel the man's hate. It was palpable. He headed to the door, avoiding eye contact as he walked past Warring. Opening the door, he glanced back just long enough to catch the dark look in the man's eyes, then quickly walked out.

He arrived, panting, at the student health clinic. He was five minutes late.

"Wait over there," said the clerk. "The nurse will call your name."

Still feeling rattled from the exchange with Professor Warring, Stats sat down and tried to regain his composure.

"Next," the nurse called. Pointing at Stats, she escorted him to a room.

"Jakob, what brings you in today?" she asked.

"I have a rash."

"Where?" she asked without making eye contact.

"I think it started on my abdomen . . . here." He pointed. "And now it's all over my back."

"Does it itch?"

"No."

"Hurt?"

"No."

"Okay. The doctor will be in shortly"

With that, the nurse left the exam room.

Stats breathed a sigh of relief. He looked forward to seeing Guildenwasser.

A gentle knock on the door, and then a small man in a white lab coat opened it slowly. Stats didn't recognize him.

"Hello, Jakob. My name is Dr. Bohrsdam." He put out his hand.

Stats shook hands tentatively. "Where's Dr. Guildenwasser?" he asked.

The man appeared empathetic and sincere.

"Guildenwasser no longer works here. I'm sorry, I was just told to come over and staff the clinic. Would you prefer another doctor?"

Stats thought about it and decided he would give him a chance.

"No, I'm fine, thank you."

"I understand you have a rash?" he said.

"Yes, and I'm worried. We just finished reading about syphilis, and, well, I hope I don't have that."

Bohrsdam chuckled, which helped put Stats at ease.

"I remember when I was a medical student," he said. "I was convinced I had leprosy, then scurvy, and eventually it was porphyria." They both chuckled.

"So let's take a look at this 'syphilitic' eruption."

Stats stood up and removed his shirt.

After a minute of careful examination, Bohrsdam said, "Jakob, given your rash, it's important that I understand some things before I can give you a definite diagnosis. You might find some of this difficult to share with me."

"Go on," Stats said, hoping not to hear what was coming.

"Well, first, I must ask—and remember, there is physician-patient confidentiality here—are you sexually active?"

Stats answered, "Yes."

"Do you have multiple sexual partners?"

"No."

"Are you heterosexual or homosexual?"

And there it was. Seven years of keeping his secret hidden away from his family and his friends. Now he was finally confronted with the question that had been so long in coming.

Stats thought carefully before he gave his answer. The few seconds felt like a lifetime.

Every repressed thought and fear, every disguised action and hidden agenda, all came back to him in a flash. The very first time he realized that he was different . . . his first kiss with another man . . . the first time he made love. All the indelibly etched memories that had waited for the right moment to be freed.

In his mind, Stats played and replayed the simple question. And, of course, he thought about the realities of disclosure. His mind ran through the possibilities, if-then scenarios, probabilities, and outcomes as he tried to gauge the ramifications of disclosure. It would be more than just social stigma and family disappointments. There were legal issues to be considered. The Reich's code paragraph 175 required the registration of homosexuals, and the creation of dossiers. He understood the implications of his answer.

It was overwhelming, and yet, at the same time, disclosure felt seductively liberating. He would be free to be himself, to be loved by those who accepted him for who he was, not for who they wanted him to be. It meant liberation from his life of lies. It was tantalizingly close. He could almost taste the seductive liquor of an honest life.

Then his survival instincts took over. Logic told him that physician-patient confidentiality was utter bullshit. It held only so long as disclosures were meaningless. As soon as there was something of value to disclose, confidentiality went out the window.

He looked at Bohrsdam again. He looked for a sign, something to suggest that he was more than a doctor. Perhaps a trusted friend, an adviser—something, anything.

Bohrsdam waited patiently for an answer. A moment of uneasy silence . . .

"Heterosexual," Stats finally answered.

"Well, then, my boy, we've nothing to worry about, have we? The condition is pityriasis rosea. I'm sure you remember, it's easily recognized by the herald patch." He pointed to the red spot on Stats's abdomen.

Stats breathed a sigh of relief and shook his head.

"Look it up. It's benign and resolves on its own." Borhsdam scribbled the diagnosis down on a piece of paper for Stats and handed it to him.

"Occasionally, sunlight will speed up its resolution. But in Breslau, at this time of year, that's not exactly an option, is it?" Bohrsdam chuckled.

"Regardless, as a doctor, you'll learn that you must always consider alternatives—the differential diagnosis, if you will." He sat back in his chair and crossed his arms. Stats watched his bedside manner.

"We must never rely completely on our first thought. We must think in terms of other possibilities. Overconfidence will result in missed diagnoses. In this case, syphilis is in the differential. And so, just to be complete, we'll order a Wasserman test and look for antibodies." He scribbled on a test order form and handed that to Stats, too. "But I really doubt it'll be anything but negative."

"Thank you so much, Dr. Bohrsdam," Stats said, taking the lab slip.

"Go back to class and finish your studies."

"I will." Stats proceeded to get up, but just before he left the exam room, he turned to the doctor and asked, "By the way, do you know what happened to Dr. Guildenwasser? He was everyone's favorite."

"Guildenwasser was replaced by orders of the Reichstag. It had something to do with his being Jewish. Apparently, there's too much Jewish influence here at the school, and, well, you know, times are changing. Good day."

Stats left the office, relieved that he didn't have syphilis. But he felt worse about himself. He had missed the opportunity to share his secret with someone. At some point, the consequences of disclosure may be less than the consequences of repression, but he knew he had not yet reached that point.

As Dr. Bohrsdam finished his note on Stats, he wrote in his chart, "Pityriasis rosea, rule out secondary syphilis." Then, in a section of the chart with the heading "Social History," he wrote, "Questionable sexual activity, suspect homosexuality." Finally, he stamped in big red letters across the note page, "JUDEN." Filing the chart, he muttered to himself, "Lying Jew," and went to greet his next patient.

CHAPTER THIRTY TWO

Over the past year, the grove had become their meeting place. They would sit on the grass and talk about whatever was on their minds. Removed and safe, it was a hideout of sorts, unknown to most people. Here, they could gossip about classmates and be cynical about teachers, without fear of being heard or watched.

Today, Rebecca had her own set of problems to deal with. She worried about how she would support her parents and still continue her education. She couldn't stomach the idea of her parents being sent to a state-run nursing home.

"Both of them are slowly falling into the abyss of memory loss," she told Stats.

Her father, Samuel Eisen, a well-known writer for the *Stettin Jewish News,* had tried hard to instill a sense of social justice in Rebecca. "He was a great journalist," she said, "and a wonderful father. But the day is fast coming when he won't even recognize me." As she spoke, she realized that the day was already here.

Stats listened.

"He made me volunteer at the soup kitchen. I hated it at first, but then I understood it. I had to serve hot lunches to the poor. How many thirteen-year-olds did that?"

"None, actually," Stats said. He sat on the grass, his back against the tree trunk.

"Exactly," she said, "He instilled a conscience." She tapped her chest. "And a heart."

He could see her lips start to tremble.

"They told me I was cut from work study for "budget constraints," but when I asked others . . ." She shook her head and wiped a tear from her eye.

"It was Professor Warring. He's the new supervisor of the work-study program."

"So?"

"He's been tasked with cleansing the program of any Jews. It's now generally accepted that if there's any work to be had, it won't go to Jewish students."

"So what are you going to do?"

"You mean what did I already do?"

"Oh, no, you didn't!"

"Yes, I did. I went to his office and pleaded with him to give me my job back. I told him I'd work for half of what they were paying me. I can't afford to lose this job."

"So, what did he say?"

He laughed at me.

"Shit," Stats growled.

"What about you?" she said. What the hell were you thinking?" She sat next to him and leaned on his shoulder. "How could you tell Warring he didn't go through medical school! And in front of the whole class!"

"Oh, fuck him. I had to go to the infirmary. What's he gonna do, kill us?"

"He might." She pulled an apple from her bag, took a bite, and handed it to him.

"Can I be *really* honest with you?" he asked.

"No, absolutely not," she said.

He looked around and took a deep breath. "How long have you known me?" he said.

"Unfortunately, longer than I'd like to admit."

She threw the apple core into the elderberry thicket behind them.

"And do you feel like you really know me?" he asked her.

"I don't like where this is headed."

"No, seriously." He looked back at her.

"I know you'd rather be doing play-by-play for the Yankees."

"And what else?" he asked.

"Is there any more than that?"

"There's a reason," Stats said.

"What."

He leaned away from the tree and turned to look at her, face to face.

"There's a reason."

"A reason for what?" she said. "You're making me nervous."

"A reason why you don't know any more about me than that."

"Okay, so what's the big secret?"

"If you'd be quiet for a minute, I'll tell you."

"What if I don't want to know?" she asked, and giggled.

"If I tell you, it might get you in trouble. It might be something about me you don't want to know." He threw a sycamore ball at a nearby tree.

"I just said that," she said.

"I'm homosexual." There. He had told someone.

Rebecca laughed.

Stats scowled at her. "Why are you laughing?"

"I'm sorry," she said, having a hard time holding back more chuckles.

"I've told no one but you. Not my parents, no one. You don't look surprised."

"If it walks like a duck and quacks like a duck, there's a good chance it's a duck," she said.

"Really? How long have you known?"

"I've only 'known' for about a minute and a half, but I've suspected it ever since we met."

She turned toward him and went from joking to serious in an instant. "You know, if anyone finds out, you're in big trouble. I'm not sure what's worse: being homosexual or Jewish." She chuckled nervously.

"In any case, you'd better keep it close to the vest. Jousting with Warring today didn't help, by the way. You can't do that and be a homosexual. You have to shut up; otherwise . . ."

"Otherwise *what*?"

"All they need is a reason to suspect you, and that'll be their reason to expel you. They're looking for reasons to hurt you, us, whatever. It's just like they did when they fired me. I'm screwed." She shook her head again.

"I'm not sure if this isn't what happened with Rosenthal."

"I know, I know, I'm careful," Stats said. "You're the only one I've told."

"Okay," she said. "Let's make a pact right now. Today. Here by this tree." She pointed her thumb at the larch tree behind them. "If, for any reason, you think you're in any sort of trouble, or someone you think has turned you in—or me, if I think I'm in trouble and you see it—let's meet back here. I'll meet you. Okay? You agree?" She put her hand out to shake.

"I say you're neurotic—and maybe a little crazy. What's going to happen?"

"Just promise. If you get in any sort of trouble, meet me here. I'm worried, that's all."

"You're overreacting," Stats said calmly.

"Really? If anyone finds out, you'll be expelled and probably arrested. You registered? No. Of course not, so they'll use that against you. And if you get arrested, you're done. I don't think a Jewish homosexual in a German jail has a lot to offer the Third Reich."

"You're blowing this out of proportion. "

"Fine, just humor me," she said.

"Look," he said. "We're both gonna finish. You'll be a great doctor. And me, I'm taking the next boat to New York City.'

"Just promise."

CHAPTER THIRTY THREE

Max waited for everyone to leave the clinic. He watched the pharmacy clerk shut off all the lights, lock the door, and flip the "Open" sign to "Closed."

He looked at his watch and decided to wait another half hour just to make sure no one was around and no one was coming back. Then he walked up to the window next to the front door and broke it with his elbow. He looked around to see if anyone had noticed. No one was around.

Reaching through the broken window, he twisted his arm around to unlock the door. It opened, and he walked in. He found a light switch and walked toward the back of the room, toward the shelves of medications.

As he neared the shelves, he heard footsteps outside the door. He searched the shelf frantically for a jar labeled "Phenobarbital."

The footsteps stopped at the front door. He looked to the front, but no one was there. Suddenly aware that he was holding his breath, he let it out and drew in another.

Finding the antiseizure medication, he grabbed as many tablets as he could, stuffed them in his pockets, and fumbled for an empty pill bottle.

At the sound of the doorknob turning, his hands shook and he spilled some pills on the floor. Taking whatever he could fit in his pockets, he looked around for an escape, a window—any way out.

Spotting a window in the back, just above him, he pulled a chair over, clambered up, and punched the window with his fist. Then he pushed out the remaining shards of glass so he could squeeze through the gap without cutting himself. His hand throbbed, and he saw that it was bloody.

Pulling himself up onto the windowsill, he pushed his head and shoulders through and wriggled. *Almost there . . .* Then he felt a hand grab his right calf.

He pulled, kicked, and jerked his leg as hard as he could to break free.

He knew he was not giving up the medications—not yet. He thrashed harder to free himself, but the hand would not release him.

Finally, he gave up. Exhausted, bloodied, and sweaty, he slid back down to the floor to face his captor.

The old man from the park was staring quietly at him.

"Turn me in!" Max shouted. "Go ahead and let the damn school kick me out. Take me to jail."

Wilhelm, the pharmacist's assistant he had befriended in the park, walked over to the bin of tablets and filled a bottle with at least a hundred more. Then he walked over to Max and handed him the pills.

"Take these pills," he said in his familiar gentle tone. "I'm not going to call the police. I'm not your judge; I'm your friend. I'll tell them I had an accident working late. I needed to come back here anyway to finish some work." He pointed to the mess on the floor.

"Sell the pills, use the pills, or give the pills away. Whatever you need them for, they're yours now." He patted Max on the shoulder and then looked him in the eyes.

"Max, they're waiting for you to fail. They're hoping you'll make a mistake. Don't give them a reason, Don't risk your future on this. It's dangerous. The world has changed overnight. The Brown Shirts are marching in the streets." He pointed out the broken window.

"They'll kill you if you're caught doing something like this. Don't let one petty theft ruin whatever future you may have left here. Go now, before the police arrive."

With that, Max scurried like a rat, out of the pharmacy. He ran and ran and didn't stop until he was inside his apartment.

Why me? he wondered. Why should the old man care? He could easily have turned the thief in. What if someone had seen Wilhelm help him? He would be jailed and publicly humiliated.

Exhausted, he collapsed on his bed. Tomorrow, sometime after school, he would visit Sasha and get her the pills. He closed his eyes and tried to fall asleep.

CHAPTER THIRTY FOUR

Marta didn't cry at her father's funeral. Quite the contrary, she felt liberated. She despised him as much in death as in life. And now she refused to speak to her mother. After all, her mother was an accomplice in the mess they were left in.

They had lived above their means, and now, with her father gone, the family had only debt and no way to make the money back. Just meeting the rising tuition costs would be challenge enough.

And yet, Marta knew she would stop at nothing to achieve her goals. No, she was not mourning the loss of her father. She was *scorning* him. She owed no one anything, and despite what the German banks might tell her, she would not let herself be fettered by her father's debt.

There was a knock at her front door.

"I heard," Max's voice said. "I'm sorry about your father."

She opened the door and hugged him, weeping.

CHAPTER THIRTY FIVE

Rebecca was failing her parents. She was now two weeks late on their house payment. The landlord had lost patience.

She scrounged through her keepsakes and found the diamond necklace her father had given her when she turned 13. She picked it up and gazed at it. Memories from the past reminded her how she had planned to wear this necklace at her wedding. Until now, she had saved it for that special day.

A sign in the window read, "We buy your jewelry." She opened the door, took a few hesitant steps inside, and paused. She looked again at the necklace in her hand.

"May I help you, young lady?" a man asked from behind a counter.

"I'm here to sell my necklace," she said. She looked around. The store was eerily empty of other customers. A disheveled, overweight woman sat in the corner of the store. She wore a loupe and seemed to be removing a diamond from a bracelet. She didn't look up at Rebecca.

"Let me see it," the man said, and reaching across the counter, he grabbed the necklace. His fingers were stained yellow from the cigarettes he smoked.

"It's very beautiful," he said, and then handed it back to her. "But we don't need any more of these. I have ten just like it in that display." He pointed to his right.

Rebecca looked at the necklaces he was pointing at. None were as nice as hers.

"But you must," she said. "This one's very valuable and very special to me. It's rare, please take another look."

"Sorry, not interested."

"I need your help," Rebecca pleaded. "Please, take another look. This necklace is different."

Without missing a beat, he said, "Doris, darling, take a look at this young lady's necklace and let me know its value."

Doris sat up for a moment, didn't speak, but waved Rebecca over to her. She opened her palm, and Rebecca cautiously placed the necklace in it. Doris took it quickly, threw it under a lamp, and pushed the loupe down over her eye. She handed it back to Rebecca and looked over to the jeweler, shaking her head.

"I'm sorry" he said. "We just can't buy this from you."

"But you must be mistaken. I know its value. The gold is eighteen karat, and the diamonds were purchased from Cartier in Switzerland. My father paid a fortune for this twenty years ago."

"I'm sorry," the man said, and held up his hands.

"Listen," Rebecca said, "you must buy this. Please. I need the money. I need this to help my parents."

"Young lady, times are tough all over. Look around you. Do you see anyone lining up to get in here? Everyone has their problems."

"Please, I'm begging you."

"I can give you five Reichsmarks." He turned away and filed some papers.

"It's worth twenty times that," she said.

"Not in today's market. That's the best I can do, really."

Rebecca looked at the necklace, and tears welled in her eyes. "Fine."

The man behind the counter handed her the money, and she gave him the necklace and walked out of the store.

CHAPTER THIRTY SIX

Max saw Marta in front of the school, but before he could say hello, he felt a sharp blow between his shoulders. His head snapped back, his books fell, and he wobbled to the ground. Confused, he felt himself about to black out, only to feel a crushing kick to his abdomen. He doubled over and fell flat on his stomach.

Managing to look up for a brief moment, he saw his attacker's face. It was Hermann. The recognition didn't last long, for a third devastating blow caught him under the chin.

Max woke up in a completely different place, with Stats and Rebecca standing over him. A cold wet washcloth was folded over his right eye.

He squinted at them. "Am I hungover?"

"Not exactly," Stats said.

He looked around to find that he was lying on a couch. "Where am I?"

"My apartment," Stats said.

"What am I doing here?"

"For some reason, Hermann pummeled you," Rebecca said, picking up the cold small towel off his head and replacing it with a new one.

"You didn't put up much of a fight, by the way. We found you blacked out."

"What about class?"

"We missed it."

"What did I do to Hermann? I don't remember fighting with him."

"Well, I wouldn't exactly say you *fought* him," Stats said. "To put it more accurately, he kicked your ass. And then he and Marta just walked away."

"*Marta* was there?" Max asked.

"Yeah, she's a piece of work." Stats wore a pained expression.

At that moment, a tallish fellow in his twenties walked into Stats's apartment. He greeted Rebecca with a kiss and walked over to Stats.

"Max, I've got to tell you something," Stats said.

"What?"

"It may come as a surprise."

"Try me."

"Can you keep a secret?"

"Probably not,"

"Meet Herschel."

"Your boyfriend?"

"How'd you know?" Stats replied.

"Really?" Max laughed. "I thought everyone knew."

"How would anyone know, if I never told anyone?"

"You're not serious. Was that really your big secret?"

"Yeah, it was going to be."

"I have a much bigger secret," said Max. "One you won't believe."

"You're homosexual, too?" Stats gaped at him.

"No. This is serious. I need you and Rebecca to come with me. There's someone we have to meet."

"Who?" Rebecca asked, giving Stats a sideways look.

"I can't tell you yet." Max stood up from the couch.

"Where?" Stats asked, and looked at Rebecca.

"I can't tell you that, either." Max started toward the door.

"Then why'd you bring it up?" Stats asked.

"Better that I show you."

"Yeah?"

"Listen, I've got to get home," he said. "I'm sore, but I need to clean up and drop something off for my sister. You and Rebecca meet me at my apartment tonight."

"You're in no condition to walk home," Herschel said.

"I'll be all right." He took a few deep breaths, walked toward the door, and said, "Meet me at ten tonight in front of my apartment."

CHAPTER THIRTY SEVEN

Rebecca approached the infirmary window, where the nurse told her the doctor would see her without a scheduled appointment. After about twenty minutes, the nurse called her back. She heard a knock and watched as the door opened.

"Hello, Rebecca. I'm Dr. Bohrsdam," the doctor said. He held her chart on one hand.

"Hi," she said tentatively.

"Can you tell me the problem?" He remained standing and distant.

"Yes. I've been feeling nauseated lately. I'm not sure why."

"I see." He sat down.

"Have you been menstruating normally?"

"Yes."

"Is it possible that you're pregnant?"

She looked at him for a moment. "No."

"Does it burn when you urinate?"

"No. They checked my urine. Did you see the results?"

"Ah, right here." He flipped to the page of lab results. "Urine normal, no white blood cells, no infection."

"Doctor, could it all be stress?" she said, looking at the floor. "I'm under a lot of stress."

"What type of stress?"

"My parents." She paused. "Well, everything I tell you is confidential?"

"Of course. Everything stays between us. In this room." He pointed around with the pen in his hand. "Doctor-patient privilege. You know that."

"Good. It's my parents—they've lost their independence. I'm worried about them." She looked at him. He sat silently and jotted some notes in her chart.

"And I don't know . . . I think they don't really recognize me anymore."

"You mean memory loss?"

"Yes, both of them. At the same time, and then, at night . . . Well, they wake up in the middle of the night, disoriented. Sometimes, they wander out of the house."

"I understand."

"It's worse than that, too. I'm Jewish. I mean, *they're* Jewish. If anyone finds out, with the way things are changing, I don't know what will happen to them."

Dr. Bohrsdam scribbled on her chart. He didn't look up.

She said, "One of those awful homes, I think they'll send them there to die. They'll kill them there."

"I don't understand," the doctor said. "Why change where they are?"

"I'm the sole provider. I pay the bills, and without my money the landlord will throw them out."

She noticed him staring at her.

"Dr. Warring just terminated my work study. I used that money to pay their bills. And I'm already a few weeks behind. It's because I'm Jewish. Now I have no work, no money. I need to get my job back."

"Well, I certainly understand the stress." He looked at her. "And your symptoms. I'm sure this is all stress related."

"I really need to get my job back."

He was staring at her legs. She pushed them together. He slid closer to her. "I think I can help you," he said, and put his hand on her exposed thigh.

She looked at him innocently. "How so?"

"I know Warring well. We went to officer school together. I can talk to him for you. I can get you your job back." He slowly moved his hand up her thigh.

She looked at him in astonishment and pushed his hand away.

He said, "Or I can't. I'm not sure."

Tears welled in her eyes. Bohrsdam reached behind him with his other hand, locked the exam room door, and shut off the lights.

CHAPTER THIRTY EIGHT

Max hurt everywhere. His head, ribs, and even his eyes were a painful reminder of Marta and Hermann.

He walked past the park, and Wilhelm was not there on his bench. Max walked over to the mother at the swing set with her daughter.

"Excuse me, miss?"

She didn't look up.

He walked closer. "Excuse me, miss?" he asked again, this time louder.

She looked at him but didn't answer. It was clear she didn't want to acknowledge him.

"I can't help but ask. Every day, an old man in a long coat and black hat sits there." He pointed to the bench behind them. "Over there. He's gone. You must have seen him before.

She looked around with wide, scared eyes.

"What is it?" Max asked.

"I have to go," she said. And picking up her daughter, she started away.

"Wait, wait! Can you tell me what happened to him?" he asked.

She looked around, then turned back to Max and, as she walked away, put her finger to her mouth.

Just then Max noticed two Brown Shirts walking toward him. He turned back to look at the woman, but she was gone. Acting as if he hadn't seen them, he quickly walked away from the park.

Without turning around, he sensed he was being followed. At his apartment, fumbling with his keys, he nonchalantly turned around. The two Brown Shirts were gone.

The keys fell to the door stoop. He bent down and picked them up and inserted the door key into the lock. The door swung open. It was unlocked.

He peeked cautiously inside. The apartment was ransacked, completely destroyed. His clothes were everywhere. Glass was broken, furniture turned over. He walked straight to his nightstand. Still hidden under his textbook were Sasha's medications, untouched.

The front door swung open the rest of the way, and he turned around, startled. But it was just the breeze.

He looked around again.

The bathroom door was closed, but he could hear a *clack* and then a rattle from inside. He went to the door. Unsure whether to open it, he stood there for a moment. The rattle grew into a fast *rat-a-tat,* stopped, then started again. He tightened his grip on the doorknob, swallowed, and yanked the door open, ready for a confrontation.

The window shade flapped lazily over the open window, where the intruder had left.

Max went to the front door and locked it from inside. Then he went to the refrigerator, took out a pitcher of cold water, poured some onto a rolled towel, and put the towel around his neck. Then, with a drink of schnapps in hand, he sat down on the couch, propped his feet up on the overturned coffee table, and closed his eyes.

The knock on the door grew louder.

"Shit," he said as he looked at the medications on his nightstand. He had forgotten to bring them to his mother.

The knocking turned into pounding.

"I'm coming," he said. Grimacing from soreness, he unlocked the door.

"What the fuck happened here?" Stats asked.

Max rubbed his neck and said, "I have no idea."

"You're in a heap of shit," Stats said. "Someone doesn't like you."

Rebecca looked detached and unaffected.

"Thanks for the good news," Max said. "Look around." He pointed to his apartment. "I don't know what's going on, but you can leave now if you don't want to get involved."

Rebecca said, "Listen, we're all dealing with our own problems. And we wouldn't have come here if we didn't want to."

"Okay, follow me," Max said. "There's something you have to see." They locked the door behind them and left the apartment.

CHAPTER THIRTY NINE

Max soon noticed that they were being followed again. It was the same two Brown Shirts he had seen earlier in the park.

"Don't be obvious," he said, "but we're being followed."

"Are you shitting me?" Stats said.

"Just shut up and act normal," Max said. "Follow me. I have a plan."

He led Stats and Rebecca back inside the school.

The Brown Shirts followed them but stopped just past the gas lamps that illuminated the arcade and the courtyard that led to the main academic building. Five minutes later, Rebecca emerged by herself. She walked away from the school, headed south. Three minutes after that, Stats emerged. He walked north.

One of the Brown Shirts followed him. Ten minutes elapsed, and Max waited inside. Watching from a window corner, he saw the remaining Brown Shirt look around and then enter the school through the main entrance.

Stats walked at a brisk pace, two blocks ahead of his follower. As soon as he saw the opportunity, he ducked into an alleyway, where the Brown Shirt couldn't see him.

He slid in between two buildings. At the sound of approaching footsteps, he slid deeper into the recess.

The Brown Shirt walked slowly past him, deeper into the alley. Stats kept still, and eventually, the Brown Shirt moved on.

Max went down the stairs on the other side of the school's entrance, then out a window and through a fire escape, before the Brown Shirt could find him.

The three rejoined each other under the old larch tree.

"Okay, we should be fine now," Max said. "I don't see anyone, so let's go." And off they went. They hopped a neglected old wooden fence, crossed briefly on to someone's private property, and then left it to walk down a vacant dirt road.

The road ended at a large, open fallow field. The moon was a mere sliver, but it was enough for them to follow the narrow dirt path.

"There." Max pointed across the field to a tumble-down old barn. They walked toward it.

Outside the barn door, Max looked at a twig wedged between the door and the frame. "We're fine," he said. He opened the door. The twig fell from the frame. He picked it up and placed it in his pocket.

The place looked abandoned except for the light of a flickering candle in the far corner. Behind it, the dimly lit figure of a man sat under the hayloft.

CHAPTER FORTY

Stats could scarcely credit his own eyes. But then, it had been a long, crazy day. He turned to Rebecca. "How can this be?" he whispered.

Rosenthal stood up. He looked better than they remembered him. He had a beard now, but he didn't look scruffy.

"Hello, Jakob, Rebecca," he said. "I'm sure you're a bit surprised to see me."

"Surprised?" Stats said. "You might say."

"I'll explain." He sat back down on the dirt and leaned against an upright supporting the hayloft. "I tried warning you. I did. That night at Hofbrau, I knew the Nazis were taking over the school. Every day, someone else got fired. I knew I was next. And then it happened."

"What?" Stats asked.

"A bunch of thugs beat the hell out of me. The night of grand rounds. I had no choice." He grinned. "So I committed suicide." He looked at Max. "Max helped me. He knew the plan the whole time."

They looked at Max. He shrugged.

"Our plan was simple. The key was to keep people out of the classroom while I was hanging there. I had a special collar that the noose was tied to. The noose was never really around my neck. It just looked that way from a distance. Max was instructed to give people only glimpses through the glass pane in the door—no close-up views." He stopped for a moment.

Rebecca said, "Are you serious?"

"The two men who took me to the morgue were part of the plan. They're part of an underground. They took me down and put me in the body bag. It had holes so I could breathe. It worked perfectly. And do you know why it worked?" He paused. "It worked because people saw only what they wanted to see: a disgraced teacher, a Jew who committed suicide. No one cared to look any closer."

The candle was down to a stub, and when it started to gutter, Rosenthal lit a fresh one with it.

"Once in the morgue, they took me out of the body bag and put another body bag, filled with potatoes, in the crematorium. I was cremated. I'm dead. I don't exist. Thanks to the underground, here we are."

Stats and Rebecca gaped in disbelief. This was all too much, too fast.

Finally, Stats looked at Max and said, "Okay, Houdini. What happens now?"

Instead of replying, Max just turned to Rosenthal.

"Resistance groups," Rosenthal said. "They started in response to the chaos, to set up rescues." He picked up a twig and scratched on the dirt floor of the barn, with the same scrawling hand he once used on the chalkboard.

"The underground is now organized. It consists of mostly Poles. There are some fringe groups of Danes and French, but they're less organized." He scratched circles in the dirt floor representing each group. "But most of the groups are Poles."

He looked up at each of them to see if they listened. Stats shook his head in disbelief. Rebecca looked away as if distracted.

"Pay attention." Rosenthal snapped his fingers in front of Rebecca.

"These fighters"—he pointed to the scratched circle representing the Poles—"they just want to beat the shit out of Brown Shirts. So whenever they hear about an incident, when a Jew is attacked, they stage an ambush and get revenge."

"What's the point here?" Stats asked. "Is someone else about to rise from the dead?"

"Here's the point . . ." He scribbled "ZWZ" in the dirt and underlined it. "This is Związek Walki

Zbrojnej—the Union of Armed Struggle. The underground, and Stefan Rowecki commands them."

"So what?" Stats asked impatiently. "I'm still not getting the point of all this."

Rosenthal gave him an annoyed look.

"It's rumored he has a direct line of communication with Roosevelt."

"I'm sure," Stats said, "And next you're going to tell us he walks through walls."

"Anyway, I had no idea how to contact him. After poking around some, I got information through some colleagues at the University of Warsaw. Some of the professors there were 'strategic consultants,' if you get my meaning."

Stats rolled his eyes.

Max turned to Stats and said, "Would you settle down, please."

"I informed a contact that I was being targeted. Thankfully, he believed my paranoid predictions, and I became one of their rescue projects. I knew I was being set up, and I knew I had to be smuggled out before they could get to me. I just had no idea *how*."

"This is a bit much," Rebecca said. "Max, are you buying all this?"

"There's more," Rosenthal said. "Rowecki was the first to help me. He worked through some Jews in New York, and they created a well-funded underground rescue effort. They stated their mission quite simply: Find the scientists and physicians." He nodded to each of them. "Rescue them and bring them to New York. Academic appointments in New York will be arranged."

He cleared his throat. "We . . . we're their first project. This effort had to be staged immediately. Otherwise, I . . . well, who knows what would have happened."

"I'm sorry," Stats said, rubbing his head. "You can understand how we might have a hard time believing this."

"So why are we here?" Rebecca asked.

"It's coming," Max said.

"I'm getting to that." Rosenthal drew another figure and scrawled "US" under it, then drew a line connecting it to Europe.

"The mission's very clear: smuggle me out of Europe. It would require many drop-offs and pickups, all orchestrated by strangers."

"We get the point." Rebecca nodded to Stats and Max. "But I still don't see why we're here."

He ignored the comment and scratched a stick figure into the dirt floor. "A Polish farmer will hide us and then take us to another location." He connected the stick figure to another stick figure. "A German housewife will help next. We move only at night.

"One mistake, and the entire mission could be blown and the escape route compromised. Everyone, including the underground helping us, would be killed. Everyone." He put the twig down and looked up for approval.

Stats said, "Escape routes? Farmers? German housewives? This is crazy." He looked to Max "What did you get me into?"

"Max," Rebecca said, "this is crazy. You think I'm doing this? Is *that* why you brought us here?"

Rosenthal interrupted. "I'm sure this must seem overwhelming, but wait. I need to explain more."

"I can't listen anymore," Stats said, "I'm really going to hang myself if I have to hear any more of this. A *real* hanging—none of this pretend bullshit."

Rosenthal sighed. "I'm not doing a good job of explaining."

"Damn right you're not," Stats said.

"Okay, listen. A formalized escape plan has been set in motion. It's to rescue me and others like me—like you . . . and you, and you."

"No, no, no!" Stats said, pointing back at Rosenthal, then Max and then Rebecca. "No way."

"Yeah, you can forget it," Rebecca said.

Max remained quiet while Rosenthal picked up the stick and began drawing a map with X's and lines and circles.

"Enough with the drawings," Stats said.

"The escape route starts in Memmingen . . . right here." He pointed with his stick.

"From Memmingen to Innsbruck."

"*Austria?*" Stats asked.

Rosenthal continued, "From there, we cross into Italy over the Brenner Pass. From Italy, back over to Spain. And, finally, from Spain, we cross the Atlantic to New York."

"That's insane," Stats said. "Count me out.

"If all goes according to plan—"

"And, of course, nothing ever does."

"We'll cross the Atlantic as stowaways on a cruise ship." Rosenthal laid the stick down and sat back. "You have to trust me."

Rebecca said, "Trust *you?*"

"A lot of people have gone to great risk and expense to set this route up for us. I've already provided your names for the underground. If you're in, you must meet me in two days in Memmingen." He circled the area in the dirt. "Listen to me." He stared at Rebecca and Stats. "If you want to get out, this is your chance—maybe your last chance."

They looked at each other.

"One more thing, and this is critical. You can tell no one. If you want out, it's that simple. I'm sorry."

Stats and Rebecca looked at each other in disbelief.

"I'm dead already," Rosenthal said. "No one would believe I'm alive. It'll be much easier for me to get to Memmingen unnoticed."

"I've had enough," Stats said, standing up. "Come on, Rebecca, let's go."

"Think about it," Rosenthal said as they walked to the farmhouse door. "Memmingen. Forty-eight hours."

Before they walked away, Max took the twig from his pocket and replaced it between the barn door and the frame.

They walked quietly home together.

Rosenthal had set something in motion that could not be undone. Their lives had been changed, and each seemed to know it.

CHAPTER FORTY ONE

Hermann and his cronies huddled together in that same familiar alley where they had brutalized the innocent old Hasid. Garbage cans and debris were strewn all around them.

"What do you mean, you lost them?" he asked his two brown-shirted comrades.

Hermann flung a glass bottle against the wall and stamped his foot, like a child having a temper tantrum. "He's a criminal. He stole from the pharmacy. That means he stole from Germany. He must pay. Any Jew who commits a crime must be punished to the fullest extent of the law!" He waved his finger in the air and moved about as if addressing thousands of people.

"We followed them into the school," one Brown Shirt said, "and then we lost them."

"Just like that?"

"Yes."

"They vanished into thin air—*poof*?"

"I'm sorry, but it happened."

"This happens, too!" Hermann took out his sheath knife and held it up to the Brown Shirt's throat while holding his neck with the other arm so he couldn't break free. The Brown Shirt didn't move. Hermann turned the knife into his skin and made a small cut, just enough to make a thin trickle of blood.

"I should kill you." Hermann looked at him with disgust.

He pulled the knife away from his neck, bent down and picked up a discarded rag, and wiped the blade clean, then slid the knife back into its sheath.

"We have two days before Goebbels visits Breslau. The university must be cleansed before he gets here. I want him to know I did it. I'll speak to Warring about this. He can help us."

CHAPTER FORTY TWO

Dr. Jessner was visibly shaken. He had lost his two best professors: Jadassohn first, to resignation, and then Rosenthal, to suicide. On his desk lay an unopened letter, its envelope stamped with a red swastika. He stared at it, willing it to vanish. He had opened at least twenty such letters over the past few months—more of them lately.

He could recite the letter without reading it. It was the same old party line, and he was tired of being the bearer of bad news to his colleagues. Every letter meant another firing.

He had to explain that a younger, "more committed" professor had been selected to replace them. "What am I to do now?" or "What will I tell my wife?" or "Where will I go?" or some variant of the question was the whimpered response.

"Science is passing you by," he would say, not believing it for a minute. "You're not publishing enough, and the budget demands that we keep only published faculty. It's not me who decrees these changes."

They knew they would never work again in academia, that their life's work was over and their achievements nullified.

He lied and said, "It'll be fine. You can look for a position at another university; you have a solid résumé"—even though he knew that it was only a matter of months before any publication they had written would be officially denounced by the state as fraudulent. They would be branded as plagiarists. A letter to the editor would specify an SS officer as the original author of the work.

Jessner knew the motions and knew that he had a hand in them. He was an accomplice, and his own high reputation in the halls of academe legitimized lies as truth.

Everything he held as sacred was destroyed, and he couldn't wash his hands of it. He felt weary of seeing research, scientific methods, textbooks, and journals replaced by propaganda. He was a pawn of the "new intellectualism." The guilt was taking its toll.

To make matters worse, the past few weeks, he had been stripped of more and more of his authority. Foolishly, he had thought that he would be spared. He had even told his wife that "given the scope of my work," they were not at risk.

He defended his being the hatchet man terminating the other doctors, as necessary for budgetary reasons. Just today, he had explained to his wife that in this economy, they "can't keep tenured professors who don't create research revenue. It's that simple."

He told his children that no one was to worry, that if the university was to remain an academic world leader, he was a critical component of that objective.

The only problem was, he no longer believed his own lies. His position as dean had become irrelevant. Staff no longer reported to him. It had become clear to him that his position was expendable. He was the last remaining Jew on faculty, with no else to fire.

He stared at the unopened envelope on his desk, knowing that this time, the bells tolled for him.

CHAPTER FORTY THREE

By the time they returned from the barn, it was morning. With little time before Warring's class, Stats headed straight to school. The thought of making a decision with such little notice seemed foolhardy. Just thinking about it made him feel queasy. For now, it seemed that the best decision was no decision at all. So he went to class.

Rebecca sat down beside him.

"Headache," Stats muttered.

"Want to talk about it?" she asked, and gave him a grim smile.

"Not now. Belly, too." He put his hand on his stomach.

Rebecca rolled her eyes, "After class?"

He massaged his temples and shook his head.

Max walked in and sat down nervously.

"What's wrong with you?" Stats asked.

"He's here," Max said, sliding down in his chair as if to make himself inconspicuous.

"Who?"

"One of the Brown Shirts who followed us yesterday. He followed me to class, and he's standing in the hall, outside the door."

Stats glanced casually through the window in the classroom door. The Brown Shirt was staring into the room.

"What are you supposed to do now?" Stats asked Max.

"I don't know." Max was visibly shaken.

Stats whispered to Max. "I can't do it. I can't make a decision without more time. I just can't get up and leave in the middle of the night."

Max glanced back out at the Brown Shirt.

Professor Warring walked into class thirty minutes late, looking strangely unkempt. He placed his books on the teaching podium, pulled his shirt and coat straight, and then pushed his hair back and started lecturing.

He scrawled a picture of a kidney on the board and tried to explain "ion fluxes of sodium and potassium through the kidneys and the loop of Henle." But the material appeared to be too much for him, and he quickly erased the chalkboard and started again.

"The ion fluxes through the loop create a balance of hydrostatic pressure, hydration, and then urination maintains blood pressure and the body's balance of fluid and electrolytes . . ." Stats knew he had it all wrong. He thought about correcting him but decided against it.

"At the end of the week, there will be an exam, so you must understand this." Warring pointed to the arrows showing ion fluxes.

"What about you?" Stats muttered to Rebecca under his breath.

Warring gave him a hard look, then sat down at his desk for a few minutes, reorganizing his lecture notes. At last, he stood up and said, "Class dismissed."

They stood up in front of their seats.

"I don't think I can do it, either," Rebecca said. "How am I supposed to leave without even telling anyone? This is all so overwhelming . . ." She stuffed her book and notebook into her purse. "My parents would be lost. They'd have no idea. They can't survive without me. And besides I think I'm still getting my job back. Bohrsdam said he would help me."

"The clinic doctor?" Stats groaned. "Don't hold your breath."

"Well, what if something happens to them because we've left?" Rebecca asked Max.

By now most of the class had got up from their seats and left the classroom.

Marta walked past Max and stopped just inside the door.

"Obviously that's a risk," Max said. Then he called out to Marta and jogged over to her.

"It's not one I'm willing to take, asshole" Stats called out after him, annoyed at seeing him run back to Marta like a trained dog to its master. "Dumbass," he muttered as he and Rebecca squeezed past Marta and walked away.

Marta said, "What's wrong with him?"

"Forget him," Max replied. "Lets talk about why Hermann would want to hurt *me*."

"I can't say why he does what he does," she said. "You know Hermann. He can be very difficult."

"Actually, I *don't* know Hermann and difficult isn't exactly the description I would use."

"C'mon, let's get a cup of coffee and discuss, " she grabbed his arm and led him out of the classroom.

Max looked over his shoulder and out of the corner of his eye, he saw the Brown Shirt following them. They walked through the line in the cafeteria and ordered coffee. Max paid for both.

"That's not necessary," she said.

"I know."

They found a quiet corner table and sat.

"Why?" Max asked.

"I don't know. He can be strange . . . difficult. I don't understand everything he does. I don't think I even want to."

"Well, how about because he's fucking *crazy*? One moment, he's a friend; the next, he's pounding me into the dirt." He looked at her for a sign of understanding.

She looked back at him with no more empathy than a china doll. She held the coffee mug with both hands and sipped.

"I don't know if it was because I know he cheated, or what," he said, fishing for her to offer some insight.

"Why don't you let it rest?" she said. "Forget about it. He probably already has."

"Honestly, I'm scared of him." He paused. "Anyway, I have other things to worry about."

"What do you have going on that we don't?" She put her coffee down and looked at him.

"C'mon. You must see, it's different for me than for you."

"What do you mean?"

"This school's turning upside down. Look at Warring. He has no idea what he's doing. How is he our teacher? It's a joke. They get rid of Rosenthal and replace him with some Gestapo monkey. You've got to be kidding me."

Marta looked around as he spoke. "No one got rid of Rosenthal . . ." She looked around them. "You might want to keep it down," she said. "Listen, Max, even if you're right and everything's changed, it does you no good to worry about it. You can't control it, so you might as well adapt. I am."

"It's easier for you."

"Not really. I'm in no better place than you. My father left us with nothing but debt. My family name's a liability." She sipped her coffee and looked away. People are passionate about what's happening, and the consensus is, it's for the better."

"Consensus? For the *better*? Are you serious?"

"This is much bigger than you or me," she said. "It's not about medical school anymore."

Max watched her as she spoke. He was still hypnotized by her beauty.

"Adapt to a changing environment," she said. "If we don't adapt, we die. I'm adapting."

They both sat quietly.

"Okay," Max said, "but there's something that I need to tell you—something you won't believe."

CHAPTER FORTY FOUR

After class, Stats went to the infirmary to follow up on his lab test.

"Hello," he said. "I'm here for my test results. My name is Jakob—"

Before he could give his last name, the receptionist interrupted him. "Yes, of course. Please have a seat for a moment. The nurse will be with you."

She acted with an eerie familiarity. Stats looked around at the empty waiting room. The nurse didn't come out, but Bohrsdam did.

He was brusque today. No smile. He said, "Come with me."

In the exam room, Bohrsdam slammed the door behind him.

"Sit down," he commanded. "Do you take me for some kind of fool?"

Stats sat speechless.

"You lied to me. "You're a homo." He looked at Stats and laughed. "A Jew queer. What were you thinking?"

Stats was shaking.

"You must have made Warring mad as hell, too."

Stats felt as if his body were weakening and falling to the ground.

"He issued orders, and men were sent to your house. But you wouldn't know that, would you? Oh, yes, you're a lucky one. You weren't home last night, so relax, you're fine."

He stood close and whispered into Stats's ear, "But they found a friend of yours. I have his dossier right here."

He picked up a file folder from the desk. The flap read "Herschel Stern," in red ink.

"What did you do to him?"

"It's not what *I* did to him. I did nothing. I'm a physician. I help the weak and heal the sick."

Stats asked again, "What did you do to him?"

"Did you not hear me the first time? I understand he slept in your bed. He was still in his pajamas. They woke him up looking for you, but asked him a few questions instead."

Stats stared straight ahead. He said nothing. He looked at the exam room door. It was closed and locked. He was trapped in the room. The only thing on his mind was Herschel.

"He gave them all the answers they needed."

"What did they do to Herschel?"

"They left him there. He's at home. I don't think he's going anywhere."

"What'd you mean?"

"You had a Louisville Slugger in your house. That's right, isn't it? One of those bats from American baseball? A number thirty-three, I believe." Again he whispered. "They mentioned that the crack of the bat against his skull sounded more like a double then a home run." He smiled and sat back in his stool.

Stats stared as Bohrsdam pulled three black and white photos from the folder.

"Here you go. Here's a good picture. You can see right here . . ." He pointed. "Right over the temporal artery, that's just where they hit him."

Stats stared at the image of Herschel lying on the floor, in his pajamas, curled in the fetal position. The floor was bloody. Stats started to cry.

Bohrsdam said, "You started this. You know, I really think this was supposed to be you." He held the photo up as if admiring it. "In an odd way, you should be happy you weren't there. You missed all the excitement. I guess some things happen for a reason." He paused, as if struck with an idea. "So tell me, where were you?"

CHAPTER FORTY FIVE

Rebecca gently pushed aside the thinning gray hair around her father's sunken temples and kissed his forehead. Then she turned to look at her mother. Only white wisps remained of her once beautiful thick brown hair. Her varicose calves looked like a road map, and the rusty speckling had grown darker.

They both sat silently, scarcely aware that Rebecca had entered the room. Almost robotically, her mother got up from her chair, poured her father a glass of cold milk, and brought it to him while he sat and stared at his paper.

He smiled and continued to read his paper, as if all were well. Rebecca hugged her mother and received a blank stare and a weary smile.

She watched the paper list and fall onto his lap as he began snoring softly.

A tear rolled down her cheek. She felt her mother's hand catch the tear just before it reached her jaw. Feeling the loving touch, Rebecca closed her eyes and pulled the hand close. She put it over her heart and wept.

Her mother put her other hand behind Rebecca's head. "What's wrong, honey? Don't worry, it'll be all right." As if her mom somehow knew what she was going through.

"I just love you so much."

"We love you, too, honey."

She placed her hand on Rebecca's, and they passed a few quiet minutes together. Then her mother looked back at her as if seeing her for the first time today. "What's wrong, honey?" she said. "Don't worry, it'll be all right."

CHAPTER FORTY SIX

Hermann and one of his cronies stood in front of the school. He was ready to attack again, and this time it wouldn't be for thrills. This time it would be serious.

"He's with Marta now, in the cafeteria," the Brown Shirt said.

"Marta knows what she has to do," Hermann replied. "She'll do it."

In the cafeteria, Marta put her finger up to Max's mouth to shush him. "I want to tell you something first," she said. "Let's leave here."

They got up from the table, and she took him by the hand and led him to the staircase. In the stairwell, she pushed him back into a corner. No one was there. She kissed him passionately on the lips. In that moment, all Max's pent-up tension became a part of that kiss. Her lips and her touch were overpowering. He closed his eyes, and for a moment he was somewhere else. When she pulled away, he pulled her closer. She kissed him once more, pulled away, and ran up the stairs and out the door.

Max, drunk on that long, delicious kiss, followed. But as soon as he opened the door, he caught a blow to the base of the jaw. His head snapped back, and he reeled with the impact, back against the closing door of the stairwell. The next punch caught him in the diaphragm, and he gasped for breath. Then he took a punch to the kidney and arched backward in pain.

He saw his attackers through a corner of his eye. The two Brown Shirts stood above him, laughing. His legs gave out, and the world went dark.

CHAPTER FORTY SEVEN

Max awoke tied to a chair, his hands bound behind him. Everything hurt, and he couldn't hold his head up, so he stared down at the rough wooden floor. His chair wobbled.

A familiar voice started talking. He heard the sound of a chair sliding closer to him. He smelled a cigarette and heard feet shuffle on the floor.

"There was this nice country house," the voice said. "The house sat on a hill. The hill sat above a valley. The valley was illuminated by the sun."

A puff of cigarette smoke enveloped him.

Hermann spoke again. "By outward appearances, all was normal in this house. It was a storybook house, and inside was a family. The family was beautiful. There was a mom and there was a sister. All was well."

Max summoned his strength, raised up his head, and looked directly at Hermann.

Hermann studied his cigarette. "But if you looked closely, if you could peer inside the house, maybe through a broken window, you might notice that something is terribly wrong. Something is missing. Some*one* is missing. The mother and her daughter are weeping. Now, here's the best part. Listen carefully. I'm not sure you'll understand this . . ." He stood up and walked behind Max, then came back around and leaned down, close to his face.

"Imagine that the house can be lifted up—just picked right up off the ground and held in my two hands." He cupped both his hands. "And then imagine that I can shake it. I shake it up and down, this way and that." He moved his hand as if shaking imaginary dice. "Everything and everyone inside the house gets turned upside down. The furniture gets thrown all over, clothes spill out of dressers, the china breaks, and the people inside . . . well, you know what happens to the people inside. They get tossed all about like a salad. Bruised and beaten. Their house and their world are shaken. There's no foundation, no relief."

"Why?" Max asked. And he felt a tear roll down his cheek.

"Wait. I'm not done yet. Or maybe I am. I stop shaking the house. I put the house down." He mimed placing something down gently on the floor.

"And I rest for a few minutes. For a moment, the house is back in its perfect place, right on the hill, overlooking the valley. The family is relieved, but they're hurt, and are they ever scared!"

Neither spoke, and in the silence, Max heard a slow drip of water onto a hard surface.

"I know you weren't in your apartment last night, and you obviously weren't at home. We did look for you, though. We had to, you know. So we asked the next best person: your sister, Sasha. That is her name, right?"

He waited for Max to answer. Again, silence.

"So sweet. So innocent. She and your mom were trembling. 'We don't know,' they said. So we asked them again, 'Where's Max?' This time we weren't so friendly, and I finally realized that your sister and your mom really had no idea where you were." He sat back down and pulled his chair up close.

"That's when your sister started shaking and jumping and, whatever we want to call it—convulsing, choking, gagging? *Seizing.* Yes, that's it."

We just sat there and laughed. We laughed and laughed. It was so funny. I think she urinated on herself. I do. I really do.

"Your mom watched, too. Well, maybe, at first, she tried to help, but I think she regretted that."

Hermann scratched the back of his head as if puzzling over something.

"Maybe if you had been there, it could have been different, but when your mom tried to butt in, then I lost my temper."

Max felt his breath quicken. He rocked the chair from side to side. It creaked with each movement.

"Listen, don't blame me. I didn't kill your sister. I think she choked, or something. Probably gagged on her own vomit. Whatever it was, she passed out, stopped breathing. Your mom did yell something about her medication, but with all the commotion, I really couldn't understand her."

Max's head drooped again, and he felt his lower lip quiver. His mouth was dry, and he couldn't swallow. The room spun.

"You may think the blood is on my hands, but I'm afraid it's on yours. If you'd been home, this would never have happened. It's your fault. Your sister and your mom, well, they're both gone now."

Max turned his head and vomited. "Just kill me," he murmured.

"Hmm?" Hermann said. "I'm sorry, did you say something?"

Max didn't speak.

"Maybe, maybe not," he said, answering himself. "I need to think about this a bit more. Decisions, decisions. I'm not sure yet." He took one last puff of his cigarette and ground it out on Max's forearm. Max gasped from the pain.

Hermann walked out of the room. He shut off the light, and Max heard the door lock click behind him.

CHAPTER FORTY EIGHT

Stats sat in silence as Bohrsdam continued his rant. The words blurred together and became background noise. He mentally removed himself from the confrontation. Now he watched Bohrsdam as if he were watching a movie. Bohrsdam became an actor on the screen, flat and two-dimensional, not real, not *here.*

Stats closed his eyes and willed everything to be gone. But when he opened them, he felt the walls of the tiny examination room close in on him. He needed to get away.

He could not shake the image of Herschel's body, lying bludgeoned on the floor.

Again he became aware of the man in a white lab coat, sitting there on his little round examination stool. Bohrsdam was small and thin. He was a bastard, all right, and probably a killer, but he was no soldier. All he had to compensate for his physical frailty was his position and an arrogant, pompous attitude.

Stats's eyes darted around the exam room. While Bohrsdam continued to speak, he noticed things in his immediate environment: a half-filled glass syringe on the counter, with a metal hub and a four-inch 20-gauge steel needle. Next to it sat a beaker of alcohol, used to cleanse the skin before administering the shot.

Then he saw the rubber-headed reflex hammer that Babinski, a brilliant French neurologist, had created in 1912 to elicit central nervous system reflexes. The handle was solid metal—a potential weapon.

While Bohrsdam ranted on, Stats concluded that the hammer had too much rubber to be useful as a weapon. But also on the counter, beside the hammer, was a stethoscope. He knew what he would do, but he had to act fast.

As Bohrsdam continued to rail about how the Jews and sexual deviants—and Jewish sexual deviants—were destroying the Fatherland, Stats reached over to his right, picked up the glass syringe with the long metal needle, and jammed it into the side of Bohrsdam's neck.

Taken completely by surprise, Bohrsdam reached up to grasp the syringe. His eyes were wide with fear, anger, and astonishment. But before he could pull out the syringe, Stats had the stethoscope and whipped it around the frail neck. With the headset in his right hand, the tubing and diaphragm in his left, he pulled hard.

He heard the soft snap of throat cartilage, and a gasp as Bohrsdam's knees buckled. Without letting go of the stethoscope, Stats caught him as he fell. Bohrsdam's eyes rolled backward, and his breathing stopped. After knotting the stethoscope to keep the blood flow from Bohrsdam's brain, Stats left the examination room, nodding to the receptionist on the way out.

Walking nonchalantly down the stairs, he forced himself to go slowly and left the building as if he hadn't a care in the world. There was no going home, so he went to the only safe place he knew.

CHAPTER FORTY NINE

As evening fell, Marta sat alone in her apartment and read the letter a third time: "For exemplary work for the Fatherland, you have been accelerated through your academic curriculum. The position of chief resident of surgery awaits you upon completion of your clinical rotations."

Marta smiled to herself. She had done it. Hermann had delivered. She had kept her end of the deal, and he had kept his. She wished her father could see this. She would have liked to show him how she didn't need him. She could manage on her own. She didn't need *anybody*. Whatever she needed to do, she did. That was life. The strong survived because the strong saw the opportunity and seized it. She was strong. She had survived. Sure, it was at someone else's expense, but then, she hadn't created this situation. What was wrong with taking advantage of it?

She poured herself a drink and lit a cigarette. Hermann was supposed to meet her here in an hour. She drained the vodka with one gulp and thought about Max for a moment.

What a fool, tricked by a kiss. She poured herself another glass of vodka.

Not as proud of herself now, she felt alone and a little sad. She looked at the letter again and remembered the last kiss with Max, this time with a tinge of guilt. She thought about Hermann. The idea of him coming over disgusted her. She felt dirty every time he left. She drained the glass and looked out at the darkening city.

CHAPTER FIFTY

Stats hoped that Rebecca would remember the promise she had made him give her. Almost twenty-four hours had passed since he met with Rosenthal, and if he was to make it to Memmingen in time, he had one day to travel 603 kilometers.

This could be a challenge. It would take just over six hours by train, but Rosenthal was not leaving from Memmingen until midnight, so Stats actually had almost eighteen hours.

He sat back against the old larch tree and waited.

He heard movement a few yards away. A twig snapped, and leaves rustled as footsteps drew near. A fox, perhaps. No, something larger . . . a deer—or Brown Shirts. They must have seen him leave the school. Maybe they know he had killed Bohrsdam.

He pressed himself back against the tree, wishing he could melt into its bark. He could see nothing, so he focused on the sounds. The steps came closer. He closed his eyes tighter and held his breath.

Out of the darkness, a hand touched his shoulder.

"Shit!" he gasped.

"What the hell are you doing?" Rebecca asked.

"You scared the crap out of me," Stats said.

"Who were you expecting?"

" Brown Shirts."

"What happened to you? You look like you've seen a ghost."

"You won't believe it if I tell you," he said. "Anyway, we don't have time. Where's Max?"

"I don't know. I went by his apartment to find him. He wasn't there . . ."

"Well, what are we supposed to do? We don't have a lot of time."

"I checked the train schedule," she said. "There's one that passes through Drowzec Glowney at five a.m. and makes it to Memmingen by noon. That gives us five hours to find Max and get aboard."

"So where do we find him?" He threw up his arms in frustration.

"I don't know. Think of something. When we left him, he was with Marta at the cafeteria."

"We need to go to her apartment." He started walking and then stopped. "But wait. It's almost midnight. She'll think we're crazy."

"Do you care?" Rebecca said, and walked away.

Marta heard a knock on her door. She wore a long nightshirt with nothing underneath. Hermann would go wild.

She opened the door and stood seductively behind it.

"What are you doing here?" she snapped.

"Marta, we need your help," Rebecca said.

She tried to close the door on them, but Rebecca blocked it with her foot.

"We need to find Max."

Marta didn't invite them in. "Why should I help you?"

"Listen, Marta, we don't have time," Rebecca said. "We think Max is in trouble. Do you know where he is?"

She giggled, swayed, and put her hand against the wall for balance. "You know, Hermann will be here any minute."

"We don't care about Hermann," Stats said. "Do you know where Max is?"

She looked him up and down, detesting him. She laughed again.

"Marta, you need to help us," Rebecca said.

Marta looked her over and then looked at the clock on the wall. "Fine," she said. "Come in."

She sat down at her kitchen table. An ashtray was filled with cigarette butts. One was still smoking. She gestured to them to sit down at the table. "Drink?"

Both guests shook their heads.

"Your loss." She giggled again. "Max is a really good guy," she said. "Really good guy. He kissed me tonight."

"Where is he?" Rebecca pleaded. "Marta, help us."

She ignored Rebecca's plea. "I kissed him back." She paused, picked up the bottle, and shook it. It was empty.

"Hmph!" She put the bottle back on the table. "Hermann's a bad guy. R-r-really bad guy." She giggled nervously. "Do you have any idea of the things he's done? I do. I know everything. Oh, shit. He's going to be here any minute." She touched her hair and adjusted her nightshirt.

"Marta!" Rebecca shouted, putting her arms on Marta's shoulders. "We don't have time. We need to find Max. Do you know where he is?"

"Please tell Max I'm sorry. Tell him I didn't mean to do it."

"Do what? Is he in trouble?"

"Yes," she said solemnly.

"Where is he?"

"I can't tell you. Hermann will hurt me. He'll hurt me!"

"Marta, if Max is in trouble, we can help him," Rebecca said.

"You don't understand . . ."

"Marta!"

Marta started to cry. "I didn't want anything to happen to him."

She grew distant again. "I'll be chief resident next year." She thrust the letter from Warring in front of them.

"Marta, is Max hurt?"

"It's my fault. Please tell him I'm sorry. I hate myself." Again tears started to well up in her eyes.

"Where is he?"

"I can't tell you."

"Marta, you can still help him. Tell us where he is."

"Hermann will kill me." With her palms, she wiped the tears from her cheeks.

"Marta, please help us," Rebecca pleaded.

For a brief moment, Marta felt sorry for them. She thought of Max and felt a pang of guilt and self-loathing. In those few seconds, she tortured herself with right and wrong, empathy and ambition. She heard many voices: her father yelling at her, Hermann's threats and empty promises, Rebecca's pleas.

The vodka helped, and she relented.

"Go to St. Maria Magdalena. Do you know where that is? It's the church a block south of Rynek. There are two towers. He's in one of them—the north, I think. I'm not sure which."

"You'll have to walk across the Bridge of Witches. Really, that's the name. You cross it to get to the north tower. Try the south tower first, just in case." She checked the empty vodka bottle again and held it up to the light. She saw again that it was empty, and put it back down on the table. She turned her attention back to Rebecca. "I'll keep Hermann occupied as long as possible. Go. Now. Back door."

CHAPTER FIFTY ONE

"Bridge of Witches," Stats murmured as they walked toward the church. "I hate bridges and I hate heights—not too fond of witches, either, come to think of it." He knew the legend of the bridge that wavered like a tightrope between the two towers, and that it was also known as the "suicide bridge."

"Maybe he's in the South Tower," he said to Rebecca.

"We can start there."

"I really don't want to cross that bridge," he said.

"Maybe we won't need to," Rebecca said. "Now, walk faster."

"Why couldn't he be at St. Elizabeth's?" he muttered. "It's got only one tower and no bridge."

"Can you stop worrying?" she said as they strode past the market square, known as Rynek.

Approaching St. Maria Magdalena, Stats looked up at the small bridge joining the two towers. "It looks like a damn tightrope. Are you sure this is the right place?"

"This is it," Rebecca said.

"What if she was lying?"

"There's only one way to find out." She nodded toward the stairs of the south tower. "Let's go."

In the dark stairwell, they started up the high, narrow steps.

Breathing hard, they reached the top, and Rebecca looked around them. "Okay, he's not here," she said. "We have to cross the bridge to get to the north tower."

"You go," Stats said. "I'll wait here. I'll guard the bridge for you."

"Get on the bridge!" Rebecca said.

CHAPTER FIFTY TWO

Marta and Hermann lay in her bed. She could feel the room move whenever she closed her eyes, so she did her best to keep them open.

"I'm going back to the church," Hermann said. "I have a plan that must be finished tonight, before Goebbels arrives in town tomorrow."

"Don't rush back. You'll have plenty of time."

"No. Max must hang from the bridge. Everyone in Rynek will see him. He'll be a symbol of Jewish humiliation. He'll hang like a flag, reminding all Jews that they are not safe here. He's a criminal and, even worse, a Jew and—" Hermann started to get out of bed.

"Stay a little longer," Marta said, running her hand over his chest.

He pushed her down. "I don't have time."

"Please . . ." Kissing him, she slid her hand from his chest down toward his groin.

Hermann fell back down into the bed, and she slithered over on top of him and kissed him some more.

CHAPTER FIFTY THREE

Stats crawled along the bridge, both hands keeping a death grip on the railing.

Rebecca shook her head in disbelief. "Let's go," she called from the north tower. "Get up and walk. Hermann will be up here soon."

She wasn't waiting any longer. She walked through a maze of fifteenth-century hallways until she reached a closed door. She tried to pull it open, but it wouldn't budge. She banged her fist against the door. "Max, you there?" No response. She banged harder. "Max? Can you hear me?"

No answer. She waited a few more seconds, then resumed her search through the labyrinthine halls at the top of the North Tower.

Stats finally made it across the bridge. He stopped and looked back the way he had come, then turned and yelled, "Rebecca?"

Several yards down a narrow corridor, he came to a door and tried to pull it open. No luck. He pushed, but it didn't budge. Backing up to the corridor's opposite wall, he ran at it as hard as he could and rammed the door with his shoulder. The impact of his burly frame hitting the door broke the small bolt that kept it locked, and the door swung open.

There in the middle of the room, tied to a chair, sat Max, slumped with his head down. Stats ran to him, removed the gag, and untied his hands and feet. Max looked up and managed a smile.

"Come on we don't have much time!" Stats hissed, hauling him up out of the chair.

Max held on, limping as best he could, and they made their way back down the hallway.

Stats called out to Rebecca, "Got him!"

They met in the central hallway, just off the bridge. Rebecca hugged Max, then cried when she saw how badly he had been beaten. Quickly wiping away her tears, she said to Stats, "We've got to go. Ready?"

He looked at the bridge. "Do I have a choice?"

With Max between them, they started across the bridge. It swayed a bit in the wind.

Halfway across, Rebecca said, "Hold on." She looked down to the street below them. There stood Hermann, illuminated by the full moon.

"What are we gonna do?" Stats said, hands locked around the steel cable handrails.

"We have no choice," said Rebecca. "We have to go back and hide."

"But the north tower has no exit to the street."

"If we go down the south tower, we'll meet him on the stairs. We go back to the north tower, hide, and with luck, we miss him. Then we go back up the tower and cross the bridge without him finding us."

"There's no way Max is strong enough to do that," Stats said.

"Do you have a better idea?"

He looked down to see Hermann enter the south tower.

Turning around, they recrossed the bridge to the north tower and descended the stairs. At the bottom, they found themselves in a large courtyard set about with old planters that looked eerie in the moonlight. Water-stained concrete benches, spotted with lichen from years of exposure, were arranged about an empty fountain. In between the shadows, tall weeds had grown on the courtyard floor, and the whole place was in a state of neglect.

On opposite sides were two storage sheds of concrete block, roofed with terra-cotta tiles. Each had a weathered door and a single window. Inside, it was dark, but enough light shone through the window to reveal some old furniture and broken planters.

Stats ran across the courtyard and looked into the other shed. In it were hoes, rakes, and other garden implements. He looked for some sort of exit, but the courtyard was completely enclosed by an eleven-foot wall.

"I'll go here," Rebecca said, entering the shed with the garden tools. "You hide with Max there." She pointed across to the other shed. "As soon as Hermann passes your shed, take Max back up the stairs. I'll wait and make sure you're in, and then follow right behind. If we're lucky, I can lock the door behind us so, even if he sees us run in, he'll be locked out of the tower and stuck here in the courtyard."

Stats started to argue, but he didn't have a better plan, so he and Max hid in the shadows underneath an old broken desk. They couldn't see anything unless they stood up and peered through the shed's only window, so they had to rely on their hearing.

The door leading from the staircase of the North Tower creaked open, and Hermann stepped into the courtyard.

"Max?" he called. "Where are you? I know you're here. Make this easy for both of us."

Stats held his hand over Max's mouth.

"Where are you, *mein Juden*? You have no place to run, my little rodent."

Hermann opened the door to the shed. Then the door closed, and it sounded as if he had left the shed to walk across the courtyard.

Stats waited another few moments, knowing that this was their chance. He pulled Max up and partially opened the shed door.

Peeking out, they could see Hermann's back as he headed toward the shed where Rebecca hid. They bolted out the door and ran as fast as they could to the steps of the North Tower.

Hermann turned around, and ran back toward them. Stats closed the door behind them and pushed Max up the stairs. And somehow, Max found the strength, with the support at his back, to limp back up the stairs on his own. Stats remained below long enough to find the door hasp, close it, and drop a bolt through it. Then he raced up the stairs after Max.

Hermann pounded on the door, and Stats heard him kick it. When it didn't budge, he ran at it again, and this time the hasp gave. Stats heard the door bang open, then Hermann's boots pounding up the stairs after them.

As they climbed, Max stumbled. He stopped and clutched his ribs. "Go ahead," he said. "Go. Don't wait for me." With Hermann gaining on them, Stats bent down and slung Max over his back in a fireman's carry, left arm over his right shoulder, left leg over his left shoulder, and pounded his way up the remaining stairs. At the landing at the top of the north tower, gasping for breath, he put Max down.

"Come on, Max. He's right behind us. You have to get up."

"Go on without me. I can't . . ."

"No chance. Let's go," Again Stats squatted down and slung Max over his shoulders. "We have to cross this damn bridge. Trust me, I don't want to do it any more than you."

"Stop there!" Hermann shouted as he reached the landing of the stairs.

Stats had dragged Max halfway across the bridge. "Keep going, Max," he urged. "Don't turn around."

"I'll give you one last chance. Stop now, or I'll shoot!"

At this point, Stats and Max had gotten three-quarters of the way across. Stats ignored the commands. "Come on, pal. We're just about there."

"I'm counting to three. One . . ."

"Just a few more steps," Stats panted.

"Two . . ."

"Soon as we reach the end of the bridge, I'm gonna let go of you, so fall to the ground."

"Three!"

Hearing the shot, Stats turned back to see Hermann, sprawled on the landing. Behind him stood Rebecca, holding a yard-long two-by-four, like a batter who has just taken a swing. She must have caught Hermann behind the knees, knocking him down and sending the shot wild.

"Hurry!" Stats yelled to Rebecca.

"You okay?" she asked.

"Yes! Now, run!"

She smiled as she crossed the halfway point of the bridge.

As Max smiled back, he saw Rebecca's smile turn to a grimace. Her head rolled backward, and blood spurted from her left shoulder. She stumbled to her right and fell down. Her upper body dangled over the edge of the bridge, and one ankle was hung up between two boards, which kept her from falling the forty-six meters to her death.

Hermann still lay at the far end of the bridge, barely able to wave the pistol. He gave a triumphant laugh.

Seeing Max's stare of disbelief, Stats pushed him. "Go down now," he said. "I'll catch up with you." And he ran back across the bridge toward Rebecca.

Running toward Rebecca, Stats could see Hermann crawling toward them, one hand pulling him forward while the other held fast to the gun. She must have hit him a good one, Stats thought as he pulled Rebecca back from the edge of the bridge.

"Leave me here," she said.

"Can't do that." He looked back and saw Hermann inching closer.

Stats bent down to lift Rebecca onto his shoulders.

"Get Down!" Max yelled.

Hermann held pistol with both hands, his elbows propped on the bridge landing. He fired a shot, missing Stats and Rebecca.

"Leave me!" Rebecca yelled. "Go!"

And with a heave, she pushed herself off Stats's shoulder and fell back onto the bridge. "Go now! Leave me!"

Stats didn't know what to do. He looked down at Rebecca. Her blouse was soaked with blood. He looked at Hermann, readying to shoot again.

Max yelled, "What are you waiting for? Grab her!"

"Go!" she yelled again.

"What are you doing!" Max screamed. "No!"

Stats ran back toward Max. He could see the tears in Max's eyes as he picked him up again. He carried him down the south tower and to the train station, to catch the 5:00 a.m. to Memmingen.

CHAPTER FIFTY FOUR

Stats and Max woke to the whistle of the freight train as it started to move. They had curled up on a patch of grass in a wooded area and fallen asleep. And now, it seemed, they might miss their train.

"It's time," Stats said, nudging Max. "Let's move."

They hurried back to the edge of the woods closest to the train, though still on the side of the tracks where the train blocked them from view of the platform. The whistle blew one last time, and the train began its slow initial chug down the tracks. They watched it roll slowly past them.

As the train gathered speed, a slat-sided car approached. They looked at each other, nodded, and, without a moment's hesitation, grabbed a slat and swung up onto the outer ledge of the car.

Looking over his shoulder, Stats could see the trees starting to whip past them at a faster and faster rate. The car's wooden ledge was wide enough for only their toes. They held on to the only thing they could find: an upright board framing the side of the grated door.

The cows mooed, and the boys peered through the grates at each other. They watched as the car passed by the station.

Several Brown Shirts were on the platform, inspecting each car as it passed. He ducked down beneath one the grates.

He took one hand off the upper ledge, pressed his toes into the narrow ledge outside the stock racks, and swung his free hand around to grab the cargo door. He tried to slide it open, but it wouldn't budge. The train was accelerating faster. Evergreen branches flew past, brushing the side of the train and nearly knocking them off the ledge.

Stats felt the force of gravity and wind pushing his body away from the train. He put his free hand back on and gripped the ledge with both hands.

"How are we getting in?" Max screamed over the wind. He was shivering from the cold.

"I'm not sure," Stats said.

"I can't hold on much longer."

Stats looked up at the wide gap between the top slat of the outer wall and the roof of the car.

"We climb up through there." He cocked his chin at the gap.

"How?"

"Like this . . ."

Stats climbed up the wooden slats, as if up a ladder, then thrust with his legs to launch his body into the gap between the top slat and the roof. His upper body was wedged in, his legs flailing outside the car. Slithering forward, he pushed with his arms against the inside of the door and squeezed through. He fell on the floor of the cattle car, cushioned by straw and cow dung. He stood up from the inside.

He could see that Max would not hold on much longer. "Wait!" he yelled.

Stats found the latch inside the door and began to unlatch it.

"I can't do it . . . I can't," Max yelled in through the slats. "I'm going to let go."

"No!" Stats shouted. He could see the defeat in Max's eyes.

"Hold on, just a minute more!" He shouted as he wrestled with the rusted latch. He couldn't get it free.

"I can't."

"Can you climb through like I did?" He yelled back at Max.

"Can't . . . not strong enough."

A branched brushed against Max, and one hand peeled away from the slat where he clung. His feet slipped on and off the ledge as his right hand somehow held fast.

As Stats went back to work on the latch, Max gave him an apologetic look. He bent his knees, ready to launch himself clear of the moving train.

At that moment, the latch broke free. Stats looked up to see Max crouched and about to jump.

Stats flung the door open, grabbed Max, and hauled him into the car.

They both fell back down onto the straw and dung.

CHAPTER FIFTY FIVE

Hermann was on crutches, but he still managed to stand at attention as Goebbels spoke to him.

"You did well," Goebbels said. "You really want to stay in this school? "

Hermann shook his head.

"You're a soldier. A student would never do this."

"Yes sir." Hermann stood up as straight as he could, ignoring the pain in his knees where the Jewish bitch had hit him with the board.

"We could use someone like you. There's an opening. I'm not sure you would want it, but—"

"Sir, I'm not interested in medicine. I'm committed to Germany in whatever way I can contribute most."

He could see Goebbels assessing him.

Hermann straightened his back, pushed his crutches off to the side, and ignored the pain in his leg that came with standing at attention.

"Very good, then. Reichsfuehrer SS Himmler sent me orders to urge you to join the SS. It won't happen right away. You'll have to prove yourself."

Hermann nodded eagerly.

"First, we'll assign you for clerical in Intelligence, but only for a short term. If you excel, a promotion awaits. The details of such promotion will be determined later."

Hermann smiled to himself.

"I would like to make it clear," Goebbels said, looking him in the eyes," it is Himmler's very definite desire to promote you. We're proud of you."

"Of course," Hermann said, and he threw his arm up in a Nazi salute. "Heil Hitler!"

"Heil Hitler." Goebbels waved his hand away, and Hermann quickly relaxed.

"You'll be assigned to *Abwehr*—Intelligence. We're working with a number of operatives who have been inserted into American cities. Several of these operatives are physicians and scientists. Without going into too much detail, we believe that with your medical background, you'd be of value as a liaison working with them from this side. Would this be acceptable?" he asked.

"Yes sir."

"Good. We're done here."

"Heil Hitler." Hermann gave the Nazi salute again.

"Incidentally, the young lady you delivered us has been sent to Stadelheim for illegally assisting criminals and enemies of the state," Goebbels said.

Hermann smiled.

"If she survives your gunshot, she'll need all her strength. She's scheduled for transfer at Dachau."

CHAPTER FIFTY SIX

Max awoke to the glare of morning sun and the warm splash of steer urine on his feet and ankles. Then he realized that the train had stopped.

"We're here," he said, nudging Stats, who sat beside him, slumped against the slatted wall. He pointed to the sign, barely visible through the slats. "Memmingen. Let's go before it leaves."

Sliding the heavy gate open just enough to squeeze out the door, they jumped out of the car on the side opposite the station. They lay there behind the berm and watched as the train started moving again. Finally, the last car passed them.

"You stink," Stats said to Max.

"And you smell like rose water?" Max asked.

"We need to find Rosenthal."

"He said he'd find us at Memmingen," Max said.

The station was busy with commuters and also police, marching around in green uniforms. There were five different tracks and three different platforms.

"We need to go there—the busiest one," Max said, pointing to the platform on the other side of the tracks and just over an old iron bridge. The bridge connected to the main station building. There was a water tender for steam locomotives, and an accommodation building just to the east, opposite the main station building.

They walked over, slowly at first, past the Orpo, then faster to blend in with the throng of travelers. Somehow, despite their rank smell and begrimed appearance, they found the bathroom without being noticed.

As they walked out of the bathroom, Max said, "Keep walking and don't look right. "I know one of those guys."

"Who?"

"Those two—other side of the shoeshine. Red hair, eyebrow like a privet hedge." He tilted his head toward two men walking through the station.

"Never seen 'em before," Stats said.

"I know I know them. Follow them."

The two men walked down Kalchstrabea, a commercial street, then turned off toward an old churchyard cemetery. The boys trailed them inconspicuously.

Max noticed that the cemetery had been vandalized—tombstones knocked over and broken. Such disrespect for the dead shocked him. Then he thought of Rebecca, left on the bridge, and felt an overwhelming sadness.

Cutting through the churchyard, he could no longer see the men they were following.

"Where'd they go?" He asked Stats.

"I thought you had them. Now what?"

"Let's get out of here," Max said.

Turning around, they started retracing their steps between the tombstones. They passed a large monument with several people, each with the same surname, inscribed below a large crucifix. All had perished on the same day—in a fire, perhaps.

Out of nowhere, a burly arm wrapped around his neck. In the same instant, the tall red-haired man he had recognized in the station planted his foot in the back of Stats's knee, buckling him to the ground, and had his head back as if he meant to snap it off.

He put his mouth up to Stats's ear and said in a gritty whisper, "*Vie gait es eich?*"

No answer.

Max watched as again the man asked Stats, "*Vie gaits?*"

Still no answer.

Max could see that Stats didn't understand the question.

The fat man pulled Max's head back and whispered into his ear, "*Vi ruft men eich?*"

"Max" he replied.

"Vuhin gaitsu?"

"Vuhin gaitsu?" the man repeated at Stats.

"It's Yiddish." Max yelled at Stats.

"Bagegenen a fraynd."

The man asked, "*Velkh iz zayn nomen?*"

Max looked at Stats again.

"Max!"

"Jacob," Max said, and tilted his head as best he could toward Stats.

"He's asking our names. It's Yiddish."

Then it hit him. These were the two men who had taken Rosenthal to the morgue.

Of course the Jewish underground would speak Yiddish. It was a safe test since every Jew in Germany—except, perhaps, Stats—could speak it.

The man smiled and motioned to his comrade to let Stats go. Stats pushed him away, rubbing his neck as he caught his breath. Max did the same. Both men smiled and began speaking in German.

The tall, skinny one said, "I'm sorry, but we had to make sure we had the right guys. I'm Meier." He put his hand out to Stats.

Stats didn't shake it. "Next time you decide to put the death grip on me, you better finish the job or I'll cut your balls off," he said.

"I'm Moses," the thickset man said. "Rosenthal asked us to pick you up at the station. We don't have much time. There was a third person, a woman. Where is she?"

"She didn't make it," Stats said.

"You left her," Max said.

"Fuck you. I knew that was coming. You son of a bitch, I saved your life."

"I would have been happier dead than leaving her."

Moses and Meier watched them argue. Then Moses said, "We don't have time for this. You're behind schedule."

"Where's Rosenthal?" Max asked.

"Just outside Memmingen," Moses said.

Moses and Meier led Stats and Max to the city's outskirts. They all walked separately.

One at a time, at roughly ten-minute intervals, they entered an old granite tower, through a door marked "Bismarck Tower—Maintenance Only." They walked down a flight of stairs to the basement. There, in a cavernous room of bare granite walls, they saw Rosenthal for the second time since his "suicide."

"I'm sorry about Rebecca," Rosenthal said, embracing the two boys.

"It was terrible," Max said. "Hermann shot her."

"I know." Rosenthal shook his head in sorrow.

"Life's been a blur for us the last twenty-four hours," Stats said. "We haven't slept. I don't know where we are or what we're doing here."

"I understand," Rosenthal said. "You must stay focused. If we are to make this work and get out of here, we can't dwell on what has already happened. These are difficult times."

Stats rubbed his neck and looked at Max. Max stared away.

"Gestapo are stationed at every border. Not only do they want to catch Jews before they leave, but they want to catch any of their own who are helping Jews leave."

"Are we just going to forget about Rebecca?" Max asked.

"Listen to me," Rosenthal said. "I know it's painful, but this mission had its risks. That was a risk. There's nothing you, I, or anyone can do to change that."

Max said nothing—just glared at Stats.

"I was saying, every border is alive with undercover German security.

"Yesterday at the German-Austrian border, they caught a German—not a Jew—leaving, seeking asylum. He was branded a traitor and burned alive. His family were imprisoned and tortured. So—"

"We get the point," Stats said.

"Do you? No one gives a shit about you, and no German is going to risk his neck for you. That's my point."

"I got it. What's the plan now?"

"Rowecki will meet us at Mittenwald before we cross into Innsbruck. At the border, he'll have Nazi uniforms for us to wear. We'll meet our contact at a violin factory. We'll be escorted together across the border as part of a German public relations effort."

"You couldn't conjure up anything better than a fucking PR campaign?" Stats leaned against the coarse granite wall.

Rosenthal said, "The German border patrol will be informed that the escort is part of a German propaganda exercise to foster goodwill between the two countries."

"All of a sudden, Germany cares about international opinion?"

"The border patrol will not have the authority to challenge us."

"Will they have the authority to shoot us?"

"As soon as we cross into Austria, the Austrian border patrol will take us into their offices. There, we change back and exit separately as three differently dressed civilians. We'll have a few hours before the guard realizes that the officers aren't coming back."

Stats clasped his hands over his head and narrowed his eyes.

Rosenthal continued, "After we leave the Austrian border, we won't meet again until we cross over into Spain. You'll have to make it to the Innsbruck main station on your own. Here . . ."

He reached into his coat pocket and handed each of them documents and money.

"The Underground has provided each of us with enough shillings to pay our way. You must travel alone. And if we see one another, don't bat an eyelash. Once you arrive at the station, buy a second-class ticket to Verona. The Brenner Railway is the line connecting the Austrian and Italian railways. We'll take the Brenner Pass over the Wipp Valley, descend the Eisack Valley to Bolzano, and end up in Verona."

Stats groaned. "Do I need to know all that? Just tell me where to end up."

"Can you stop interrupting?" Max hissed.

"Verona Porta Nuova—the main railway station in Verona. You'll have to change trains to reach Genoa. We board a ferry. It'll take us to Barcelona."

"How long?" Stats interrupted again. He was tapping his feet.

"Eighteen hours. So use that time to get some rest. Once we're in Barcelona, we can meet again."

"That's the cruise ship?" Stats asked.

"Yes. The *Rex.* Once we make it aboard, we should be safe. Now, get some rest. We leave in three hours."

The boys were so exhausted, they lay down on the hard floor and closed their eyes.

CHAPTER FIFTY SEVEN

"C'mon, honey, it could be a lot worse."

Rebecca didn't look up from the cold floor of the prison cell.

The guard spat on her face. "Hey, I'm talking to you, honey."

Rebecca wiped the spittle off her cheek and raised her head.

"When I'm talking to you, look at me."

She looked up at the uniformed woman standing above her.

"It could always be worse. You could be in Dachau." The guard laughed. She was strongly built, with square legs, thick ankles, and a severe face.

"What, honey? You don't like what you see? Well, you're going to."

Smiling, she grabbed Rebecca's hair so that she could not turn away.

"Lot of famous guests have come through these doors. Yup, you're in good company, honey. Real good company."

She let go of Rebecca's hair and walked to the open cell door.

"Hey, I'm talking to you," she said again.

Fighting the pain, Rebecca lifted her head.

"Not everyone ends up dead when they leave here, you know. Really. Hitler was imprisoned here, in that cell over there." She pointed across the corridor. "And look where he ended up." She laughed as if this were immensely funny.

Rebecca just listened.

"But, others . . . not so lucky. Roehm was here, too. Not a good ending for him, so forget that one. And, let's see, then there was Heydebreck. Another bad ending." She closed the door of the cell and walked away, the sound of her laughter receding with the click of her heels on the concrete.

CHAPTER FIFTY EIGHT

The facade at the Neuner violin workshop in Mittenwald was as inconspicuous as the bakery next door. Its pastel colors, window boxes, and arched wooden door reminded Stats more of a fairy-tale cottage than a violin workshop. But for whatever reason, a luthier who also worked for the underground was their next important liaison.

They entered the century-old workshop, where craftsmen sat at workbenches crowded haphazardly in small rooms. Violins hung everywhere: on windows, below windows, on any bit of free wall space. The shop master greeted the three visitors while the other craftsmen, apparently accustomed to having guests, went right on with their work. He led the visitors, one by one, into a back room, and a few minutes later, each emerged dressed in a Nazi officer's uniform.

They walked around the workshop unnoticed and, in a matter of moments, left without having spoken or made eye contact with anyone. A car waited for them beside a fountain just outside the workshop.

When they reached the border, the three of them got out of the car and made their way to the border patrol office.

"These officers are here as part of a public relations mission—direct orders from the führer's office," the Nazi officer said to the border patrol guard.

"Here are the orders." He handed the border guard a folded document bearing official stamps. "You're to escort them across the border. They will inspect the Austrian side. This mission is part goodwill and"—here he winked—"also information gathering. You understand, don't you?"

The border patrol nodded in agreement.

"We need to confirm that no one on their side is stashing weapons or getting up to mischief. Make sure the borders are not compromised. "Public relations, okay?"

"Of course, understood," the border guard replied.

He took the papers, looked through them in a perfunctory manner, and handed them back to the Nazi officer.

"They are to be accorded every courtesy. Understood?"

The border guard gave a crisp Nazi salute, and Stats, Max, and Rosenthal clicked their boot heels, returned the salute, and said, "Heil Hitler!"

"When their inspection is complete, the Austrian patrol will escort them back to you." The officer clicked his heels, gave them a vigorous "Heil Hitler," and left.

The checkered red and white border gate was raised, and the three men in Nazi uniforms walked across to the Austrian side. There, a border guard in drab green trench coat and round gray helmet, with a rifle strapped on his back, escorted them to a small office.

They walked into the office, where a man in a three-piece gray suit, with a white pocket square in a three-point fold, sat on a worn olive-green sofa. The only other furniture was a wooden desk, bare except for a telephone and an ashtray full of butts. The man in the suit sat with his legs crossed, looking perfectly comfortable in his shabby surroundings. He took a last puff of his cigarette, walked over to the desk, and crushed the butt out in the ashtray, then stuck out his hand.

"Anselm Grand."

Rosenthal shook his hand. "Rowecki?" he asked.

"Yes, of course, who else? I'm Frontmiliz. We work with the Poles, and we're all connected to keep the bastards from winning." He walked over to the window. "We bought an hour. After that, he comes back in." He nodded toward the border guard. "By then, you'd better be long gone."

"Our clothes?" Rosenthal asked.

"There." He pointed to a small bathroom in the corner. Beside the toilet lay a large unopened suitcase.

"Thank you," Rosenthal said, walking over and opening the suitcase. He threw Max and Stats their clothes.

They quickly shucked off their Nazi uniforms, put on their civilian clothes, and stuffed the uniforms back in the suitcase.

Grand said, "You're all set, then," and walked to the door. "Godspeed"

"Wait," Rosenthal said. He handed him the suitcase with the Nazi uniforms.

Grand took it, opened the door, and walked out.

Rosenthal said to the boys, "We wait a half hour and then leave, one at a time, at five-minute intervals."

The three of them sat in silence as twenty-five minutes ticked by on the wall clock.

Stats turned to Max. "How you doing?"

"Not so good."

"I know."

"I could have done more." He looked down. "I should have done more. My sister . . . my mom . . . Rebecca."

"It wouldn't have mattered," Stats said. "Listen, this isn't your fault. Everything's crazy. Nothing's normal anymore. They'd want you to get out. It's what they'd want. Otherwise, their pain, their suffering—well, it just doesn't matter."

Stats put a hand on his friend's shoulder. "Remember, no one gives a shit about us. No one cares. We have to get through this. Somehow get lucky."

"I don't know," Max said, and looked away.

Rosenthal walked over to them. "Shilling notes for the trains." He handed them each an envelope. "And peseta notes when you get to Spain."

The boys took the envelopes and put them in their pockets.

"Be careful. You're on your own now. Trust no one. And don't draw attention. I'll see you in Spain." He started to walk away, then turned around.

"We'll share a drink on the ship. You're almost there. Good luck, boys."

Rosenthal had a sparkle in his eye and a confident smile as he walked out the door and was gone.

"You're next," Stats said to Max. "See you in Barcelona."

Max said, "Rosenthal says he'll get us into a medical school in New York. We can still be doctors."

"Whatever gets you to the other side of this crazy world."

They got up and embraced.

"See you on the other side," Stats said to Max.

Max turned around, smiled back at Stats, and walked out the door.

CHAPTER FIFTY NINE

Admiral Wilhelm Franz Canaris's silver hair and aristocratic features suited him well for politics, but perhaps even better for espionage. He never gave off the slightest clue to what he was thinking, and this kept Hermann constantly on guard. At any time, those blue-gray eyes could shift between icy and caring. Meanwhile, his brilliant success as a spy had given Hitler little choice but to promote him to chief of the Abwehr.

"Have you heard of the Amerikadeutscher Bund?" Canaris asked Hermann.

"Sir?" Hermann asked politely.

"Your desk will be over there," Canaris said, ignoring Hermann's reply. He pointed to a small desk in the corner of the room. "Deputy Führer Hess authorized

Heinz Spanknobel to form an American Nazi organization: the Friends of Germany."

"Is that the Bund?" Hermann interrupted.

"Excuse me?" Canaris glowered at him. "Spanknobel was tasked with helping us counter American Jewish boycotts of German businesses in German neighborhoods in the US. Obviously, this is unacceptable."

"Of course it is," Hermann said. He walked over to the coffeepot on the corner cabinet. "May I?"

Canaris nodded. "The American Congress concluded that Friends represented a branch of the Nazi party in America. This tied our hands. Hess ordered all German citizens to leave Friends and asked for its leaders to return to Germany. Spanknoble is gone now. We're sending Fritz Kuhn to replace him. From this office, we'll be a resource for them. You'll assist me with those communications . . . among other things."

"I got it."

"Do you? Kuhn is forming the German-American Bund. He's set up training camps. We are to communicate with American leadership in those camps."

"Americans?"

"Yes. Americans sympathetic to our cause." He pointed to the pen and paper on Hermannn's desk. "Take this down. Ready?"

Hermann put his coffee down, slid into the desk chair, and grabbed the pen.

"Six camps: Camp Nordland in Sussex County, New Jersey; Camp Siegfried in Yaphank, New York; Camp Hindenburg in Grafton, Wisconsin; Deutschhorst Country Club in Sellersville, Pennsylvania; Camp Bergwald in Bloomingdale, New Jersey; and Camp Highland in the Catskills. Stop." He walked over to Hermann, picked up the paper, read it, and handed it back.

"Budget for flags, posters, arm bands needed to be sent to above. Need approval."

Hermann transcribed as fast as he could.

"Underline that," Canaris said, pointing to the last line on the paper.

"Yes sir."

"Okay, let me see."

He reached over and took the letter and scanned it. Then he walked over to his desk, folded the letter, put it in an envelope, and stamped and sealed it. He handed it back.

"Walk this over to Himmler's office."

"Of course," Hermann said, thrilled to be sent to the great man's office.

"Give it to Hedwig."

"Hedwig?"

"His secretary."

Hermann finished his coffee and stood up from his desk.

"If ever asked, we don't support the Bund. Is that clear?"

"Yes sir."

"Hitler's in the midst of appeasing the US president, and so, "officially," Germany must distance itself from the Bund."

"But . . . ," Hermann interrupted.

"But?"

"I mean, sir, is this an official request?" Hermann held up the letter.

"No, it's an unofficial request. You understand?"

"I understand," Hermann said, unsure whether he really did.

Canaris said, "Listen to me. I need a good assistant, and I can see you're ambitious, eager to please. Maybe *too* eager, in fact. Rein that in a bit."

"Of course. Yes sir." Hermann got up and put his empty coffee cup back on the corner cabinet, then left with the letter.

CHAPTER SIXTY

Max watched every person who walked by. Just as Rosenthal had instructed, he suspected everyone. At the Mittenwald station, he paid for a second-class ticket to Innsbruck. He boarded the train, and the conductor punched his ticket. No problems so far. He found a seat, closed his eyes, and tried to sleep.

The images of Hermann tormenting him played over and over in his mind. Half asleep, he dreamed that he was back in the north tower of St. Maria Magdalena, tied to a chair. Hermann yelled at him, then ground a cigarette out on his forearm. He cried in pain and woke up breathing hard and sweating.

His cry turned a few heads in the train car. He looked down. This was not what Rosenthal had meant by not drawing attention. Again he closed his eyes, and again he dreamed. In slow motion, he saw Rebecca getting shot on the Bridge of Witches, but this time, through the head.

In his dream, he ran over to her and wiped away the blood on her forehead. Then he picked her up, slung her over his back, and walked her off the bridge. As they walked, Hermann laughed loudly and shot her in the back several more times. Each shot made her body jerk. Max continued walking her off the bridge. She smiled at him, unaffected by the bullets. He kept walking, and eventually he was just dragging her limp body across the bridge. He pulled her across the bridge, and then her body just vanished and he was left grasping nothing but air. He woke up crying quietly. The rest of the train ride, he didn't let himself fall back asleep.

CHAPTER SIXTY ONE

Stats chose a circuitous route to Innsbruck Station. With his backpack slung over one shoulder, he looked more like a college student on break than a refugee on the run.

He walked through Mittenwald via Obermarkt, a narrow old street of pastel-colored homes with roofs that joined together to form a series of wooden gables. Stats thought, how could such festive colors line the streets when Europe was in such chaos? It was as if Breslau existed in a black and white world, and Mittenwald was in Technicolor. The beauty inspired Stats, so that for a moment he forgot why he was here and what he was doing.

As he left Obermarkt, he began a modest ascent up the Laintal Creek. At the top of the rise, he headed down to the Elmau Valley.

At Innsbruck Station, he noticed two men, both in black uniform with the red swastika arm band.

He walked into the bathroom to evade them. Inside, a man stood at the sink washing his hands, while a small boy used the urinal. Stats found an empty stall and closed the door. In that same instant, he heard the outer door's hinges squeak as someone else entered.

Peeking out from under the stall, he saw black boots. He climbed on top of the toilet seat to keep his feet from being seen beneath the stall's partial walls. The man and the young boy had left.

The black boots moved down the line of stalls, and he could hear each door swing open.

Stats stood in the stall in the far corner. He held his breath as someone pulled forcefully on his door, but the latch held. Someone tugged again, harder this time. The bathroom door squeaked again, and new set of heavy footsteps clomped in. The black boots went back to the sink, to give the appearance of washing up. Stats exhaled.

The new arrival went to the urinal. A moment later, someone else walked in, and Stats heard the click of the bolt on the bathroom door. He counted four men in the bathroom.

Stats peered through the space between the stalls. The black boots belonged to the same men he had seen outside the bathroom. Both Nazis turned to look at the latest arrival. The man by the urinal had already slipped behind the unsuspecting Germans, turned his back to them, and was reaching down to his boot. A moment later, Stats heard gagging and gurgling sounds, and both Nazis fell to the floor.

"*Aroyskumen zayne bsholem,*" one of the attackers said.

Stats didn't understand. He stood frozen on top of the toilet seat.

"*Zayne bsholem,*" the other repeated.

He still didn't understand, and he didn't move.

"Come out. It's safe," the man said, this time in German.

Stats saw the two Nazis lying on the floor and knew he had no choice. He climbed down off the toilet and opened the stall door.

One of the men approached him and put out his hand. "I'm Rowecki. We're helping whenever we can. Be careful. You're a wanted man now. They know you killed Bohrsdam—nice work, by the way! And they know you've escaped."

Stats just stood there. He didn't know what to say.

Rowecki looked at his watch. "You have five minutes to catch the Brenner Pass train. We've got a little mess to clean up here. Good luck." Stats walked out of the bathroom, unsure what had just happened. He bought his ticket, boarded the train, found a seat, and fell asleep.

He woke up briefly to look out at snow-covered Alps.

CHAPTER SIXTY TWO

No one had any inkling Rosenthal was still alive, and no one had trailed him. He went, as instructed, to Genoa's St. Lawrence Cathedral.

Rowecki sat disguised as a congregant, praying in one of the pews at the front of the church. Rosenthal sat next to him. Both men stared ahead at the altar.

"Max and Stats are making their way out of Austria," Rowecki whispered while gazing worshipfully at the crucifix that hung over the pulpit. He genuflected and looked down.

"When you arrive in Barcelona, the customs agent is one of ours. He'll ask questions that verify your identity. Answer him, and you'll pass through customs without interruption. Good luck."

Rowecki stood up and left the pew. Rosenthal stayed for another ten minutes, then left and boarded the ferry to Barcelona.

CHAPTER SIXTY THREE

The port, once a quiet pass-through for tourists and businessmen, was now crowded with military guards who walked around with scary-looking German shepherds.

The customs officer stood at a turnstile, ready to question the new arrivals. Rosenthal spotted other armed guards positioned just beyond the customs kiosk. They were the last obstacles to anyone entering Spain, even if only for a few hours' layover.

Rosenthal reached the front of the queue.

"What is your purpose here: business or pleasure?" the customs officer asked.

"Pleasure."

"What ship did you arrive on?"

"The ferry from Genoa."

Most of the people coming through customs did not arrive on that ferry, because it was a cargo ferry. The answer triggered the next question from the customs agent.

"Welkh iz der yidish nay yor?"

Rosenthal replied, "Rosh Hashanah."

With a smile, the officer stamped his passport. "You may pass."

The customs agent looked up at the armed guards in front of him and waved them off as Rosenthal passed by.

Rosenthal walked quickly, though not *too* quickly, down another hallway to the embarkation area for passengers waiting to board the *Rex*. There he waited patiently for the two boys to join him.

An hour later, Max walked down the gangplank from another cargo ferry in Barcelona. He approached a customs officer who looked nothing like the one Rowecki had described. The officer asked to see his documents. As Max began fumbling in his pockets, a different officer tapped the agent on the shoulder.

"Break's over," he said.

Max had no idea what was happening.

"What's your purpose here: business or pleasure?" the officer asked.

"Pleasure."

"What ship did you arrive on?"

"The ferry from Genoa."

"Welkh iz der yidish nay yor?"

Max looked at the agent and said, "Rosh Hashanah."

"You may pass." The agent didn't look at him and didn't smile.

Max joined Rosenthal in the embarkation area. "Where's Stats?" Max asked.

"He should be here soon."

A half hour later, Stats arrived at the port to find guards pacing about with dogs.

"What's your purpose here? Business or pleasure?"

"Pleasure—all pleasure," Stats replied.

"What ship did you arrive on?"

"The bus from Genoa"

The agent didn't look up.

"Welkh iz der yidish nay yor?"

Stats didn't understand. He didn't answer.

"*Welkh iz der yidish nay yor?*" the guard repeated, still looking down.

Stats had no idea what he asked.

This time, the agent looked for a clue that Stats was part of the group. He peered into the young man's eyes. *"Yenik are`du traveling mit?"*

"My name's Jakob. I'm traveling to meet my friends.

Wrong answer, apparently. *"Yenik are`du traveling mit?"* he said in a soft voice.

Stats smiled and extended his hand. "I'm here to meet my two friends. I know some Yiddish but not enough . . ."

This was not the answer the officer was looking for. He waved to the guards in front of him. Seconds later, two guards came over and grabbed Stats by the arms.

"Wait! Where you taking me?" Stats asked.

The guards didn't answer, but pulled him into a windowless room just off the corridor.

Stats sat alone at a table in a warm, dimly lit room. A ceiling fan turned slowly above him. He stared at the rotating shadows the paddles made on the tabletop. A fat, sweating customs officer, who seemed annoyed with his task, began asking questions in Spanish—a language Stats understood little of.

Every question got no answer. Worse, they were interpreting his silence as disrespect. The questions seemed friendly enough at first but soon deteriorated into yelling. In despair, Stats put his face in his hands and closed his eyes.

Meanwhile, Max and Rosenthal waited at the embarkation area, knowing that the *Rex* was due to arrive any minute now.

"He should've been here by now," Max said.

"I don't know," Rosenthal said, "but the *Rex* is here." He pointed out the window to the tugboats pushing the ship into dock. We can't wait. We have to assume he'll make it and meet us on the ship."

"Is there any way we can find out?" Max asked. "Can't the underground help us?"

"Not really. I don't know where to find them or how to contact them. They usually find us."

"What are we going to do?"

Rosenthal picked up his bag. "We have to get on. If we miss this ship, we aren't going. Everything's arranged. This is our only chance, and we have to take it."

"I need to find Stats," Max pleaded.

"Listen to me. You can't do anything. I don't know where he is. *You* don't know where he is. He could still be in Genoa, for all we know. You knew the deal. Any one of us could have missed this ship. We took that chance. If you go back there . . ." He glanced toward customs. "You'll compromise this plan. You'll put me at risk. You'll put yourself at risk. And you'll put the whole damned underground at risk. You just can't go back. I'm sorry."

"I can't leave him."

Rosenthal grabbed him by the shoulder. "You can't go. Don't you get it? You don't think I want to help?"

Max gave him a hard look.

"Listen to me. If he's not here now, then something's up. Something's happened, and in all likelihood, there's nothing we can do about it."

"So we just leave, that's it?"

"That's it."

Max sat for a moment, staring at the cracks in the concrete floor.

"We have to board," Rosenthal said. "Let's go." He started out of the embarkation area, toward the dock.

Max stood up. He looked back at the customs area one last time. Then he looked pensively down to the ground for a few seconds. Finally, he looked toward the *Rex* and the receding figure of Rosenthal.

A man approached him and shook his hand. He handed him an envelope.

Ignoring Rosenthal's wave to hurry it up, Max turned around and walked back toward the customs officer.

"Did you see him? Did my friend come through here?" Max asked. The customs agent looked right through him.

"Tell me, please, did you see my friend?" He grabbed his arm. The agent pulled his arm away and gave him a stern look.

Max looked around him. Guards were everywhere, and now they were noticing him.

He went up to a guard and tried to speak in broken Spanish. *¿Ha visto yo amigo?* he asked. *"Es grande, fuerte."* He flexed his biceps. "He's about this tall. Big man, small beard." He scratched at his chin. No answer.

"Anyone? Please. Help me. I'm looking for my friend. Has anyone seen my friend?"

One of the guards stood up to apprehend him, and just before he could do so, Max felt a hand on his arm.

"Shut up and come with me."

CHAPTER SIXTY FOUR

Stats listened as his interrogator grew more irate. He didn't notice the new guard enter the interrogation room. He did notice, however, that the questions had taken a different tone. He looked up. The first interrogator was gone. The new guard smiled at him. "*Damn,* but you make things tough," Rowecki said. He was dressed as a customs agent. Stats, stunned and relieved, broke into a smile.

"You don't have time. The *Rex* is leaving in a few minutes. I'm taking you out of this room. Keep your head down and your yap shut." Like a veteran policeman, Rowecki handcuffed Stats. He tucked the key to the cuffs into Stats's trouser pocket and hurried him out, pushing his head down with one arm and holding his left arm with the other as he led his prisoner down the hallway.

CHAPTER SIXTY FIVE

"Just shut up and don't bring any more attention to us than you already have," the familiar-looking man with the bushy, continuous eyebrow said to Max. He, too, was dressed in a customs official's uniform. He walked Max toward Rosenthal.

"I'm not leaving, not without him. I can't—"

"Right. You're not. Now, shut up or I'll throw you in the harbor and do us all a favor."

Max looked ahead toward the ship and saw Rosenthal's smile. Then he saw Stats and a man who fit Rowecki's description. He breathed a sigh of relief, and when he looked again, the man was gone. The "customs officer" with the fiery hair and the long eyebrow escorted Max to Rosenthal.

"Can we go now?" Rosenthal asked as he opened the envelope and handed each of them a bogus third-class ticket. He held his real boarding pass in his left hand. Rosenthal was registered as a passenger; the boys were not. They just needed to get aboard the ship and stow away in Rosenthal's stateroom.

The ship's horn bellowed, and they watched through the porthole as the dockhands freed the massive braided yellow hawsers from the rusted mooring bollards.

CHAPTER SIXTY SIX

Rebecca knew her only as Sophie. She was pretty, blond, and didn't look like a criminal.

"My father died here," the girl said, "and now I'll follow in his footsteps," she said.

She sat down, leaned back, and crossed her legs, apparently resigned to her fate.

"You'll die here, too. Everyone does. This place is a death factory." She pulled her hair back.

"Why?" Rebecca said, feeling her lips tremble.

"I've been sentenced to death. Treason. It's bullshit, of course, not that it matters. What's your heinous crime?"

"I helped friends, other Jews, escape. Or I don't know."

Sophie didn't respond. Her eyes hinted at an intelligence beyond her years.

"What'd you do?" Rebecca asked.

"My brother—he's here too . . . someplace." She waved her hand to indicate some other place.

"We wrote leaflets and handed them out."

"What sort of leaflets?"

"I guess, the sort that land you in here."

Rebecca stared at her.

"Sorry." She looked down, rubbing her forehead as if in disbelief. "We wrote what everyone else was thinking but didn't have the guts to say."

"You Jewish?" Rebecca asked.

"No, born Lutheran, like half of Germany. But now my religion—ah, what does it matter? My religion is a 'theology of conscience.'"

Rebecca could hear the passion in her voice.

"Have you heard of the Lion of Münster?"

"No."

"A Catholic bishop. His sermons inspired us. That's why we did what we did. Fuck the Nazis."

Rebecca could see her bold front collapse into fear.

"I couldn't live with myself if I did nothing," she said, and held up a fist.

Trembling, Sophie wiped away a tear.

"Now I'm good and fucked."

"Maybe it won't happen," Rebecca said. "Maybe they'll delay. You know, bureaucratic bullshit. There's still plenty of that."

"How long you been here?"

"I'm not sure."

"What happened to you?" She looked at the injured shoulder, which hung in an abnormal position.

"I was shot. It's kind of a long story."

The guard called her name. "Sophie, your turn."

"I guess, no time for long stories," Sophie said.

"She just got here," Rebecca protested.

"Don't be a fool," the guard said, and pushed Rebecca back down to the floor.

"I'm fine," Sophie said as she again wiped away a few proud tears. "If, by what *we* did, we woke just one person up from the narcotic slumber of complacency, then fuck them and fuck the guillotine." She raised her fist defiantly in the air as the guard pushed her out of the cell.

CHAPTER SIXTY SEVEN

"I gotta get out of this room," Stats said. "I'm going crazy." He looked around him in the cramped cabin, at the two stacked bunks on either side. He took two steps and bumped into the small white porcelain sink that hung from the wall on the hull side of the room. Bending down, he peered through the porthole just above the sink and then banged his head on the small wooden shelf, just above it, holding a water pitcher and white ceramic bowl.

"See?" He rubbed his head. There's more room in a jail cell!

"We can't," Max said.

"C'mon, he's asleep." He glanced over at Rosenthal, snoring softly on the opposite bunk. He walked to the door. "Nothing will happen. We've been cooped up here for three days. I think he's paranoid."

"He said no one is to know we're on board."

"I'm claustrophobic, and these cabins are like closets. I'm going, with or without you."

Max took the water pitcher from the shelf and walked over to the sink. Pouring water into his hand, he splashed some on his face. "Fine," he said, blotting his face with a washcloth. "I'll go. But just for a few minutes."

"Fine, a few minutes."

"And no one can see us."

"Right-o," Stats replied, giving a sailor's salute.

"Don't," Max hissed as Stats sauntered up to the bar on the main deck.

"What drink can I get you gentlemen?" the bartender asked in Spanish.

"Scotch, single malt?" Stats understood enough Spanish to answer that question.

Max looked furtively about to see if anyone had noticed them.

The bartender poured their shots. "You guys tourists?" he asked.

Max didn't answer.

"Sort of," Stats answered. "Students. We're on holiday."

"From where?"

"Breslau."

"Never been. Enjoy," the bartender said, and went to the next patron.

"I couldn't help but overhear—you two from Breslau?" said a stranger in German with a Spanish accent.

Max shuffled uncomfortably.

Stats smiled. "Yup."

"I know it well. Haven't been back in a few months, though. I miss the Hofbrau House."

"As do we," Stats said.

"So, what brings you to the States?" the stranger asked, sliding his chair closer.

His silver-rimmed glasses reminded Max of intellectuals back at Breslau. His olive Mediterranean complexion contrasted nicely with his white suit.

"We're on holiday," Stats said. "We're both medical students."

"You know, I have a pain, right here in my neck. What can you tell me about it?" He chuckled, rubbed his neck, then slapped Stats on the back. "Just kidding, Doc."

Stats laughed along with him, and Max patronized him with a cautious smile.

"So, what do you think of what's going on over there?" the stranger asked.

"What do you mean?"

"I hear they're kicking the Jews out of that place."

"It's about damn time," Stats said, and smiled at Max.

"Let's see," the stranger said. "I know a few of the professors there. Ah, damn it . . ." He snapped his fingers. "What *is* his name?"

"There are too many to know them all," Max finally interjected. "But we're on holiday, so we'd rather forget about school."

"Sure. Of course. Right."

"Anyway, I'm Dr. Oteiza. I'm a surgeon at the University of Barcelona."

They shook hands.

"I'm Hans, and this is Hermann," Stats said. "What brings you to New York, Doctor?"

Max shot Stats a warning glance.

"I've been invited to speak at Columbia's grand rounds. I pioneered a new approach to cholecystectomies."

Max couldn't help noting the tone of self-adulation.

Dr. Oteiza sipped the last of his drink and set the glass down dramatically on the bar. "Why don't you two join me for dinner tonight? I'm eating alone."

"Thank you, but, we can't," Max said.

But before he could give a reason why, Dr. Oteiza added, "I'll put the dinner on my room tab. It doesn't matter; Columbia's paying for it.

"That's very generous, but we can't—"

"Nonsense. I insist." He took a pen out of his pocket.

"What room are you in? I'll send you my table and time."

"Deck five, stateroom five thirty-one," Stats replied.

"All right, then. I'll send the confirmation and see you this evening. Looking forward to it."

Dr. Oteiza got up from the bar and left.

"Are you an idiot?" Max hissed. "What happens when he finds out it's not our room?

"What? We just don't show up. He doesn't know our last names, so he can't check the passenger manifest. Relax. It's not a big deal."

They finished their drinks and went back to Rosenthal's stateroom.

CHAPTER SIXTY EIGHT

In the ship's dining room, the finest Lennox china sparkled on starched white tablecloths as the Swaroski crystal chandeliers shimmered with the ship's motion. Red-vested waiters, a white napkin dressed just so over a bent forearm, glided about, doting on each diner. The headwaiter, in a black dinner jacket, went about the room, introducing himself at each table while surveying his staff.

"Three glasses?" the sommelier asked Dr. Oteiza.

"Yes," he replied, pushing his empty scotch glass to one side.

"You asked for our finest Bordeaux." The sommelier held the bottle up for Oteiza's inspection. "This Mouton Rothschild is magnificent."

"Of course," Oteiza replied. I know the vineyard quite well. In Pauillac—lovely little village just north of Bordeaux. Excellent choice."

"Very good, sir. Your guests will have quite a treat." He opened the bottle and poured it into a decanter. "Here, we'll let that breathe."

Dr. Oteiza looked at his Patek Phillipe. His guests were twenty minutes late.

The sommelier said, "May I get you started while you wait, sir?"

"Yes, why not?" Dr. Oteiza said.

The sommelier returned ten minutes later. "Well, what do you think?"

"Beautiful."

"Thank you," the sommelier said with some satisfaction. "May I pour you another?"

"Please."

Dr. Oteiza stared back at his watch. The boys were forty-five minutes late. He looked around the dining room.

The sommelier said, "Should I call a waiter to the table, sir?"

Oteiza looked at his watch again. "Ah, what the hell. Send the goddamn waiter over." He placed his dinner order, finished another glass of Bordeaux, and motioned to the sommelier to fill it up again.

The Mouton Rothschild was indeed a splendid vintage. Dr. Oteiza finished his dinner and the bottle and wobbled just a little as he stood up. Leaving the dining room, he fished the card out of his coat pocket and read his scribbled note.

Room 531. Little bastards—he would have a word with them.

He took the elevator to the fifth floor.

CHAPTER SIXTY NINE

Max watched as Stats and Rosenthal finished their dinner in the cramped stateroom. He had no appetite.

"We need to talk about what happens next," Rosenthal said.

Stats rolled his eyes.

"You are going to have to change your names. The laws in the states have not made this any easier. Ever since Congress passed Johnson-Reed, they shut the doors on more Jews coming in."

"Johnson-Reed?" Stats asked. He took a final bite of his dinner roll.

"It's a quota on how many Jews can immigrate per year."

"How many?" Stats asked while chewing.

"Obviously, not enough. They exceed that number within a few weeks and basically shut the door. So here's the deal: You can't be Jews anymore. It's that simple. If they find out you're Jewish, you're on the next boat out."

"Do they have the legal right?" Max asked.

"Of course they do. There's precedent. Don't worry, you'll have papers ready with your new names." Rosenthal reached into a bag hidden under his bed. "But regardless, take these. Wear them."

He handed Stats and Max each a crucifix on a silver chain.

"You're kidding, right?" Stats said.

"Do you see me laughing? Get used to your new name, too." To Max, he said, "Pleased to make your acquaintance, Maxwell Door." He turned to Stats. "And yours, Jimmy Blake."

"I actually like that name," Stats said. "Can you schedule a rhinoplasty for me, too?"

"I keep my name," Rosenthal said.

"Of course, you do," Stats said.

Rosenthal gave him an annoyed glance. "I get citizenship because of my academic work. There are a few loopholes in the law—academic reciprocity, so they can accept intellectuals, professors, scientists . . ."

"Just not your run-of-the-mill Jews," Stats said.

CHAPTER SEVENTY

Dr. Oteiza knocked on the door of stateroom 531 and got no answer.

He looked around, adjusted his sport coat and his ascot, and knocked again.

"Get your asses up!" he yelled. "I want to talk to you!"

A couple walked by and stared, but no one came to the door.

This time, he banged with his fist continuously a full minute.

The door opened. A tired elderly woman in a nightgown opened the door halfway, blinked sleepily, and said, "Can I help you?"

Oteiza blanched. "Pardon me, madam. I apologize. I must have the wrong stateroom." He looked down at the card, then again at the number on her stateroom door. Even after a bottle of wine, there was no mistaking. They both clearly read "531."

The woman slammed the door.

"Is there a problem here?" a voice said over his shoulder.

Dr. Oteiza turned to find the ship's purser. "Yes, there's a fucking problem. I'm looking for two little weasels that gave me this stateroom number."

"It's late. Why don't we call it a night, Mr. . . ."

"It's *Doctor.* Dr. Oteiza."

"Excuse me, Dr. Oteiza," the purser said. "Maybe I can help you. Why don't you come back to my office. I have a passenger list there. They should be easy to find."

CHAPTER SEVENTY ONE

"Please, Doctor, have a seat," the purser said, gesturing to a chair in his office.

"May I get you a coffee? You prefer black?"

"I do." Oteiza looked around the tidy cubicle. On the oak desk with a center inlay of faded maroon leather rested a worn copy of Gill's *Textbook of Navigation and Nautical Astronomy*.

"Okay, give me a moment." Squeezing between the desk and file cabinet, and the purser left his office.

A few minutes later, he returned with a cup of coffee.

"Okay, let's see . . ." He sat down behind his desk and opened the ship's passenger manifest.

"Who did you say you're looking for?"

"Two young men. Harold, Henry . . . No, that's not it." He snapped his fingers. "*Hans.* And Hermann. Yes, that's it."

"I see. Any last names?"

"No."

"A bit of a challenge. Probably need a last name, but let me peruse the list and see if I can find anyone by those first names." He ran his finger down the list. "Nope. Sorry."

"That's it?" Dr. Oteiza asked.

"That's it." He closed the book. "Time to call it a night." He got up from his chair.

"Wait a minute. That's not it. Can't you search by age?"

The purser thought for a moment. "Yes, actually, we can. Do you have their ages?" He sat back down.

"No, not really."

The purser looked at Dr. Oteiza. "Then I'm afraid that's it. Look, it's really late."

"Hold on. Hold on. They were about twenty-one, give or take a year or two. There can't be too many on the ship that age."

"Oh, that's easy. Don't even have to look. There's no one on the ship that age—unless, of course, they're staff and work in the kitchen. Or the engine room." He refolded the manifest.

"No. These guys don't work in the engine room. Are you sure you have no passengers that age?" Dr.

Oteiza leaned forward, regarding the purser with raised eyebrows.

"I'm positive. The passengers are my responsibility. I'd absolutely know. Are you sure they weren't older?"

"I don't know. Maybe. I guess. No. They were students. They can't be much older than that." Dr. Oteiza paused. "What does it mean if they're not on the passenger list?"

"Probably that they're not passengers."

"What?"

"Look, it's late and you've had a few," the purser said. He picked up the folded manifest.

"Listen, I'm not drunk. And I'm not crazy. I wasn't hallucinating. I know what I saw . . . Wait a second. They ordered drinks. Go ask the bartender."

"Drinks? Are you sure?

"Yes."

"Then there's one other possibility."

"Go on," Oteiza said.

"Stowaways."

"Seriously?" The Spaniard's eyes narrowed.

"Yes. We're supposed to be on the lookout for this. People fleeing to America."

"They're not stowaways. Why would they come to the bar and have a drink?"

The purser looked at Oteiza.

"I don't know. Anyway, that's the only thing I can think of. There are no passengers of the age you describe. No passengers with the first name you gave. And it's late. I'll look into it in the morning." He opened the door to his office.

"We arrive in New York Harbor tomorrow afternoon. If there are stowaways aboard, I'll need to alert the authorities. We'll do a stateroom search in the morning. If I find anything, I'll let you know. Good night, Doctor."

CHAPTER SEVENTY TWO

The next morning, the purser and two of his crew inspected the ship. First, they searched all the common areas. They walked past the lido deck, library, and card room, then searched the pool deck and the promenade.

The purser asked his two assistants, "Where have you checked?"

"No one in the engine room, staff quarters, or laundry facilities, sir," the first assistant said.

"Nothing in the dining room, card room, or library, sir," the other assistant said.

"Okay, we muster in an hour. The staterooms will be empty; we'll search them then. We'll start aft and port and move forward and starboard."

The ship's captain's voice came over the public address system. "Attention, all passengers and crew. There will be a muster drill in five minutes. The staterooms must be evacuated, and all passengers must go to their assigned muster stations. This drill is required by international maritime law. All passengers, with no exceptions, must be present for this muster drill. Thank you for your cooperation."

A series of seven short blasts from the ship's horn followed, then one long blast.

"I have to go upstairs for muster," Rosenthal said. "Then I'll settle the shipboard account. You both stay here."

Just as Rosenthal left his stateroom, the purser passed him in the hallway. Rosenthal waved, and the purser greeted him with a smile.

The purser knocked on the aft stateroom doors. At each door, when no one answered, he used his master key to enter and briefly inspect each stateroom. Then he moved forward to inspect the next one. Each inspection was one stateroom closer to Rosenthal's.

CHAPTER SEVENTY THREE

Being cooped up in the stateroom was dreadfully boring.

"Do you wonder if she's still alive?" Stats asked.

"She took a bullet in the back. I doubt Hermann rushed her to a hospital."

Stats went to the door and turned the knob.

"What are you doing!" Max said. "We need to stay here."

"I need fresh air."

"You can't go out. You know what Rosenthal said."

"Listen, it'll be five minutes. I need a quick walk around the deck, that's all. Just to get some sea air. I'm going stir crazy in here."

"Five minutes?" Max held up his fingers. He could see his angst.

"Yes, five minutes. Don't worry."

"Okay, I'm going to jump in the shower. Be here when I'm done."

From the shower, Max heard a sharp rapping on the stateroom door. Then, to his surprise, he heard a key in the lock, and the door opened.

"Dr. Rosenthal?" a deep male voice asked.

Max stood still.

"Dr. Rosenthal?"

"Yes, may I help you?" Max said in a deep voice..

"It's the ship's purser. We're inspecting the staterooms for two stowaways. I'm sorry to intrude, but you must go to muster. Really, this is required by law."

Max remained in the shower. He didn't answer.

"Okay, then. I'm leaving, but please make sure you finish, and go right away."

"Of course, thank you," Max mumbled.

Returning early from muster, Rosenthal met the purser in the corridor and bade him good morning.

"Hello," the purser replied, and climbed the companionway to the promenade deck.

Rosenthal went to his room.

"Damn, that was close," Max said upon seeing him.

"What?" Rosenthal answered.

"The purser. He just left here a minute ago. He thought I was you. I was in the shower. He said he's inspecting the staterooms, looking for two stowaways."

"How could that be?" Rosenthal asked. "No one knows you're on the ship."

"Oh, shit, Stats is out there."

"Where is he?"

Stats watched the purser come off the companionway to the starboard side and walk toward him. He quickly turned and walked farther aft. At the stern of the ship, he turned to port and hopped over the rail. The glossed teak railing coursed along the entire stern, above the steel transom that kept passengers from slipping off the deck and into the sea. He knew that if he squatted low enough, the sheet of steel was large enough to hide him from the purser. Balancing on the thick braided cable that coursed through a series of chocks welded to the hull just below deck level, he glanced down five stories to the boiling cauldron of white froth generated by the propellers.

Stats heard the footsteps stop as the purser reached the stern. He felt his right forearm ache with fatigue from holding on to the pad eye. His other hand held fast to the stringer plate jutting just off the deck's ledge. The purser, meanwhile, took his time looking around, clearly unaware that the stowaway was mere inches away, holding on but starting to lose his grip.

Stats knew he couldn't hold on much longer. He looked down into the maelstrom created by the propellers.

Suddenly, the ship's horn gave seven short blasts, followed by one long blast. The captain's voice came over the speaker system.

"Thank you for your cooperation. The muster drill is over. You may return to your staterooms. All staff, please return to your posts."

The purser looked around once more, saw nothing but passengers, and went back to his office.

Once he was gone, Stats pulled himself back over the railing and walked back to the stateroom.

CHAPTER SEVENTY FOUR

Rosenthal had stolen the white jumpsuits with "*Manutenzione*" stenciled in large black letters on the back. Max and Stats, now dressed as maintenance workers, moved from inside their stateroom to the deck, where they stood outside on the promenade, cleaning the ship's railings.

They worked diligently as the *Rex* steamed into New York Harbor, and they stayed at their task until the last passenger had gone down the gangplank and into the customs office. Then they started cleaning the gangplank, working their way from top to bottom.

Once they were fairly sure no one had noticed them; they entered the customs building and went straight into the bathroom. A strange man locked the bathroom door behind them, and Rosenthal handed them each a change of clothes.

"Congratulations, boys," the stranger said. "You made it." He stuck out his hand. "I'm Varian."

Max remembered Rosenthal's description of Varian Fry, but he seemed much less imposing in person. A journalist by trade, he dressed like an intellectual: shirt and tie, pale green V-neck sweater, and over that a faded brown twill coat with tan patches sewn over the elbows. He looked nothing at all like a covert rescue operative.

"Trust me, this was no easy feat," he told them. "Here's your papers, stamped and ready." He handed each of them a folded passport with stamped visas between the covers. "Just hand them to the customs officer as you past through the turnstile. And here's some money—you'll need this to get you started." He handed an envelope to Max and one to Stats.

"I managed to find a family to board both of you," he said. "Here's the address."

He turned to Rosenthal. "You're much simpler. Columbia's really excited about the possibility of your joining the faculty."

After Max and Stats had changed out of their white maintenance-worker jumpsuits and stashed them in their duffels, Varian unlocked the bathroom door, and the four of them walked out into the concourse of the shipping terminal.

The concourse was buzzing with New Yorkers, tourists, and businesspeople from all over the world. Max had never seen so many people going in so many different directions.

"So this is America?" Stats said.

"Look." Max pointed up to the vaulted ceilings adorned with a herringbone pattern of Guastavino tiles.

"A shipping port like a cathedral," he said, marveling at the polished Tennessee marble on the floors.

"C'mon, stop gawking," Stats said, pulling him by the arm through the crowd.

"Forget Columbia," Rosenthal was saying to Fry.

"What are you talking about?"

They stood in line waiting for their turn to hand their papers to the customs officer.

"Don't play me for a fool, Varian."

"You mean Luther—that incident? It's nothing."

"Why do you care where I go?" Rosenthal said. "NYU is fine."

"Because Butler asked me personally, and I told him I'd get you over to see them before NYU gets you."

"What do you get for that? "

"Are you *serious*? After what I've done for you, you're gonna ask me that? He's the president of Columbia. He wants you there."

"I don't care if he's the bloody *pope*," Rosenthal said. "He just invited the German ambassador to speak in defense of Hitler!" He handed his papers to the customs agent. *"At Columbia."* The agent waved him through. Fry was next and did the same, and both of them left the terminal. They walked outside, onto the Westside Highway at Thirteenth Street, on the busy sidewalk just in front of Pier 54's doors.

"That's academia," Fry said. "It doesn't mean any sort of endorsement."

"How so?"

"It's the Ivies. Deans just want to broaden their students' exposure to more than one worldview, but it's meaningless. You know, let 'em see the good and bad."

"Then what about Klein? Rosenthal said.

"What about him?"

"Jerome's been blackballed." He looked skeptically at Fry. Then he turned away, looking west in between the piers, at the Hudson River and Hoboken behind it.

"Papers?" the agent asked Max.

Max handed over his papers, and the agent inspected them, then glanced down at the crucifix necklace. He glanced back up at Max and handed him back his papers, and Max passed through the turnstile.

"That's Butler's answer to free speech," Rosenthal said as the cars on the Westside Highway blew past them. "Klein's dismissed for protesting an invitation to a Nazi. I'm sorry, but I can't be a party to that. It's a matter of principle. The only reason they want me on the faculty is to pacify the complaining New York Jews."

"No, they really want you," Fry said.

"What about me?" Max interrupted.

"It won't be Columbia," said Rosenthal.

"Why?"

"Quotas," said Fry.

"You can thank Butler for that, too," Rosenthal muttered.

"I'm not sure I'm following," said Max.

"He's right," said Fry. "Columbia created Seth Low to—"

"To divert the overflow of Jewish applicants," Rosenthal interrupted. "It's nothing but a bogus community college."

The customs agent looked at Stats. "Citizenship?" he asked.

"American," Stats replied in his best English accent and handed him his papers.

The agent looked at Stats, then again at his papers. He waited to hear more, but the young

American was silent. After a few seconds, the officer waved him on.

With an effort, Stats forced himself to walk casually through the turnstile, then stepped quickly to catch up with the others.

"What is it with you and customs agents?" Max said, laughing. "They ask you something in Yiddish?" Or maybe it's your accent?"

"Fuck you," Stats said in English. "How's was my accent there?"

"If you're on the faculty, you can help fix what's broken," Fry said.

"Do you have any idea what I just went through?" Rosenthal said. "Look, I have no interest in changing Butler or anybody else at Columbia. I'm tired of academic politics."

"It's the most prestigious school in New York," Fry said.

"I'm well past that, Varian," Rosenthal said with a thin smile.

A horn blew, and Max jumped back from the curb as a taxi swerved to miss two men in business suits who were walking blithely across Thirteenth Street, against the light.

"Watch were you're going, assholes," the driver yelled out the window as he sped past.

"That's freedom!" Stats crowed, grinning. "That's what it sounds like."

"What are you going to do?" Max asked Rosenthal, ignoring Stats.

"I'm going to accept an appointment at NYU."

"Whatever you decide is fine," Fry said. "Just let me know; I'll tell Butler." He looked at the traffic in front of him and turned back to the boys. "Anyway, this is where I say good-bye and good luck." He started away.

"Wait," Stats called out.

Fry turned back toward him.

"Are you in communication with the underground and Rowecki?" he asked.

Fry's silence answered the question.

"Can you inquire about Rebecca? Can you find out if she's still alive?"

"I'll see what I can do," he said, walking away, "but I can't make any promises." And like that, he was gone, vanished in the horde of pedestrians moving along the streets and sidewalks.

"And what about us?" Max said.

Rosenthal looked east across the highway and up at the Empire State Building. "That's us: the new." Then he pointed downtown to the Woolworth building. "And that's the old. We've got to move from the old to the new. And in keeping with that, I'm going to accept the chair in neurology for polio research at NYU, not Columbia."

"Lucky them," said Stats. "Congratulations. You deserve it."

"Thank you, but there's a doctor on staff—Charles Cooper. He's volunteered to help me get acclimated, and at the right time, I'll ask him to help both of you."

As they stood inadvertently blocking the sidewalk, people hurried past, occasionally bumping into them and throwing them cross looks and even a few words.

"How long before you can ask?" said Max.

"As soon as I can. Cooper has a research lab. I was told he needs a lab assistant. You'll get paid, and you'll need his recommendation to get into medical school there. Maybe in the next few days? Again, be patient."

"How do you know he'll do it?" Max persisted.

"I don't, but I'll ask," Rosenthal said, waving down a cab. "For right now, you both have some money to last for the short term. Better yet, you're alive, and no one's trying to kill you. Be thankful. Go meet your new family. Get a good night's sleep. I'll be in touch." He got in the waiting cab.

CHAPTER SEVENTY FIVE

Canaris smoked a cigarette in the corner of his office. He cracked the window to let the smoke out. He seemed nervous.

Hermann poured himself his usual cup of coffee and held the pot up to Canaris. "Coffee?"

Canaris waved his hand away, then picked up some papers from his desk. "Please file these for me."

Hermann put down the coffee, took the papers from his boss, and walked over to the file cabinet. He pulled out the drawer, riffled through the files until he found the right folder, and dropped the papers into it.

Canaris paced the floor, then walked to the window and threw out the cigarette butt. He said, "I'm going to let Himmler know you've been a great help to me. There may be a promotion sooner than you had hoped. Who knows?"

"Really, Admiral? "Hermann stepped back from the file cabinet. "That would be splendid, sir! I don't know how to thank you enough."

Canaris said, "You'll thank me by doing a first-rate job. Anyway, I need a few minutes for a private call. Do you mind?"

"Of course not, sir." Hermann walked into the hallway. Waiting just outside the door, he heard the lock click.

CHAPTER SEVENTY SIX

Dr. Charles Cooper sat behind his desk, reading the new issue of *Social Justice.*

"Hello Curt," he said without putting down the paper.

"Good morning, Charles," Rosenthal replied as Cooper peered at him over the paper, and then laid it down on his desk and stood up to greet him.

Cooper was tall and handsome, with a full head of youthful blond hair, parted neatly to the side. He wore a necktie in a full Windsor and looked more playboy than scientist.

Rosenthal had done his research before the meeting. Cooper was a Michigander. Born in Detroit, he had spent a privileged youth in Grosse Ile and summered with the Fords in Harbor Springs. He was educated in Ann Arbor, and though a Midwesterner born and bred, Cooper liked to think himself a Connecticut blue blood.

"Charles, I have a favor to ask of you," Rosenthal said.

"Anything. Name it." He folded the paper and placed it precisely on his desk.

"There's a young foreign medical student. He moved to the States, and he's an orphan. He wants to volunteer, work—he'll do anything to get lab experience."

Rosenthal turned around and pointed to the lab area just outside Cooper's office door. "I'm sure he'd clean the droppings out of the rat cages in your lab, if need be. He needs experience. A bright boy. Any way you can help—he needs a leg up for his applications."

"Sure, I can help," Cooper said. "Have him come here tomorrow. There's always a job for someone willing to work."

CHAPTER SEVENTY SEVEN

The lab was filled with flasks, retorts, beakers, and half-open journals. Mice rustled about in their small cages. A Bunsen burner stood beside a double sink, and behind it hung a chalkboard scrawled with mathematical operations.

Dr. Cooper put his arm around Max and walked him over to the other lab technician. "Max, meet Virginia," he said.

"Hi," Max said. "Happy to meet you."

"This lab," he said, raising his arm, "is where I do all my research. We use pigs and mice to study pancreatic enzyme extracts. It's fundamentally neuroendocrine research." Reaching into a cage, he picked up an albino mouse by the tail and held it in his palm, gently stroking its back with his thumb.

He put it in front of Max, and Max reached out and felt the smooth, velvety fur. Then Cooper returned the mouse to the cage and closed the gate. "Neuroendocrine research deals with how the nervous system affects hormone release. We stress mice and quantify the enzyme extract production that results."

Cooper put his arm back around Max.

"In essence, we simulate what happens when humans are stressed or, say, put in less-than-desirable situations."

"What's this?" Max asked, looking at Virginia's lab station. Cooper took his arm off Max and picked up a pipette from the workstation. He held it up to the light and examined it.

"Virginia takes each pipette, quantifies the extract, and places it in this centrifuge. Then she spins it down and weighs the sediment." He put the pipette down in the holder. "Virginia, look at this for me," he said, frowning. "I'm not sure it's looking right."

Virginia kept working as Dr. Cooper spoke. She glanced back at Max momentarily. He couldn't help but notice the lovely curves beneath the white lab coat. Her long, dark hair was done up in a bun.

"Anyway," he said to Max, "there's always work to be done, and you can start by helping Virginia. She'll tell you how you can best help her. This research is important, Max,"

He put his arm around Max again and whispered, "If we get the results I expect"—he darted a look at Virigina—"I'll include you as a coauthor on our next paper." He patted Max on the shoulder. "That's all you'll need on your résumé to get into medical school, here or anyplace else." And he walked to his office in the back of the lab.

CHAPTER SEVENTY EIGHT

Stats couldn't shake the image of Rebecca's face on the bridge. Lately, she haunted his thoughts more than ever.

"Waiter, can you please get me some water?" an elderly patron at Carnegie's yelled from across the room.

"Right away, sir," Stats said.

He brought the water to the table.

"The sandwich isn't the way I ordered. It's cold. Send it back." Stats took the plate with the half-eaten pastrami sandwich.

"He doesn't think I know, he eats half first and then complains about it," Stats said to the cook as he tossed it in the garbage.

The cook grunted and handed him a new sandwich. Stats brought it to the customer.

"More water," he demanded, lifting his empty glass up with one hand while taking a bite from the fresh sandwich with the other.

Stats started to pour, but a piece of ice got stuck in the mouth of the pitcher. When he shook it slightly, the trapped ice cube came dislodged, and the water gushed out onto the table and onto the customer's pants.

"You imbecile!" the man shouted.

Stats turned and looked at his manager, then back at the customer. "Fuck this," he said, and poured the remaining ice water in the customer's lap.

The customer swore and jumped up from his seat, brushing the remaining bits of ice off his pants. Covering his groin with both hands, he hurried out of the diner.

Stats set the pitcher down on the table and walked out of the restaurant.

On his way home, Stats walked past Ferrara's. He walked in, paid a nickel for a cannoli, and walked toward Central Park. He wandered past Bethesda Fountain, where parents played with their kids, musicians busked for pennies, and madmen tried to convince the unbelieving about the next impending apocalypse.

He sat on the edge of the fountain and unwrapped the cannoli, enjoying the treat one slow bite at a time. He hated that damn job anyway.

His mind returned to thoughts of Rebecca. If he could do it again, he would never have left her. He would have dragged her off the bridge even if it meant getting shot by Hermann. He shook his head, but the sense of guilt would not leave him.

He took another bite of cannoli and threw the empty wrapper in the fountain.

CHAPTER SEVENTY NINE

Hermann could see a tear well up in Canaris's eyes as he sat slumped at his desk, face buried in his palms. He never showed any emotion. Clearly, something was awry.

"Hermann, take this down. I need a draft to send to Himmler."

"Yes sir." Hermann took out a pen and began transcribing.

"Attention, Reichsführer SS Himmler, from Admiral Canaris, Chief of Abwehr: At this time, I would like to recommend the promotion of General Oster to deputy head of Abwehr. The promotion is well deserved. As you know, he served bravely on the Western Front in the last war, and more recently, he has worked with Göring and the police. His background would be invaluable to Abwehr's needs." He paused. "You got that?"

Hermann scribbled, "Western Front in the last war." He read it back aloud as he transcribed. He stopped, took a sip of his coffee, and set the cup back down on his desk.

"Come on, Hermann, speed it up. Leave the damned coffee alone."

"Yes sir. Can you repeat after 'the last war?"

Canaris repeated, "And more recently, he worked with Göring and the police. His background would be invaluable to Abwehr's needs."

"Got it."

"Good. Bring it here."

Hermann watched as Canaris stopped and stared for a few minutes at the sealed envelope.

At last, he said, "Deliver this to Himmler," and handed it off. Then he turned away and stared out the window.

CHAPTER EIGHTY

Max walked into the lab and went to the closet, where he took off his jacket and replaced it with a white lab coat. He went to the sink and began washing dirty beakers.

"So how'd you get started here?" he asked Virginia as he reached for another beaker to wash.

"Well, it's a long story, really." She stopped placing test tubes in the centrifuge and looked at him. "You don't want to hear it."

"Sure, I do."

He watched as she held a pipette up in the air, measured it, drained it into a test tube, and recorded a value in her lab book.

"All right. So my family's from Michigan. And they happened to work for Cooper's parents in South

Haven. His family owned one of those huge blueberry farms, you know? His parents, grandparents, great-grandparents—typical old Michigan money."

She stepped back from the centrifuge and went to the sink.

"Here, let me show you." She took the beaker from him, reached up to the shelf above them, and grabbed a sponge.

"Use this," she said.

Max took the sponge and began swabbing out the beaker.

"Anyway, Cooper worked in Ann Arbor during the week but would come on Saturdays to check on the farm. His parents were getting too old to manage it."

She gently took the beaker and sponge out of his hand.

"No, like this." She scrubbed the beaker differently, rinsed it, and put it in the drying rack. "Place them upside down so no soap stays inside."

She went back to her lab bench.

"So, I guess, one of those Saturdays, my parents must have let Cooper know I was studying to be a doctor. There was no way they could afford to send me to medical school. Maybe they were thinking he'd help."

She opened a drawer and pulled out a wire pipette brush and handed it to Max. "Use this."

"Thanks."

"I don't think he really cared too much about me. Think about it. My parents were just farm staff. So not really sure why they told him, but . . ."

She rubbed her brow with her arm to avoid touching her face with her hand and stared into her lab book.

"Hmm," she said. "That's funny." She scratched her head while looking at the data in the lab manual.

"Anyway, one day, when I finished my final exams at East Lansing, the provost of the school called me into his office. He informed me that there was a fire in the farmhouse where my parents worked. They both died."

Max put down the flask he was washing. "Oh, my God!" he said. "That's awful. I'm so sorry."

She grabbed a test tube and a pipette and removed some extract from the test tube.

"I'm fine now, really. That was three years ago already, but that's when Cooper contacted me and said he'd make sure I got into medical school."

She took another pipette and again, held it up to the light, carefully inspected it, placed it back in its rack, and scribbled more notes in her lab book.

"Yeah, something to the effect that he was moving to the city, and if I wanted to come with him, he would pay me as a lab tech through his research grant's funding. And at the same time, he'd make sure I got accepted to NYU's medical school."

"Wow."

"Yeah, pretty amazing, right?"

Max placed the cleaned pipette in the drying rack and picked up another one.

"Look, you do know how important this is, don't you?" she asked.

"I just treat everything like it's important," he said, putting the last pipette in the drying rack and wiping his hands on a dry towel.

"For the grants to continue, his work must be published. Without the grants, my job goes away—probably yours, too. But . . ." She shook her head wistfully. "I won't be able to pay my way through medical school."

"When will you know if it's publishable?" Max asked.

"We don't. We just hope to get the results we're looking for, that's all." Then she smiled. "That's it. You've got it down now. Now, don't get too good, or you'll take my job away."

CHAPTER EIGHTY ONE

Rebecca didn't recognize her own arms. They looked skeletal compared with those of the young woman who had just been thrown into her cell. She found herself staring at the girl's hair.

"Oh, you can see I cut it short," she said with a sad smile.

She couldn't be more than 17, and she looked even younger.

"I did it because I work for the underground."

"For who?"

"Rowecki," she said. She walked nervously around their small cell and peered between the bars, trying to see down the hall. "I was with two others. Did you see them?"

"No," Rebecca said quietly.

"I'm Masha. Are you Jewish?"

"Yes."

The stocky woman guard with the thick ankles came in. "You," she said, pointing her rifle at Rebecca. "And you." She pointed it at Masha.

"Turn around," she said to Rebecca. Leaning her rifle against the bars, she tied Rebecca's hands together behind her back.

"Now you," she said to Masha. After trussing the girl, she picked the rifle back up and pushed the muzzle against Masha's back. "Out. Both of you, walk. Now."

They walked out of the cell, getting alternating pokes in the back with the rifle muzzle as the guard marched them down the passageway toward the rear door.

"You . . ." She pointed to Rebecca. "Watch. She goes first." She pushed Rebecca's head against the barred window.

Rebecca could see into the street. Spectators had gathered around the town square as if expecting a show. To the center of the crowd stood a post with a short horizontal beam projecting from the top, like an upside-down L, and a sturdy rope with a slipknot hung from the beam.

The guard pushed open the door to the street and put her rifle to the back of Masha's head. "You're first. Walk."

For the first time, Rebecca noticed that Masha wore only a scarf, a light-gray coat, and underpants. Her legs were bare. Rebecca watched from the window as the barefoot girl walked slowly past the staring townspeople. Winter had come early and killed whatever color once flourished in the town square. Nothing but bare branches remained on a few small trees.

Masha's teeth chattered with each hesitant step she took on the uneven cobblestones. As she walked closer to the gallows, Rebecca turned away. But the guard pushed her head back to the window and said, "Watch."

Masha took three steps onto the scaffold, and two soldiers hoisted her onto a stool beneath the beam. A man put the noose around her neck and hung a sign on her that read "*Juden*."

Some of the spectators laughed, and one even took a photo of the girl on the stool.

When Masha looked up and stared back at her, Rebecca felt the tears come. She could see the fear in the girl's eyes. Then a command was shouted, and the executioner kicked the stool over. Rebecca turned away again, but the rifle muzzle nudged her back.

"Watch," the guard commanded. She watched as Masha's legs flailed about and she lost control of her bowels and bladder.

"Now it's your turn," the guard said. And grabbing Rebecca by the arm, she marched her to the closed door. There they waited for several minutes. Then the guard turned her around and walked her back to the cell.

"Not today," she said, laughing. "But soon."

CHAPTER EIGHTY TWO

Cooper was dressed for the weekend: plaid shorts, loafers without socks, and a pink dress shirt. A white argyle sweater was draped loosely over his shoulders, and he wore a new pair of oval tortoiseshell glasses.

"I want to see the latest numbers," he said to Virginia.

Max handed Virginia the lab book.

"Here." She opened to the page. "These are the most recent results."

He looked at the book carefully. "Something's not right," he said. "The numbers aren't tracking."

"I wondered about that," Virginia said.

"Did you correct for the weight of additional solvent?"

"Of course."

"What about . . . wait. I know, did you pipette using the same scales? You didn't change scales, did you?"

"Of course not."

Max watched as Cooper grew more agitated.

"Virginia, this isn't what we expected. Did you measure the aliquots in cubic centimeters, or milligrams?"

"I did it just as you told me to," she replied.

"This can't be right," he said. "Go back and do it all again. Repeat it. Something's off. Fix it. Make it work." He thrust the lab book back at her. "For God's sake, have Max help you if you can't figure it out."

"Asshole," she said under her breath as he left the room.

CHAPTER EIGHTY THREE

General Hans Oster was shorter, skinnier, and generally less imposing than Canaris. Hermann watched as the two leaders stood by the window and spoke in whispers. He tried to hear what they were saying, but their voices were too soft. Oster's face was more revealing than Canaris, easier to read, Hermann thought.

"Hermann, give us a few minutes," Canaris said.

"Of course." Hermann grabbed his coffee and left the office.

Canaris went to the door and locked it. Then both men stepped away from the door and back near the window.

"September, he's planning Czechoslovakia," Oster said. "This must be done before Chamberlain goes public; otherwise, he'll annex it, and then there's no military operation."

"We're set. Beck, Von Weitzelbaum, and Hoepner—all ready," Canaris said.

"If Chamberlain louses it up, we lose their support. We must move before . . ."

A knock on the door interrupted Oster.

"Who's there?" Canaris asked.

"Hermann, sir."

"What is it?"

Hermann put his mouth up to the door. "I left some files on my desk. I need them so I can work while I wait."

Canaris looked at Oster. He nodded, and Oster walked over and unlocked the door. They watched as Hermann grabbed the files on his desk.

"I'm done; this what I need. Sorry."

Hermann sensed that something very odd was happening. He hurried out of the office, closed the door behind him, and stood in the hallway. He heard the door lock behind him. He looked around. No one was in the corridor, and he could hear no footsteps. So he put his ear against the door to hear the conversation inside.

CHAPTER EIGHTY FOUR

Virginia opened the lab journal and said, "These are the most recent results."

Ignoring the lines of data, he took a pipette from the rack and held it up to the light. She could see the stress in his tired eyes.

"Virginia," he said, "I'm about to receive the most prestigious grant in NYU's history. We've got to get our numbers right."

"Dr. Cooper, the numbers don't lie," she said.

"Yes, I know this. Do you take me for an imbecile?"

Virginia was taken aback. He had never spoken to her that way.

He slapped the open journal at her workstation. "Review these books, find out where the discrepancy is, and fix it."

She pointed to the journal. "Doctor," she said, "I've been over these books ten times. There's no discrepancy. The hypothesis is shot; the theory doesn't work. You've got to scrap this project." She looked down at the terrazzo floor.

"Virginia, *we* are not scrapping this project. If it gets scrapped, I lose my funding and you get scrapped. You lose your job—and any chance of getting into this medical school."

"Well, I can't change what is into what we wish it were. I can't just make up data."

He looked at her in silence.

"Oh . . . I see. You want me to cook the numbers."

He looked at her again without speaking.

"I'm sorry. I won't do that."

"Listen to me, and don't be a smart-ass. You took my help when you needed it; now I need *your* help. This is not the time to get all holier than thou."

Virginia shook her head. "I won't do it," she said. And closing the lab book, she walked out.

CHAPTER EIGHTY FIVE

Stats was surprised to see Varian Fry standing at the front door. A cap hid his face, and his arms were tucked into the pockets of his unbuttoned trench coat.

"Let's talk," Fry said.

Stats turned around and looked inside the house. No one was home. He motioned for Fry to come in.

"Outside," he said, and looked over his shoulder to the park across the street.

Stats went to his room, grabbed his jacket, and walked across the street to join Fry.

He sat down on the park bench. The park was quiet except for a mother pushing a stroller on the narrow gravel path.

For a moment, Fry looked at him and said nothing.

Stats stared back, waiting for an answer.

He looked straight ahead, as if Stats were just another stranger. "She's still alive."

Stats burst into tears.

"She's in Stadelheim," Fry continued.

Stats took a deep breath and said, "How do you know?"

Fry looked around them and said, "Rowecki."

"Here's the problem . . ."

Stats brushed away the tears and said, "What problem?"

"She has ten days; then they're moving her to Dachau."

"But . . . she's as good as dead there," Stats said.

Fry got up, but Stats followed him. "Can you get her a message?"

"She's in Stadelheim," Fry repeated.

"Rowecki can do it. I need you to get her a message."

"No. I'm sorry, I can't. Look. I got what you asked for. That's all we can do. It's out of our control."

"What about Rowecki?" Stats pleaded. "Can I talk to him? I need to talk to him."

"Look, I don't know when I'll hear next from Rowecki. It just happens when it happens; I don't initiate it. If I hear anything, I'll let you know." He patted Stats on the shoulder.

Stats just looked down at the winter-brown grass.

"This conversation never happened," Fry said, and he walked away.

CHAPTER EIGHTY SIX

Every time Oster came to Canaris's office, Canaris asked Hermann to "give us a few minutes." And it was occurring with a disturbing increase in frequency.

"I just finished with Himmler," Canaris said. "The Gestapo's identified some resistance fighters. They've caused all kinds of headaches for the SS. They're our agents."

"How many?" Oster asked.

"Seven Jews."

"I'll talk to Rowecki and see what he can do," Oster said.

"You need to get them out now, before Himmler gets to them."

"I know." Oster stepped over to the office door, unlocked it, and walked out, passing Hermann just outside the door.

"Excuse me," Hermann said as he bumped into Oster.

Oster looked at him oddly and walked away.

Hermann went back into the office, sat down, opened some files on his desk, and resumed his work.

He watched as Canaris walked to the window, opened it slightly, and lit up a cigarette.

"Admiral, any news with the Bund?"

"The what?" Canaris said.

"The Bund. The Americans."

Canaris put out his cigarette and went back to his desk. "Ah, yes, Hermann, how's that going?"

"Excuse me?"

"Sorry," the admiral said. "Just a bit distracted today. I'll keep you posted on the progress. I'm quite pleased, though, with the job you're doing."

CHAPTER EIGHTY SEVEN

Cooper knew as well as anyone on the faculty that Dean Wyckoff was too principled to tolerate unethical academic behavior. Only this month, he had expelled eight students from the medical school for cheating on a relatively trivial quiz. There was no discussion, no warning, just no tolerance. They were gone. "If they cheat now, they'll cheat later," Wyckoff had said to Cooper. "I won't graduate them. It's that simple."

They sat in Wyckoff's spacious office. On the wall were pictures of the dean shaking hands with the young Democratic governor, Franklin Roosevelt, and with Mayor Jimmy Walker.

"I get it, Jack," Cooper said, "but let's be honest here. Everyone's feeling the crunch. The university's not paying you enough to put up with this bullshit. By the way, how's Elizabeth?"

"Mean as ever," Wyckoff said, smiling, and Cooper chuckled. "Look, Chuck, I didn't take this job for the money. I took it—"

"Jack, stop. Spare me the bullshit, please. You still need money. Your wife still likes a nice dinner out, a show now and then." Cooper sat down in the chair across from Wyckoff's desk, took out his pipe, and tamped a load of tobacco down in the bowl without lighting it.

"We're doing fine." His eyes shifted ever so slightly from side to side.

"All right," Cooper said, the pipe clamped in the corner of his mouth, "Look, I just thought . . ."

"What is it?" Wyckoff asked.

Cooper took an envelope from his coat pocket and laid it on the desk.

Wyckoff picked up the envelope. "What's this?"

"All you have to do is certify them. It's fine. If they look normal, certify them as normal; if they don't, then just certify them as abnormal. You're doing nothing wrong here."

Wyckoff opened the envelope and pulled out electrocardiogram reports. He thumbed through them and then put them back in the envelope.

"They need a cardiologist's stamp of approval, so I thought of you; that's all. If you don't want it, I'll take it back." He reached out for the envelope.

"But for each read, you get a hundred dollars. That's a lot of first-run Broadway tickets for Elizabeth."

"Sorry, Charles." He handed the envelope back.

"Okay, your call." He put the envelope back in his coat pocket. He stood up from the chair, tapped the unsmoked bowl of tobacco into a wastebasket, and put the pipe back in his coat pocket.

"You've worked hard, Jack, and you're a damn good cardiologist."

"I have ethical guidelines," Wyckoff said.

"Look I'm doing this for you, Jack," Cooper said. "I don't get anything out of it. I don't see any ethical dilemma here." He reached back into his pocket, pulled the envelope out, and put it back on the desk. "Tell you what: if you want it, it's here. If you don't, just toss it there." Cooper pointed to the wastebasket, then turned and strode out of the office.

CHAPTER EIGHTY EIGHT

Max was excited to be invited to the department meeting. He watched in anticipation as Rosenthal cleared his throat, then picked up his teaspoon and banged it lightly against his champagne glass.

"I want to thank all of you for taking time to celebrate," he said, then waited for the murmurs to fade.

"I'm tremendously honored and privileged to be the chair here. It's a special night. One man's life commitment to bench research has benefitted all of us." Rosenthal raised his champagne flute. "The largest grant in US history has just been awarded to our own Dr. Charles Cooper."

During the eager applause, Max watched Dr. Cooper's expression of feigned humility.

"I'd like to read the letter from the National Institutes of Health," Rosenthal said. He took the letter from his coat pocket and pushed his glasses down on his nose. "This grant pins the hopes of the entire country on the groundbreaking work of Dr. Cooper. The promise of a cure for debilitating diseases will one day be within reach. In these times of economic uncertainty, the NIH is certain that these funds are well allocated."

Rosenthal put the letter down.

"What does it mean for us?" He looked around the room. "Well, Dr. Cooper's grant affects everyone in this room. Half goes to the department, half to Cooper's lab."

Applause again filled the room.

"Hold on. There's more. This grant makes NYU's the highest-funded department of neurology in the country. And, we're indebted to Dr. Cooper for making this happen."

All present gave a rousing final applause. Cooper smiled and raised his drink in acknowledgment to his colleagues. Max plastered on a fake smile and raised his drink. It occurred to him that he hated these dog-and-pony shows.

CHAPTER EIGHTY NINE

Max looked up at the waitress as she poured their coffee. She started to put two breakfast menus on the table.

"Not necessary," Max said. "Two over medium, piece of toast, just for me. Thanks. She's not eating." The waitress scribbled on her notepad, smiled, and walked away.

"You missed quite a meeting last night," he said. "Cooper was the man of the hour. It was a disgusting display of vanity."

Virginia took a sip of her coffee. "I've decided to take a break from the lab for now."

"Just like that?"

She looked out the window at the people hurrying past on the sidewalk. "I did research because it would help me get into med school. Now that I'm accepted, I need to refocus."

"What about Cooper? What's he gonna say?"

"What *can* he say? Dean Wyckoff let me know last week he had a spot for me. I'm supposed to start next month. I can't do both."

"Does he understand?"

"I don't really care."

"A bit touchy this morning, are we? Really, what is it?"

"Nothing."

"What about the tuition?" Max said. "What are you going to do?"

The waitress brought his plate. He picked up the ketchup bottle, tilted it, and smacked it with his palm.

"I don't know. Apply for loans."

"And what about the research?"

"Cooper will figure it out."

"Hah!" he said, his mouth full of eggs and toast. "I can't help him."

She looked up at the clock behind the counter.

"Wait, then what about me?" he asked.

"It's getting late. I need to go." She got up and hugged Max. "Sorry I don't have time to stay while you finish your breakfast."

"You didn't answer me," he said.

"I know," she said, and off she went.

He pushed away his plate. Suddenly, his favorite breakfast didn't taste so good.

CHAPTER NINETY

Varian Fry walked alone through Central Park. It was dusk, and the park was quiet. He strolled past Bethesda Fountain and glanced casually at a streetlamp nearby. His eyes tracked up the lamppost and then down to the small x chalked four feet from the bottom. Appearing to lean on the concrete post, he wiped away the x with his elbow. He walked over to a bench fifty yards away and sat down to watch the model sailboats in the pond. He reached under the bench and pulled out a *New York Times*. Taped inside was a small white note.

> *Tunnel still open. Lieutenant Van der Stok on board. Will need one more to help retrieve package. Recruit, meet, and educate. Clock ticking. Must be immediate. Fondly, Row.*

Fry got up from the bench, folded the paper, and walked over to a garbage can, ripping the note into tiny bits and dropping them as he walked.

CHAPTER NINETY ONE

Hermann knew he was taking a gamble, but then, risking was the only way to get ahead. He approached Himmler's office, straightened out his uniform, took a deep breath, and knocked on the door.

The secretary, the voluptuous Hedwig Potthast, opened the door. "May I help you?" she said.

"I don't have an appointment, but I would like to speak with the Reichsführer."

She looked him over. "No appointment? He's in meetings. You won't be able to see him."

Watching her turn around, he almost forgot his mission. Everyone knew about Hedwig and Himmler—everyone, that is, except for Margarete, Himmler's wife.

"I'll wait," he said.

"I can't guarantee he'll see you, but you're welcome to do whatever you want," she said, and went back to work behind her desk.

CHAPTER NINETY TWO

Rosenthal straightened in his comfortable leather chair and stared into his colleague's eyes. "Tom, do you have any idea what you're saying?"

"Of course" Tom Debeer replied. That's why I look like this—I haven't slept in days."

Tom was a neurology fellow who worked in the lab next to Dr. Cooper's. He was tall and thin, with a perpetual two-day beard. It never grew, and he seemed never to shave it. His strong cheekbones and reddish-blond curls somehow put Rosenthal in mind of a willowy, rather effeminate Viking. Rosenthal knew that Tom and Dr. Cooper had been at odds ever since Cooper shot down his proposal for studying the effects of blood sugar on peripheral neuropathy.

"You do know what everyone will say?" Rosenthal asked.

"Oh, yeah, I know."

Rosenthal said, "You know he's the most prestigious researcher in our department—single-handedly responsible for putting us on the map, getting me my job, paying my salary and those of probably half the researchers in this department."

"I know. But I'm telling you, the numbers don't add up. I tried to reproduce them. Nothing works. It's not an error; it's impossible."

Rosenthal leaned back in his chair. "I just can't risk it, Tom. He's too important. I'm not going to say anything. "

"You have to."

Rosenthal cocked one eyebrow. "I beg your pardon?"

"Listen, I mean no disrespect, but you know as well as I do, if his numbers are bogus, you need to do something about it."

Rosenthal pounded his fist on the desk. "God damn it, Tom, you're talking about a career researcher of the highest caliber. I just can't accept this. I won't!"

"You won't, because it'll compromise your own prestige?"

Rosenthal looked at him. "You're out of line."

"Am I, Curt?"

"Everyone knows you have it in for Cooper. It's no secret around here."

Tom crossed his arms defiantly. "You know damn well this has nothing to do with my issue with Cooper." This is about giving false hope to a country desperate for a cure. It's about NIH funding. I'm telling you, something's not kosher here."

Rosenthal retreated back into his chair. "I'll tell you what. Let me do some poking around and ask someone else to run the numbers. You have no credibility anyway—everyone will just think you're trying to shoot him down for spite."

"Okay, look, it's not my problem anymore. I did what I needed to do. Take it for what it's worth." Tom stood up and walked toward the door. "And just for the record, I do hate that pretentious son of a bitch."

CHAPTER NINETY THREE

Hearing the knock, Stats opened it and was surprised to see Varian Fry standing on the stoop.

"Let's take a walk," he said to Stats.

Stats grabbed his jacket, and they both walked down Houston Street.

They turned onto Orchard. Street vendors with pushcarts peddled their wares in front of run-down tenements. Orchard was thick with pedestrians as they continued their walk toward Chinatown.

Fry said nothing for three blocks, and then looked around them and said, "I heard from Row."

"Who?" he asked.

"Rowecki."

"Yeah? And?"

"They're going to try."

"Try what?" They both kept walking.

"Come on . . ." He looked around. "Retrieve the package."

"You mean Rebecca?" Stats said.

"Can you *please* use some discretion," Fry said, glancing around them for possible eavesdroppers.

"We have an asset. He's made a few runs—escaped twice already. He's going back."

"Who?"

Fry waited for a young couple to pass them on the sidewalk and get out of easy earshot, then said, "A lieutenant, Royal Air Force—works with underground. "

Stats stopped walking and pretended to look at some bad rugs. "Is this possible?"

Fry turned away and murmured, "Look, this guy's done it before. Of course, it's not easy. He's smart, gifted with languages, knows the countryside, but . . ."

"But?" Stats asked.

"He needs someone to accompany him back into the Beehive. He won't do it alone. It's easier in packs of two. Not only for his cover—he'll need help."

"So who? What about Rowecki?" Stats asked.

Fry looked straight ahead and said, "Watch your tongue, dumb shit."

"He doesn't do the missions. He coordinates them, puts the plan in place."

Stats looked up to the sky. The gray cloud cover had burned off, and it was blue and bright again.

"So who, then?"

"I'm looking at him."

CHAPTER NINETY FOUR

Himmler's office was paneled from floor to ceiling. A burgundy leather couch was positioned conveniently next to a wet bar. His small, steely eyes peered out from thick wire-rimmed glasses.

"Would you like a drink, Hermann?" he said.

"No . . . thank you, Reichsführer," Hermann stammered.

"Well, then, you've told me enough," Himmler said. "I'll look into it." He poured himself a brandy. "If it pans out, you'll be a hero, young man."

"Reichsführer, sir, I don't really care about all that," Hermann replied in what he hoped was a modest tone.

CHAPTER NINETY FIVE

"You wanted to see me?" Dr. Greer asked.

"Yes, I need a favor," Rosenthal said. "And I need you to keep it quiet. He leaned forward with his elbows resting on his desk.

"What is it, then?"

Rosenthal reached into his desk drawer. "I want you to validate this." He slid Cooper's abstract and grant proposal across his desk.

Greer picked up the pages and thumbed through them. "What do you mean?" he asked.

"Just what I said: I want to independently verify his numbers."

"Why? You doubting them?" Greer asked.

"No. I just want to make sure they hold up."

"How would I do that?" Greer placed the paper back on Rosenthal's desk.

"That's his abstract and his NIH proposal. Take it and run the numbers. Make sure it works. Use my lab. I'll cover the expenses."

Greer picked the paper back up and looked at it again. "You sure?" he asked.

"Just do it as quickly as you can and report back to me."

"Yeah, I guess, but . . ."

"No buts. And remember, no one, not a soul, is to know about this."

"Got it."

CHAPTER NINETY SIX

The thin mattress did little to cushion Stats from the stiff wires underneath. Each time he turned, the cot squeaked as he tried to find the position where nothing dug into his back. He looked over at Max, envying his ability to sleep in any conditions. Stats folded the worn pillow over his ears to dampen the snores coming from across the little bedroom.

No luck. The snoring grew louder.

Stats threw his pillow, catching Max on the face.

"What the hell was that for?" Max asked.

"I can't sleep—your snoring is killing me."

Max threw the pillow back and growled, "Leave me alone. I'm trying sleep, asshole."

"I need to talk to you," Stats said. He sat up in his bed.

"Tomorrow. I need my sleep."
"I spoke to Fry today," Stats said.
Max sat up.

CHAPTER NINETY SEVEN

With his office at his back, Canaris looked up at the street sign, Prinz Albrecht Strasse, and then looked east toward Wilhelmstrasse. It was a typical gray Berlin day, and he wore gloves and a thick winter trench coat.

Taking his gloves off, he stuck them in his coat pocket, took out a cigarette, and lit up. He was alone. He looked up at the Museum of Decorative Arts, then at the Martin Gropis Bau next to it.

Their headquarters had taken over the museum, and now his office, Himmler's office, and the Reich's main security office all operated from there.

He watched as Oster left the building. Then he walked on down the street, toward Stresemannstrasse neat Potsdamer Platz, and waited.

"Damn, it's cold out here," Oster said, coming alongside.

"We can't talk in the offices anymore," Canaris said.

They walked together, speaking softly. "Row made contact," Oster said. This time the package is in Stadelheim. A chosen one."

"I'm not sure," Canaris said, lighting up again. "The time may not be right. Himmler seems to be one step ahead of them." Holding the cigarette between his fingers, he cupped his hands and blew into them.

"Why don't you put your gloves on?" Oster said.

"Doesn't work with these damn cigarettes."

"Is the network primed?" Oster asked.

"Yes, Gisevius. Circuits are on and electricians standing by."

"Okay. The current must flow. Seven days."

Canaris turned and walked back to their office while Oster looked in a store window.

CHAPTER NINETY EIGHT

Max walked quietly into the lab. Dr. Cooper was working at his desk.

"Dr. Cooper?"

He looked up at Max.

"Is there anything you need me to do? Virginia would have a list of daily tasks for me."

"Oh, yes, of course. Max, do me a favor. Clean up her bench. Get rid of any work she was doing. You can just dispose of it. Make her area look untouched."

Max walked over to her lab bench. He opened her journal and sorted through the pages of her work. He glanced at the formulas, and notes written on the pages, though he wasn't sure of their meaning. Her observations, though, were noted, with the time and date recorded.

"Dr. Cooper," Max called across the lab. "Are you sure you want me to throw this away?" He held up the book. "Don't you need that?"

"Of course I know what it is, and no. I've got the same numbers here." Cooper pointed down to the papers strewn all over his desk. "Just clean it up and get rid of it. We have a new tech starting, and he'll need a clean working space." Cooper pushed his glasses back up and said, "Can you be a good chap and just do that for me?"

"Of course. Right away."

"By the way, I've spoken with Dean Wyckoff about you. He's had a few spots open up—something about some students he had to dismiss. I guess bad news for them is good news for you," Cooper said.

CHAPTER NINETY NINE

Dr. Greer sat across from Rosenthal. He looked as if he had been up all night.

"I can't believe it," he said. "You were right."

Rosenthal put the fountain pen in its holder. "Go on."

Greer laid the papers down in front of Rosenthal and whispered, "The numbers don't work. I've tried every conceivable scenario. I don't get it."

"Thanks, Mel," Rosenthal said. And taking the papers off his desk, he folded them in half and tucked them in his sport coat.

"That's it?"

"That's it. I'll take it from here."

"What are you gonna do?" Greer asked.

"I don't know yet. Remember, no one knows about this."

"Yes, I got that."

"I guess I should double check. You considered all variables?"

Greer nodded.

"Effects of temperature?"

Yes, everything checked and rechecked."

"You accounted for the differences between various cell membranes? The islet cells from different species? You cross-checked it?"

Greer gave an exasperated sigh. "Curt, I ran it forward, backwards, sideways, and upside down. No matter how you slice it, these numbers are fudged. *They don't work.* I'm sorry. You'd think NIH would've done their homework."

"Thanks again, Mel."

Greer stood up and pushed the chair back. "You'll see my numbers in red. They show where the errors are."

"Nice work."

Greer walked out. As the door shut behind him, Rosenthal picked up the phone and started dialing. Then he stopped and put the phone back on its cradle.

"Damn it," he said, and buried his face in his hands.

CHAPTER ONE HUNDRED

"You wanted to see me?" Cooper asked.

"Please sit down," Rosenthal said.

"Okay, but I'm in a hurry," Cooper said.

Rosenthal moved a stack of papers from between them and said, "Charles, I wanted to talk to you about the grant."

"Sure, Curt. What is it?"

Rosenthal put Greer's notes down on the desk. "Take a look at this."

Cooper picked the notes up and thumbed through them.

"What is this?"

"It's data."

"And?"

"Come on, Charles, don't be an ass. It's data reproduced from your work. See the numbers in red."

Cooper stared at it quietly, turning the pages more slowly this time. "This isn't right," he said at last, and dropped the file back on the desk. "These aren't my numbers."

"But they are."

Cooper thumbed through them again. "What are you trying to say, Curt?"

"I'm not sure yet."

Looking him in the eye, Cooper said, "Is this something you really want to do?"

"What?" Rosenthal asked as he loosened his tie.

"This is hogwash. Whoever gave you this is full of shit. This is not my research."

"Charles . . ."

"Listen, you ungrateful son of a bitch, I got you this damn job." He pointed his finger down at the desk.

"Charles, I was just asking you for an explanation."

Cooper grabbed the papers out of Rosenthal's hand. He looked again, quietly studying it. He swallowed nervously. Then, as if struck by a lightning bolt of truth, he sat back and put the file back down.

"I didn't want to believe this," he said.

"What?"

"Well, I figured if NIH accepted it, it must be true. I was sure they would have verified."

"What do you mean? You knew?" Rosenthal asked.

"No. I didn't *know.* I guess I just didn't want to believe it, so I didn't want to look hard enough to challenge it."

"I'm listening," Rosenthal said.

"Well, my lab tech—I've trusted her with everything. I practically raised her."

"What are you talking about?"

Again Cooper shook his head sorrowfully. "I wondered why she left the lab so abruptly."

"I'm not sure I understand."

"I brought her here after her parents died. Got her the job in my lab to help me with research. Hell, I actually got her a position with Wyckoff to start in medical school next month." He chuckled and sat back down.

"I'm not sure I'm following."

"So she needed this research grant more than I did. She has no money to pay for med school."

"What are you saying, Charles?"

"She must have manipulated the numbers. She gave me false data."

"Why?"

"I don't know why. Probably to get the funding approved so she'd have a job to pay for med school. Don't ask me why someone would do this sort of shit at my expense."

"What are you saying?"

Cooper licked his lips and said, "I'm saying I'm guilty—guilty of trusting my lab tech. I should have verified the numbers she gave me, but her work was always solid. I had no need to run these numbers any other way."

Rosenthal stared at him, then said, "We have to let NIH know."

"Of course we do. I'll let them know what happened."

"That's a relief," Rosenthal said, meaning it.

Cooper picked up a staff picture off Rosenthal's desk.

"Come on, Curt. How long have you known me?"

"Look, it's not an indictment of you. You had an overzealous, unprincipled technician."

"Whatever it is, it's not what I want to be associated with." He set the framed photo back down. "You know what, though? I'm sorry for the department."

"They'll get over it." Rosenthal said.

Cooper got up to leave.

"Before you go?" Rosenthal asked.

"Yes?"

"You want me to talk to Wyckoff about this lab tech? Or do you want to? Either way, she'll never be allowed to enroll here. You know Wyckoff; he won't stand for it."

"I figured that," Cooper said. "Probably best if you tell him. I think it's too painful for me. She was like a daughter." He walked out of the office, looking grief-stricken.

CHAPTER ONE HUNDRED ONE

Rebecca had lost all sense of time. She couldn't remember if she had been here a month or a year. And with no reference point, she could gauge time only as intervals, either shorter or longer, between her brief but tragic encounters with Sophie and Masha, both of whom she saw hanged at the gallows just outside the prison door. The memory of those events punctuated the difference in time more effectively than the progression of days and nights, which had now blurred into each other. She sat alone in her cell, awaiting her own march to the gallows.

She looked around the cell and noticed the utter absence of color. The cell floor and walls were gray, the bars were black, and her clothing was gray. Colors, change, flowers, azure skies, green grass—she yearned to see them once more. Perhaps, at least, they would hang her on a green spring day under a blue sky. She hadn't yet given up hope, but she knew she should. *Hope for what?* Her parents gone, her friends gone, her life now was all about the wait.

And that was why the voice of the guard no longer surprised her, no longer threatened her. For what threat remained? Certainly not death. Even the threat of pain no longer elicited an emotional response.

"Get up," the guard said, opening the cell door. "It's your turn." It was an odd time to be woken. All the other prisoners were still asleep. She didn't move until she felt a hand clamp down on one gaunt arm. She was dragged up off the floor and out of the cell.

Rebecca was confused, but clarity came with the sharp prod of a rifle muzzle against her bony back. "Walk this way," the female guard with the masculine voice commanded, and she started the slog down the familiar hallway.

"I'll take the *Juden* bitch from here," said a strange man dressed in a Wehrmacht officer's uniform.

"Heil Hitler," the guard said, saluting the officer.

Hans Bernard Gisevius returned the Nazi salute, then pushed Rebecca down to the floor.

With no fat or muscle left to cushion the fall, she winced at the jarring, bruising impact. Hunger brought with it all manner of incidental pain.

He yanked her up by the hair. "On your feet, dog," he said.

She moved like a marionette in the hands of a tired puppeteer. He then pushed her through the same door she had previously watched Sophie and Masha pass through to meet their fate. And, now, with no family to cry to and no friends to reach out to, it was finally her turn to thrash and dangle from the gibbet.

CHAPTER ONE HUNDRED TWO

Himmler called a special meeting of his inner intelligence corps. Present were SS-Brigadeführer Walter Schellenberg and also Reinhard Heydrich, chief of the Reich Security office. Both men sat attentively on his leather couch. Conspicuously absent was Canaris.

"Coffee?" Hedwig asked.

Himmler watched as both men tried not to notice her moving seductively around the room and pouring the coffee.

Himmler moved to the window and glared outside. The buildings spoke to him. Their carved stone implied Nazi strength and reinforced his own sense of superiority.

Heinrich Himmler was not a large man, but he overcompensated for his physical limitations with cunning. His ability to anticipate the next move, whether by the enemy or by a colleague, had made him one of the most powerful men in Germany.

He backed away from the window and stared at his reflection, hating his face. The chin was weak, making him look like a baby bird. He looked at his reflection again and turned his head to the side, then came away from the window.

He stared silently through the round wire-rimmed glasses that had become his trademark. This was a tactic he always used: never speak first. The two men on the sofa, also talented and accomplished in their own right, fidgeted in the painful silence. They knew never to speak first with Himmler, for whom every encounter was a chess match.

"I have reason to believe a cancer is growing in the Abwehr," he said at last. He stared coldly at the two men.

"I want surveillance on Canaris, Oster, and Gisevius." He didn't turn around.

"I want to know everything they do, everywhere they go, every time they talk. I want to know when they take a shit."

CHAPTER ONE HUNDRED THREE

Fry met Stats at Chelsea Piers. They strolled around the docks, among the hordes who had gathered to catch a glimpse of the *Queen Mary* before she sailed out of New York Harbor.

"You sure you're up for this?" Fry asked, motioning behind him at the world's largest passenger ship.

"It's a little late for second thoughts," Stats replied.

Fry took papers out of his inside coat pocket and handed them to Stats. "Okay, here we go again." After a quick glance around, he said, "Here's your new identity." He handed him a fake Dutch passport. "If you get caught, you're Dutch."

"But I don't speak Dutch."

"Then don't get caught. Here, this is for the *Queen Mary*." He handed Stats the boarding tickets and pointed to the embarkation ramp behind them.

Stats put the passport in his baggage.

"When you get off at Southampton, RAF reps will find you. They'll bring you to a place to meet Van der Stok. He'll take it from there. "Good luck."

"Luck's a funny thing I haven't had much of," Stats said, and walked toward the board ramp.

"You're breathing, aren't you? Sounds like good luck to me."

CHAPTER ONE HUNDRED FOUR

The dean's office was considerably larger than Rosenthal's. Rosenthal glanced over to the bar area and noticed the almost empty bottle of twenty-five-year-old Macallan's. Next to it was a small wide-rimmed glass with a bare few drops of amber in the bottom.

"Jack," Rosenthal said, "I came over here to tell you about a tech in Cooper's lab. Apparently, she was the one who fudged his lab results."

Wyckoff got up from behind his desk and walked over to the bar. He picked up the whisky glass. "You?"

Rosenthal waved it off. "No thanks.

Wyckoff picked up the bottle and emptied the remaining scotch into his glass, then dropped the bottle into the garbage can below the bar. "Curt, why are you telling me this?"

"It affects all of us," Rosenthal said, staring at his back.

"What do you mean?"

"The department's going to lose its NIH funding. Cooper's data doesn't hold up. It doesn't work."

Wyckoff walked back to his desk and sat down. "So what? The NIH funded Cooper, not the data."

"Not really, Jack. The money's gone. They won't fund a bogus project."

"What about the Rockefellers?"

"We could go to them, but that's not what I'm saying. The department will be fine, but . . ."

"Then what is it?"

"It's the tech. She's supposed to start medical school here next week."

"What's her name? "

"Virginia. Virginia Wright."

"I know Ms. Wright." He picked up his glass and took a sip of his scotch.

"She fudged the data—almost sabotaged Charles's lab."

"What do you want me to do?" Wyckoff asked. He finished the remaining scotch and banged the glass down on his desk.

"I don't know. I thought you'd have strong feelings about this. I just wanted you to know."

Wyckoff leaned forward. "God damn it," he growled, "you know as well as I do, we can't permit that kind of behavior here. I can't admit her now."

"I suspected as much." Rosenthal looked down momentarily and then pushed his chair back and stood up.

"Tell Cooper to reapply with the Rockefellers. They're are anxious to fund something."

"Will do."

As Rosenthal left, Dr. Wyckoff summoned his secretary. "Mary, please get Miss Wright to my office. I need to speak to her immediately. God damn it!"

CHAPTER ONE HUNDRED FIVE

Canaris lit up another cigarette and walked over to Hermann. He put his hand on his shoulder. "You're doing a good job, Hermann."

"Yes sir, thank you, sir." Hermann said obediently.

Canaris sat down at his desk and began to scribble something on a note. Then he ripped it up and threw it in the wastebasket. He stared at the curl of smoke rising from his cigarette.

"Is there something else, sir?"

"What?" Canaris said, distracted.

"Is there anything, or should I leave?"

Canaris didn't answer. He walked over to the window and stared down at Wilhelmstrasse. He stood silent for a minute.

"Sir?" Hermann said.

Canaris didn't look back at him.

"I'm going to step out unless you need something else."

Canaris didn't acknowledge him but just continued to stare out the window.

Hermann glanced at the garbage can and eyed the ripped note. Dropping a pencil, he bent down to pick it up and grabbed the note as well. He stuffed it in his pocket and left the room.

CHAPTER ONE HUNDRED SIX

Virginia had no idea why she had been called to the dean's office. Her feet tapped nervously on the floor as she waited.

"Dean Wyckoff will see you now," Mary, his secretary, said, leading her into his personal office.

Dr. Wyckoff was on the phone. He gestured for Virginia to sit down, put his hand over the phone, and said, "I'll be with you in one moment."

She stared around the room and noticed the empty bottle in the garbage can, then saw the empty glass on his desk.

"Miss Wright," he began. "Virginia?"

"Yes."

"Is that all right?" he asked, taking a cigarette from the pack on his desk. He lit it and slowly exhaled.

She nodded her head.

"Do you know why you're here?" Wyckoff asked.

"No. Not really." She leaned forward on the chair. Her feet tapped nervously on the floor.

Wyckoff looked down momentarily and watched her nervous tapping.

"This is difficult. I'm not really sure how to tell you this. Damn."

She looked at him and didn't say anything.

He picked up his empty scotch glass and put it back down, then said, "Oh, what the hell. We're withdrawing your acceptance."

"What do you mean?" Virginia asked stunned.

"*Perstare et praestare.*" he said, pointing to the NYU medallion that hung on the wall.

He walked over to the bar, bent over, and picked up the discarded bottle. Turning it up, he held it over his glass and shook a few drops out of it, then dropped it back into the wastebasket.

"It means 'to persevere and excel.'" With his back still to her, he said, "It's the moral core of this university."

"But why withdraw my acceptance?"

"We can't accept anyone who doesn't demonstrate the highest commitment to excellence. And that means honesty and integrity. " He turned around from the bar and stared at her.

"I did nothing that was dishonest."

"Talk to Cooper; he reported you. Told us you fudged his numbers so you could keep getting paid."

"That son of a bitch," she murmured.

"It saddens me to revoke your admission."

Tears welled up in her eyes, but she said nothing. He stared silently.

"There are other schools," he said. "Just not NYU. Remember, persevere and excel."

Her hands trembled. She wiped a tear from her eye.

"Fuck this." She mumbled and got up and left his office.

CHAPTER ONE HUNDRED SEVEN

The noose hung in the spotlight on the only illuminated spot in the courtyard. The rest of the gallows stood in shadow.

Every step brought her one step closer. Too weak to walk without aid, Rebecca was half dragged. The night air felt oddly cold. Everything seemed to happen in slow motion. She remembered how Masha had resisted death, how her body flailed and convulsed as it fought a losing battle with the gallows.

A hand under each arm lifted her up onto the platform.

"Get up," the Wehrmacht officer said.

And with his help, she stepped up onto the stool.

The man reached up over her, placed her head through the noose, and cinched it with the knot to the side of her head.

She looked straight ahead, through the small window into the dimly lit prison. She made momentary eye contact with the smiling gaze of the female guard. Even from here on the platform, she could hear the loud, cackling laugh. Rebecca watched her as she turned and walked away.

Rebecca looked at the door, where another guard was stationed. He turned away in disgust as she looked at him.

Alone, with no one to watch, no one to care, no one to cry, she looked up to the sky. She saw one star shine brightly back at her, and a tear rolled down her cheek. She began to recite the Shema.

The man who had lifted her up onto the gallows and so precisely fitted the noose around her neck kicked the stool down, and it came crashing to the platform's base. In an instant, she felt the slack tighten. Reflexively she put her hands up to grab the noose. She kicked and flailed as Masha had done.

And then, just as she was about to take her last breath, she felt the stool slide back under her feet. The man removed the noose and stabilized her on the stool. She gasped voraciously for air. Confused by her continued existence, and with no time to sort it out, she felt a bag flung over her head, then saw nothing but complete darkness.

Gisevius dragged her off the platform and back to the prison. Without speaking, he dragged her, with her face covered in a black bag, past the first guard. And then he dragged her limp body through the hall of the prison. He said nothing. He dragged her up to the female guard, who stood outside the empty cell. And finally, he dragged her out to the last door in the prison, the usual entrance. He stopped for a moment, held Rebecca's body with one arm, and pulled the door to open it. He was about to pull Rebecca out when he heard a voice behind him.

"You're not going to leave her hanging there?" the female guard asked, pointing back to the gallows.

Gisevius stopped. Still out of breath from this exertions, he looked back at the guard and said, "For the crows and rats? Too much of a mess to clean up tomorrow."

He waited for an answer, then pulled her body through the door.

"Stop!" someone yelled from behind him.

He took a deep breath and turned back.

"You forgot this." The other guard handed him the dead prisoner's shoes.

"Keep them as mementos," he said.

And walking out the door, he stuffed the body into the trunk of his Mercedes-Benz 290-C and drove away.

CHAPTER ONE HUNDRED EIGHT

It looked as the workstation had never seen a day of use. Max had rearranged Virginia's pipettes, test tubes, and test tube holders. He moved her centrifuge and her scales. The lab cages were cleaned out.

"Nice job, Max," Dr. Cooper said, patting him on the shoulder. He carried his coffee into his office, then said to Max, "I heard there might be an opening in next year's class."

Max stopped sorting lab glassware and went to the door to Cooper's office. "What do you mean?"

"A spot has unexpectedly opened up. That's all I can say, but maybe . . ." Cooper sat down at his desk.

"Maybe?" Max said.

"I don't know yet for sure. Anyway, thanks for straightening up.

"You're welcome," Max said quietly.

Leaving the lab, Max walked out the street side of the building, opposite the quadrangle, to Second Avenue. Cars passed him as he walked the two blocks up to Twenty-Eighth Street, to a large granite building with white columns. Inside, he walked up a flight of stairs to the second floor and found the door with Rosenthal's name on it.

"May I help you?" Rosenthal's secretary asked.

"I need to see him," Max said. Striding past her, he barged into the office.

He stood in front of Rosenthal's desk. "Cooper told me a spot opened up."

Rosenthal said, "Yes, that's right."

"Why didn't you tell me?" he asked.

"Because I didn't think you'd want it."

"That's rather arrogant of you."

Rosenthal looked up at him. His eyes were empathetic. He sighed. "You know Virginia Wright?"

"Yes, of course. What about her?" Max asked, leaning forward with his hands on the desk.

Rosenthal just looked back at him.

"It's *her* spot? How could that be?"

"Cooper said she fudged his lab data. He fired her. Wyckoff revoked her admission."

"What!"

"Yes. There's no way he was going to admit her after that. Cooper lost his NIH grant, and the department lost its funding."

"Oh, shit." Max turned and looked away.

"I'm sorry." Rosenthal said.

"That's a load of shit. It's not fair."

"Look, I didn't create the situation."

"Yeah? Well, I don't see you doing anything to fix it, either."

Max walked over to the Lower East Side, just off Orchard and Rivington, and found the tenement building where Virginia rented a room. He walked up a flight of stairs and found the door open.

A mattress with no linens was on the floor, but the bookcase was empty and the armoire drawers were cleaned out and half open.

"Virginia?" Max called out. He looked in the apartment. "You here?"

No answer.

He walked back down the stairs, and sat down outside, on the steps in front of her building. He looked south to Rivington Street, lined with pushcart vendors and merchants selling secondhand clothes.

"What are you doing here?" Virginia asked, walking up behind him. She had a duffel bag over one shoulder, and a backpack slung over the other.

Max was startled to see her.

"You're leaving?"

She put her duffel down on the steps, shrugged the backpack off, and sat down on the duffel. She didn't say anything.

"What are you gonna do?" he asked.

"I'll find something. I'm going back home. Michigan. I don't know." She looked at him. "I guess I need some time away from this academic circus."

"You're too smart for that," he said.

"Yeah, I'm real smart."

"What do you mean?"

"You heard didn't you?" she asked, and turned away. "Just be careful of that monster you work for. He hung me out to dry to save his back."

Max listened.

"I quit working for him." She shook her head in amazement.

"Actually, that's not what I heard." He gave her a puzzled look.

"I'm not surprised. He asked me to fudge his lab data, and I wouldn't do it. So I quit. And when he got caught, he blamed me."

"*What!*" Max stood up.

"Yeah, that's right. He hung me out to dry, to save his own skin."

Max slumped where he stood. "Why didn't you say anything?"

"Oh, yeah. What am I going to say? That the famous and brilliant Dr. Charles Cooper made it up? Who are they going to believe?"

"That's bullshit."

She got up off the steps, slung the backpack over her shoulder, and bent down to grab the duffel.

"Maybe so, but that's life in the big city. I'll be fine." She kissed him on the cheek. "And I was just getting to like you." She smiled, turned, and walked away.

He watched her blend into the throng of buyers and sellers on the street.

CHAPTER ONE HUNDRED NINE

Hermann sipped his schnapps and stared at the ripped note on the table. He put the four pieces back together and smoothed them out enough to make out Canaris's cryptic scribbling.

"Meet me 2300 tomorrow, 101 Wilhelmstrasse, in front of Prinz-Albrecht-Palais, Do not discuss."

Hermann downed the last of his schnapps for courage, stood up, and went straight to Himmler's office.

Hedwig looked up from her desk, blinked her lovely eyes, and said, "I'm sorry, he's not here right now."

"I'll wait."

"I don't know when he'll be back," she said.

"That's fine. It's important," Hermann said, and sat back in one of the chairs.

Hedwig walked over to him with a pot of coffee.

"Yes, thank you," he said, admiring the view as she bent over him.

A few minutes later, Himmler walked past him and directly into his office. Hedwig followed after him.

She returned shortly and said, "He can't see you today. He said that whatever you have to discuss, do so with Schellenberg. He asked that I escort you to his office."

"Fine," Hermann said. He knew that SS-Brigadeführer Schellenberg had become one of Himmler's most trusted confidants. He followed Hedwig to the man's office.

She showed him inside, and he stood at attention. When Schellenberg acknowledged him, he said, "I have reason to believe that Canaris is planning a meeting that is, let us say, not patriotic."

Schellenberg looked at him skeptically. "You do realize what you're saying, yes?" Right hand holding the lapel of his coat, he walked in a circle around Hermann, inspecting him up and down as he might a prisoner.

"Yes." Hermann looked down.

"And I'm sure you realize the possible consequences of making such an accusation."

"I do."

"And what basis do you have for this?" Schellenberg asked.

"Well, sir, as I have told Reichsführer Himmler before—"

"Yes?' he interrupted, coming closer.

Hermann cleared his throat. "Well, as I was saying, I informed the Reichsführer that I believe something's odd, something about Canaris's behavior and his frequent meetings with Oster."

"So you, basically a clerk for Canaris, have decided that something's odd?"

He walked around Hermann some more. "Well, I think that what *you* are saying is odd. You have no basis. Why should I believe you? You're just a glorified secretary."

Hermann said, "Yes, Brigadeführer Schellenberg, I understand how it must sound. But, respectfully, I've seen things; I've heard things. I just think, well, they're suspicious, at the very least, and may be worth looking at."

"I see, and these things are what, exactly?"

"Well, it's always Canaris talking quietly or meeting with Oster or Gisevius, sir."

"And what's being said?"

"Well, sir, that's what I don't know. I can hear only the tone of their voices."

"Their *tone*?" His eyebrows rose.

"Yes, their tone. It's . . . deliberately secretive—you know, as if they were discussing something they wouldn't want me to hear."

"You're a clerk. I wouldn't want you to hear anything of importance, either."

Hermann cleared his throat. "Yes, I understand sir, but as Canaris's personal clerk, I've been privy to some classified information. It's just that this seemed different."

He stood at attention, waiting for his superior to decide how much he should trust him.

"What do you have now that is so important today?" Schellenberg asked.

"Yesterday, sir, Canaris looked troubled, not himself. He seemed nervous. I can see it. He paces, and he smokes constantly."

"Get on it with it, boy." He was growing impatient.

"Well, I saw him scribble on a note. Then he ripped it and threw it in his wastebasket. I retrieved it without him seeing, and here it is." He took it from his pocket. "May I?"

"Go ahead." Schellenberg waved his hand.

Hermann placed the four pieces of the note on his desk.

CHAPTER ONE HUNDRED TEN

Max hadn't slept all night, which made him even more irritable than yesterday.

"Good morning, Max," Cooper said, walking past him to his desk.

"Morning," Max replied as he set about his work routine. One by one, he placed the test tubes in the test tube rack. He wrote down the number of each. *Just do your job and get through it,* he told himself.

He picked up a pipette and measured extract from a petri dish. The amounts were tiny. He placed the extract in the test tube, picked up the test tube, and placed it on a holder attached to a scale.

"How are today's measurements?" Cooper called from inside his office. Max looked at the test tube, then at the pipettes. He didn't answer.

"Max?" Cooper called again.

"I can't do this," he said, and he pushed the test tubes off the counter. They broke as they hit the floor.

"Max, what's going on in there?" Cooper asked.

Max went to his desk. "How could you do that to Virginia?"

Cooper looked up. "What are you talking about?"

"You lied about her."

"Careful, Max."

"Because she wouldn't lie for you."

"You little shit," Cooper said.

"I know what you did. You made up your own lab results, and when you got caught, you blamed her. You ruined her."

Cooper got up from behind his desk. "Who do you think you are, to talk to me that way?"

Max retreated slightly. "I'm nobody. Just like she was nobody. But I'm not going to let you get away with it."

Cooper walked up to Max and jabbed a finger into his chest. "Listen to me, smart-ass. You think I don't know what you are? You don't think I know you're Jewish?"

Max glared at him. He could feel his heart pounding.

"You think I'm stupid? Just try me. You'll never get in any med school. Oh, don't worry, I'll make sure of that." He looked at the crucifix hanging on Max's chest. "You think anyone wants another Jew doctor, anyway? You've heard of quotas, haven't you?"

He grabbed the crucifix.

"Threaten me. Go Ahead. You'll be a lab rat for the rest of your life. I'll rip this crucifix from around your neck and hang you by it." He let go and went back to his desk.

"I'm going to the dean," Max said. "I'm going to tell him everything." He could feel the tears welling up in his eyes.

"Good luck. Who do you think he's going to believe? Look around you. You think this is all academic niceties? Think again. It's about money. You should know that better than most, you little Jewish shit."

Max trembled as he started to walk out.

"By the way, stir the pot, and I'll make sure Rosenthal's gone, too. His career will be over, and why? Because of a little smart-ass, holier-than-thou Jew. Now, get out of my lab."

"I've seen worse Nazis than you, asshole," Max said, and walked out of the lab.

CHAPTER ONE HUNDRED ELEVEN

Inside the trunk, Rebecca felt every bump in the road. As she jostled up and down, she opened her eyes only to find that a black hood covered her face. She wriggled until she got her arms free from under her body, then rolled to the side and pulled the hood off. Still she saw only blackness.

She felt the car stop and heard the sound of a car door opening, then footsteps approaching, then hands on the trunk.

The trunk lid swung open, and she saw the bulk of a man standing there. It was still too dark to make out his face, but he wore a military uniform. He reached in and gently lifted her out of the trunk.

She wobbled like a newborn calf, then stood upright. Her head hurt, her neck was raw, and she was thirsty.

"Come," the man said. "Follow me."

She took a few steps and then collapsed on the cold ground. The man reached down and picked her up, and now she noticed his Nazi boots.

"Why?" she said, and she cried without really knowing why.

No one was out at this hour, but she could see they were at Breslau's train station. The man propped her arm around his neck and dragged her to the back of the station, to a crawl space under the platform.

"I'm sorry, but this is where I leave you," he said. "Stay here. People are coming to get you. You have to wait—I don't know how long, but don't leave this space. They know you're here."

She crawled under the platform, not knowing anything except that by some miracle, she was still alive. She was alone and disoriented. She gazed at the gravel beneath her. Looking up between the floorboard planks, she could see the ticket office for the trains. She turned back to see the uniformed man walk away into the shadows.

She shivered for a moment and rubbed her arms to keep warm. A moment later, he returned. He bent down, "Here, take this," he said, and handed her blanket wrapped around a bread loaf and a half-full bottle of milk.

"Eat some now, but make it last. Good luck."

Again she watched him disappear into the shadows. She wrapped the soft blanket around her body and lay down on the ground.

CHAPTER ONE HUNDRED TWELVE

The three men stood in front of 101 Wilhelmstrasse, in the darkening shadow of the Olde Grande Palace. Across the street, at 104 Wilhelmstrasse, a man watched Hermann fidget nervously. He could see that Heydrich and Schellenberg were losing patience.

Standing behind a column, he lit another cigarette, taking care to keep the small glowing ember out of sight.

He saw Hermann glance back toward the two-hundred-year-old palace that had been transformed into the Sicherheitsdienst intelligence agency's office, where Chief Heydrich worked.

Both men looked down at their watches.

"Five minutes more, Hermann," Schellenberg said. "If they don't show up, don't bother us anymore."

"You've wasted our time, young man, with your grandiose delusions," Heydrich said.

"I don't understand it," Hermann said. "I'm sure something will happen."

"Young man, let me explain something to you," Schellenberg said, reaching into his coat pockets and putting on his gloves. "You get only one chance to prove your worth, and you have used up that chance."

"But . . ."

"You've made accusations against the head of the Abwehr."

"*False* accusations," Heydrich noted.

"These are grounds for imprisonment," Schellenberg said. "We don't take accusations against a national hero lightly. You'll be dealt with appropriately—this issue won't just go away."

And Heydrich and Schellenberg walked away.

As if on cue, the man stepped out from behind the column and watched as the two men left. He knew that Hermann, now alone, could see his shadowed figure, punctuated by the ember of a cigarette.

CHAPTER ONE HUNDRED THIRTEEN

Max felt nauseated. He ran to the nearest bathroom and vomited. From there, he went to Rosenthal's office.

Again he walked right past the secretary and barged in.

"What is it?" Rosenthal asked. "You look like you've seen a ghost." He stood up and poured a glass of water. "Here."

Max drank.

"What did you do?" Rosenthal asked.

Max didn't say anything.

"Well?"

"I told him the truth. I told him he ruined Virginia's life and that I was going to tell the dean."

"And what did he say?"

"He said I'll never do anything but clean test tubes for the rest of my life."

"Probably a fair statement," Rosenthal said. "Sit down, please," he motioned to the chair across the desk from him.

"He also said if I do it, he'll ruin you as well." Max walked over to the window and looked outside on to Twenty-Eighth Street.

"He's a pompous ass," Rosenthal said. "There's more bark than bite there."

"By the way, he knows I'm Jewish." Max held out the crucifix pendant that hung from his neck. "*This* did a fat lot of good."

"Sit," Rosenthal said. "You're stalking about like a madman."

Max walked over and sat down. "It felt like dealing with Hermannn all over again. I can't let him get away with this."

"Well, then, do something about it," Rosenthal said.

"What do you mean?"

Rosenthal lowered his voice to barely above a whisper. "If you don't want to let him get away with it, finish it."

"I'm not sure I understand what you're saying."

"Well, how do you want to make this thing right?"

"I don't know. I could talk to the dean, but Cooper's probably right. Why would he listen to me?"

"He probably won't . . . unless you have proof."

"What kind of proof?" Max asked.

He pinched his nose and closed his eyes, as if he were searching for an answer. "What about a lab book, a journal? Something . . ." He opened his eyes. "*Anything* that would show he manipulated the numbers."

"The only person who had those numbers was Virginia. And she's gone, and he had me throw everything away . . . Wait a second." Smacking his forehead with his palm, Max jumped to his feet. "What's today?" He was already to the door.

"Tuesday. Why?"

"Cooper had me discard all of Virginia's manuals. So I threw them in the garbage."

"And?" Rosenthal asked.

"And the garbage doesn't get carted off till tomorrow. We gotta go. Come on."

"We?"

"Yes, Professor. I need your help."

Rosenthal shook his head. "Not me."

"Come on, I helped you when you needed it. We have to do this tonight."

"Yes. He's out the door by six p.m." He looked up at the clock on the wall. "We'll have to sneak back into the lab after he leaves."

CHAPTER ONE HUNDRED FIFTEEN

It wasn't the morning sun that woke her up. It was the dust sifting onto her face from the foot traffic that shuffled above her. She looked up through the cracks and took in what she could, which wasn't much but the soles of people's shoes.

Small shoes meant children, narrow shoes meant women, and the large shoes belonged to the men. The boots belonged to the Nazis.

She sat up quietly, draped the blanket around her shoulders, and ripped a piece from the loaf. She closed her eyes and chewed. It was the taste of heaven.

She picked up the bottle of milk and removed the waxed paper lid. She could see the lip marks where someone had already drunk from the bottle, but she didn't care. She put it to her mouth and drank. It tasted like fresh cream straight from the milking shed. It was thick and delicious, but she put the lid back on and put it back on the cold ground. She had to make it last a day, anyway.

She tried to get comfortable under the platform. Looking outward, she could see not just shoes but entire legs. The legs moved back and forth, fast. Some of the little ones even ran. What must it be like to have such energy! She closed her eyes and waited.

The sound of breathing woke her up. Not human breath, but panting. She looked up through the planks. Nothing. Then she looked outside her crawlspace, into the eyes of a German shepherd. She quickly covered her face and pushed herself farther back into the crawl space, but the panting turned to barking. She pulled the blanket down just enough to peek out again. She saw the dog pacing back and forth in front of her. Quickly she covered her eyes again. The barking grew louder. She peeked out again and could see only the long tall black leather boots, four of them, belonging to two different guards. A guard bent down and looked into the crawl space. He scanned quickly, but Rebecca had scooted back into the shadows.

She watched as the boots walked back and forth, in laps that took them away and then back again. Each time they returned, the bark grew louder, and as they walked away, it receded.

She paced her breaths so that when they walked away, she could breathe, and each time they came close, she held her breath.

The dog wasn't giving up, though. The barking persisted. She stared at the bread loaf.

Scooting forward almost to the entry of the crawl space, she looked around. Then she took one fond last bite and flung the loaf as far as she could from where she sat.

In that moment, a small boy walked by alongside a woman's legs. Seeing the bread roll in front of him, he stopped.

"Mom," he pleaded.

She pulled him. "Come on, Jurgen, we'll miss the train," she said, tugging him along.

Rebecca pushed herself back as far as she could under the crawl space, covered herself with the blanket, and listened.

She heard the dog and his guards making their next circuit. This time, however, the dog lost interest in her and went straight for the loaf of bread.

She relaxed, closed her eyes, and felt herself drifting off.

CHAPTER ONE HUNDRED SIXTEEN

Max watched Cooper get in his Ninth Series 840 Packard. The whitewall spare, mounted just in front of the driver's seat, contrasted beautifully with the bold red paint job.

"Now we go," he whispered to Rosenthal.

At the lab door, Max fumbled with his keys.

"Hurry up," Rosenthal said.

"Shit!" Max said as he dropped the keys. He bent down to pick them up.

A light shone on the door, and a voice said, "Max, can I help you with anything?

"Hi, there, Tom," Max said. "No. We're fine. Just left some things in the lab. Need to pop in and get them."

"That's fine, Max. Have a good night." The security guard turned around and continued on his rounds.

Max unlocked the door, and they went inside. Rosenthal turned the lights on.

"Turn those off!" Max hissed.

"Why?"

"What if he comes back?"

"Why would he?"

"I don't know. What if he forgot something?"

Rosenthal flicked off the light.

"It's here." Max walked over to the broom closet.

Just then the door latch clicked, and the door opened. Max yanked Rosenthal into the broom closet and shut the door.

Dr. Cooper walked back to his office, turned on his desk lamp, and sat down to do paperwork.

Max peered through the cracked broom closet door, and his heart sank. Cooper must have taken the lab book out already.

After a few minutes, Cooper got up from his desk, yawned, and placed Virginia's lab book in his desk drawer. He locked the drawer and then put the key under his desk lamp, turned the lamp off, and left the lab.

They waited another fifteen minutes before creeping out of the broom closet.

Max picked up the desk lamp, removed the key, and opened the drawer.

"That was easy," Rosenthal said.

Max smiled back at him and grabbed Virginia's journal from the drawer. He opened it up to the page Dr. Cooper had just finished writing on.

"This is what the son of a bitch just erased." Max pointed to the page. "Look at her numbers. You can see where he wrote over it."

"Let's get out of here," Rosenthal said.

"Wait," Max said, staring at the page. "Why is *this* so important?" He pointed to an entry in the book.

"Not now," Rosenthal said. "Show it to the dean."

Max pushed the drawer back in its place and put the key under the lamp. "Wait," he said.

"What now?"

He took a pen out and scribbled "Fuck you, asshole," on a piece of paper, took the key out, unlocked the drawer, and put the paper back in the drawer in place of the book. He smiled back at Rosenthal.

"Can we go now?" Rosenthal asked.

Max placed the key back under the lamp, and they quietly left the lab.

CHAPTER ONE HUNDRED SEVENTEEN

Stats disembarked from the *Queen Mary* in Southampton and walked through the terminal. He had no idea who he was meeting or even what he looked like. A few minutes passed before two men in blue-gray jackets and uniform trousers approached him. Each had an RAF patch on his shoulder.

"Sir?" one of the guards said.

Unaccustomed to being addressed as "sir," Stats looked around. "Me?"

"Please. Follow us."

"Nice to meet you, too."

They led Stats to an open-air command car, parked just outside the terminal. Both men jumped in front, and Stats took the backseat.

"Where we headed?" he asked as the car sped away. Neither man answered. They just kept driving on a dusty unmarked road, through unrecognizable countryside.

"Okay, then," Stats said. He closed his eyes and tried to relax in the buffeting wind.

Fifteen minutes later, the command car came to an abrupt stop, and both men got out.

As Stats started to climb out, another man approached him.

"Good day," the man said, and put out his hand.

Stats shook it.

"Welcome to Stoney Cross." He pointed to the airfield.

"And you are?"

"Sorry, lad, thought you were prepped. I'm Van der Stok." He had a smirk that conveyed both confidence and intelligence.

Stats knew that he was supposed to be one of the best aviators in the Royal Air Force. "Really?"

"What is it, old chap?"

"I guess I expected something different."

"Like what?"

"Oh, I don't know. A little taller, maybe, more hair, maybe a bit more muscle."

He gave a deep, long laugh, shook his head, and hit Stats on the back of the shoulder.

"Come on, then. We don't have much time."

They walked over to the plane.

"There she is, a de Havilland Express. This is our baby." He rested his arm against the fuselage for a moment. The engines were running.

"Is it safe?"

Van der Stok laughed again, again hitting Stats on the back. "You're a funny one."

He walked around to the right side, where the door was. "Enough chitchat, then, time to go," he said, and climbed aboard. Then he reached down and hauled Stats in. He gave the pilot the thumbs-up and closed the door, and within moments, the plane was taxiing to the runway. A minute later, Stats was airborne for the first time in his life.

Van der Stok yelled over the roar of the engines, "Here, strap this on." He thrust a parachute and a backpack at him.

"What's this for?" Stats yelled back.

"Jumping out of airplanes," he said, strapping on his own parachute.

Stats put it down on the floor of the plane. "I can't jump."

"Don't worry, I'll grab you," Van der Stok said, handing it to him again.

"Where?"

"In the air, after we jump."

Stats said nothing.

"Here's the plan," Van der Stok yelled as he stowed supplies in his pack. "We're Dutch."

"That's it?"

"Don't worry, it'll work. I've done this run before."

Stats reluctantly picked up the parachute pack and slowly put it on.

"We drop in tonight, under radar, into Breslau. Row's said the package is . . ." He took a crumpled note from his pocket and smoothed it out on his lap. ". . . there." He pointed through the window to a small cluster of lights on the ground. "The train station. Don't worry, I know it like my sweet Jenny's arse."

"Comforting," Stats yelled back over the engine roar.

CHAPTER ONE HUNDRED EIGHTEEN

Hermann entered the Abwehr's office, greeted the secretary, and walked tentatively to his desk. "Is the admiral in today?"

"He was in earlier, at a meeting. He brewed some coffee if you want."

"Sure," Hermann called back to her, and poured himself a cup. While drinking his coffee, he did some paperwork.

Finishing the standard requisition forms, he suddenly felt queasy. The queasiness quickly turned to nausea, and he loosened his belt and looked about for a waste can to vomit in. A moment later, he began to sweat profusely. His breathing grew labored. With a shaking hand, he picked up the coffee cup and lifted it to his nose. Too late, he caught the whiff of almond. He dropped the cup on the floor, vomited, and slid off his chair. He tried to scream but did not have enough breath to utter a sound. His eyes rolled backward, and he fell facedown on the floor.

CHAPTER ONE HUNDRED NINETEEN

Rosenthal and Max walked into Dr. Wyckoff's office. It was much larger than Rosenthal's, and the wall was covered with accolades.

"Please, have a seat," Wyckoff said, pointing to the two visitor chairs in front of his desk.

"Jack, this is Max. He's a friend of mine from Europe. I got him a job with Cooper. He worked in his lab, and he has something to tell you. Go ahead, Max."

"Dr. Wyckoff, before I show you this, I wanted to let you know, I'm here on behalf of someone else." Max paused and looked at Rosenthal.

"Go on," Rosenthal said.

"Someone was wronged. And I feel an obligation to fix it."

"What is it, son?" Wyckoff asked."

"You know Virginia Wright? She worked in Cooper's lab."

"We're not dragging this up again," he said, giving Rosenthal an annoyed look.

"Let him finish," Rosenthal said to the dean.

"Okay, but it had better be worth my time."

"Dr. Cooper told Virginia to fudge the numbers for his grant."

"Please," Wyckoff said. "This is water under the bridge. I've heard this tune before."

"Different tune, Jack," Rosenthal said. "Listen. It's a catchy one."

Max said, "When she wouldn't fudge Cooper's numbers, she quit."

"Why are you telling me this? Curt, you know better than that." He glowered at Rosenthal.

"Look, she did the right thing, and it came back to bite her," Rosenthal said.

"Did you tell Cooper this, Max?"

"Of course. And when I did, he told me he'd make sure I never get into any medical school, here or anyplace else. He said he'd ruin my life."

"And you listened to him?" Wyckoff leaned back in his chair and crossed his arms.

Max didn't answer.

"Why should I believe you?" Wyckoff asked Max.

"Because I've nothing to gain."

Wyckoff leaned forward, resting his elbows on his desk. "Everyone has something to lose and something gain. What's your motive, boy?"

"Standing up for somebody who can't stand on their own."

"A noble sentiment, to be sure, but I'm still not buying it." He turned to Rosenthal. "Curt, do you understand the gravity of what you're saying? Charles is one of the best and brightest. Not just here—he's one of the top researchers in the country. You can understand why I'm having a hard time with this."

"Show him," Rosenthal said, nodding at the journal in Max's hand.

"Yes, please. By all means, show me," Wyckoff said.

CHAPTER ONE HUNDRED TWENTY

Van der Stok threw the de Havilland's door open. He turned to Stats, who had backed away, into the cabin.

"You first. Jump and pull." He pointed to the rip cord. "But not till you're falling through the air, or the whole plane goes down.

Stats shook his head from side to side.

"It's now or never," Van der Stok said.

Stats glanced down into the black void and shrank back from the door. Van der Stok sighed, reached over and grabbed him by the parachute harness, and yanked him over to the door.

Stats looked out at cold, buffeting darkness. "I can't do it," he said, holding on to both sides of the open doorway.

"That's all right, lad," Van der Stok said. "I completely understand." Then he shoved Stats out of the plane.

Stats felt his body swirling like a leaf in a wind tunnel. He repeated to himself, "Pull the cord, pull the cord," as he struggled to find it. He groped and groped in the darkness, and still nothing. He was feeling lightheaded when a hand closed on his calf.

"See? No worries," Van der Stok said as he clipped a carabiner onto Stats's harness, and then pulled his cord. Stats held on to him and then felt a hard yank that seemed to pull him back up in the air. Then, just as quickly, the wind stopped as they both drifted quietly down. Van der Stok negotiated their landing over a stand of trees and into a meadow.

CHAPTER ONE HUNDRED TWENTY ONE

Max laid the book down in front of Wyckoff and opened it to the page Cooper had erased.

"What's this?" Wyckoff asked.

"His lab journal."

"You stole it?"

"No. Well, yes. Actually, it was Virginia's, and he asked me to throw it away. I did and then went back to find it."

"Okay, so what's so special about this page?"

"Take a look. These are the actual results." Max pointed to the page. "And here's where Cooper erased the results and tried to match them to what he wrote in his proposal."

"And?" Wyckoff removed his glasses and looked over at Rosenthal.

"There's more. Show him, Max.

"And he didn't finish changing it all," Max said. "This is Virginia's handwriting, her results." He dragged his finger along the page.

"See here." Rosenthal handed Wyckoff a paper. "This is what he wrote in the grant application. They don't match up—not even close."

"I'm not sure I get it," Wyckoff said, rubbing his eyes.

"Cooper disregarded Virginia's results," Max explained. "Right here. He fudged the numbers."

"When I confronted him about the numbers, he blamed Virginia," Rosenthal said. "I took him at his word. He basically sacrificed that girl's future to save his own."

Wyckoff took a deep breath, and Max watched as he tried to figure how to reconcile this.

Wyckoff looked at Rosenthal and then at Max. "Thank you both for your time."

"That's it?" Rosenthal asked.

"That's it." Wyckoff said.

"Are you going to do anything?"

"I'll take this under consideration. I appreciate your willingness to bring it to my attention." He stood up and opened his office door. "Mary, please show Dr. Rosenthal and Max out."

CHAPTER ONE HUNDRED TWENTY TWO

Van der Stok took out his compass, looked at it, walked around a bit to get his orientation, and then looked at his watch.

"Okay, we're right on schedule," he said.

Back in the copse of trees they had just drifted over, they used the entrenching tool from Van der Stok's pack and buried the parachutes. Then they started toward the Breslau train station. In the faint light of a crescent moon, they walked along the darkened roadside, dodging off to the side whenever headlights approached.

"If anyone asks what we're doing in the woods at this time of the night, you're a Dutch worker."

"Right—one who doesn't speak Dutch," Stats said.

"Well, then, you won't be much help, will you?"

"What kind of plan is that?"

"Don't worry, just let me do the talking," said Van der Stok.

"Why did you have me come along?" Stats asked. They continued walking briskly.

"That's an excellent question. I don't usually like to travel in packs. I always say, he who travels alone gets there soonest."

"So why, then?"

"Because I'm not sure what she looks like. And even then, once we get her, I'm not sure how strong she'll be. She's a Jew who's been in a German prison—she'll likely need help walking." He patted Stats on the back "And a big, strapping lad such as yourself . . ."

"I got it," Stats said.

"And she's younger than I—more like your age. If we get stopped, you two'll be a couple. Me alone with a younger girl—though the idea appeals to me, it wouldn't look right. Or maybe I'm just getting too old to keep doing this stuff solo."

Stats understood.

They approached the railway station platform and went to the ticket window, where Van der Stok bought three second-class ticks to Alkmaar. The train was leaving in an hour.

"I'll sit here." He sat down on a bench. "You go find her."

Stats looked around. "And where might that be?"

"She's over there. Just don't be obvious."

"Where?"

"Wait. You can't let anyone see you approach her."

"I don't even know where she is," he said.

"Walk away from me, have her clothes ready, take your pack off, and sling it to her when no one's watching," he said, looking away from Stats as he spoke.

Stats looked around, still not sure exactly where Rebecca was. He saw two military police with a German shepherd patrolling the station. He looked back at Van der Stok, who had closed his eyes and was pretending to sleep. His head lolled backward.

"Over there." He cracked his eyes and shifted them toward the side door.

Stats glanced in that direction. He saw nothing obvious except people walking on the platform. Then he realized that she must be in the crawl space under the platform.

After waiting for the dog and police to make their pass, he quickly walked by, unslinging his pack as he went, and tossed it under the crawl space. He didn't stop walking and was soon back at the bench. He sat next to Van der Stok and waited.

CHAPTER ONE HUNDRED TWENTY THREE

Wyckoff walked over to Cooper's lab.

"Let's go outside," he said. "We need to talk."

Cooper looked up, saw Wyckoff's concerned expression, and followed him outside. They walked over to a bench in the quadrangle and sat facing Bellevue Hospital.

"Charles, you've really created a mess," Wyckoff said.

"What is it now?"

Wyckoff gazed out at the building gray clouds and the students walking between classes. "You've put me in a tough situation."

"I can't let this go without some action."

"You're talking about the data, Jack. You're over-thinking this."

"I don't know, Charles. I run this place by certain standards—a level of integrity that we can be proud of, I can't be a hypocrite about it."

Cooper laughed, then tightened his smile and put his arm around Wyckoff. "Aw, come on, Jack, don't be so goddamned self-righteous."

Wyckoff pulled away. "Wait a minute. What are you trying to say?"

"Well, you didn't seem to mind when I brought you the business from those disability claims. How much did you earn from certifying those EKGs, by the way?"

Cooper could see he had hit a nerve, and pressed on. "You're holding me to a different standard than yourself?"

"That's a bunch of crap. This is totally different, and you know it. This is about academic integrity."

"Is it different? You signed your name to those cardiograms." Cooper watched as Wyckoff looked down to the ground. "You needed the money."

"Not really," Wyckoff said. "Not at the cost."

"What cost? Is this how you say 'thank you'?"

"Look, I didn't do it so you could hang it over my head," Wyckoff said. "You've put me in a corner with this funding bullshit."

Cooper sat up a little taller on the bench. A fine, misty rain began to fall.

"By the way, did you happen to see the *Times* this morning?" he asked, ignoring the rain.

He took the morning paper out of his briefcase and laid the article on Wyckoff's lap. The headline read: **"Insurance Fraud by Scam Attorneys and Crooked Physicians."**

"You're kidding me," Wyckoff said.

"You have nothing to worry about, Jack." He took the newspaper off Wyckoff's lap and spread it out over his head to shield him from the drizzle.

"They don't mention you, and even if they do, you did nothing wrong."

"Maybe not legally, but certainly ethically and professionally."

"I mean, how were you to know that those EKGs were falsified by a bunch of disease fakers?" Cooper said.

"It doesn't matter. I should have realized that the abnormal waves were digitalis induced. Any good cardiologist would have." He folded the paper and thrust it back at Cooper.

"This isn't about me, Charles. It's about you—more specifically, about how you handled that lab tech."

Cooper ignored the comment and kept on coming. The water was now beginning to bead on Wyckoff's hair, and the two men's clothes were getting wet. "You did nothing wrong, nothing intentional. Anyway, no one but me knows that you read those cardiograms. And why would I say anything?"

Wyckoff gave him an appraising look. "You're trying to *blackmail* me?"

"Jack, you're being ridiculous. No one cares. The only thing you're guilty of is not recognizing the digitalis effect."

"After researching digitalis for years? Come on, no one'll buy that."

"I told you, I'm not going to say anything." He gave his best disarming smile.

"Charles, you've pigeonholed me. I really don't have much of a choice."

"Jack, you always have a choice."

"You're threatening me, you son of a bitch."

"Was there anything else you wanted to speak to me about?" Cooper stood up and brushed his pants. "We should really get out of the rain." Before walking away, he said, "Really, Jack, you're not going to let a few Jewish refugees affect our relationship, are you?"

CHAPTER ONE HUNDRED TWENTY FOUR

Rebecca woke at the sound of the small pack hitting the ground and sliding toward her. Instinctively, she backed away from it. It could be a trick, a taunt, even a bomb. Holding the blanket around her, she looked at the milk bottle. It was almost empty. She longed for a bit of the bread she had given to the inquisitive dog. She couldn't last down here forever.

She scooted forward and grabbed the pack, hoping to find food. It was clothes. One by one, she pulled out a dress, a pair of shoes, a scarf, and a jacket. She looked up through the planks of the platform. Nothing had changed. People walked about, going to and from their trains. She looked outward through the crawl space. No legs stopped in front of her. No dogs nosed about.

She undressed quickly and stuffed her prison garments in the pack, then got into the new clothes. She heaved the pack behind her, deeper into the crawl space, and inched forward. The military police were not patrolling in front of her; there was no dog. If ever there was a time, it was now. She slipped out of the crawl space, stood up straight, and was fixing her hair when she felt a man's hand on her shoulder.

"Come on, honey, our train leaves in a few minutes."

At the sound of the voice, her terror of being imprisoned again melted into astonishment.

"Stats . . . ," she gasped, and melting into his arms, she began to cry.

"Let's go," he said. "We don't want to miss our train."

He held her tightly against him, and they hurried up the boarding steps onto the train. Moments later, a man Stats seemed to know walked past, dropped a wedge of cheese on her lap, and sat behind them. Rebecca picked up the cheese and took a bite of it, and looked at Stats. "How?" she asked.

He put his arm around her and put his lips to her ear, as if to kiss her. "It's a long story. Let's get some rest. We'll have time to catch up."

She fell asleep with her head in his arms.

They arrived in Dresden at midmorning. The next train was the midnight to Bentheim, on the Dutch border.

"We need to wait," Van der Stok said, "but not here. There's a cinema over there." He handed Stats some money. "Buy tickets. I'll sit behind you. Once you're inside, get some rest. Sleep is free."

By the time Stats and Rebecca found their seats, the theater was dark and the film was playing. They dozed off until the film ended and Van der Stok gave Stats a nudge.

They waited for him outside. He walked past them, and they followed him into a beer hall. Stats and Rebecca found a table while he sat alone at the bar.

"This feels like a dream," Rebecca said. "So tell me: how?"

"How what?" Stats said, sipping his beer and looking casually around the bar for anything unusual.

"Never mind *how*, she said. *Why?*" She stared down at her beer, rubbing her finger on the rim of the glass. "Why rescue me?"

"Here." "He pushed some crackers over to her. "You need to eat."

Van der Stok walked by their table and dropped a folded paper napkin on the floor by Stats's foot. Stats picked it up, unfolded it, and read it:

> 30 minutes - meet at French brothel- just a few steps away. Sign on door reads: "Nur fur Auslanders Deutschen verboten."

Beneath the message was a crude map of the cross-roads. They finished their drinks and followed the map to their next waypoint.

Van der Stok knocked on the door while Stats and Rebecca waited.

When no one answered, Van der Stok knocked again.

"How did we pick this spot?" Stats asked.

Van der Stok didn't answer. Stats had drawn his eye to the figure of a man standing beneath a store awning across the street. "It's a safe house," Van der Stoke murmured. "From Row." They waited for the door to open. No answer. Stats turned around, and the man was gone.

When the man appeared suddenly a few yards away from them, Van der Stok moved in front of Rebecca.

"Do you have any black-market wares for sale?" the stranger asked in a Polish accent.

Van der Stok moved aside and said, "It depends. Do you know any Swedish soldiers?"

And with that, the Pole unlocked the brothel door and led them inside. Locking the door behind them, he said, "Wait here."

A few moments later, he returned with a man who was indeed a Swedish sailor.

Van der Stok said, "We need to get out, either by train or by boat." The sailor spoke not a word as he walked around all three. He stood close to Rebecca and touched her face. She felt so weak, it was all she could do to stand up. He backed away.

"A ship is leaving in two hours," the sailor said at last. "Meet me outside the docks on the Elbe." And he walked back inside.

"Now what do we do?" Stats asked.

"The way I see it, we have two options," said Van der Stok. "We can wait till midnight and hop the train to the Dutch border, or we can take the boat to Sweden now, with him." He gestured after the sailor.

"What's the safest?" Stats asked.

"Usually better to take the first way out," Van der Stok said. "The boat leaves soon. If the train is on time, we have another eight hours to wait. If it's delayed—as is pretty common—who knows?"

"Fine," said Sats. "Let's get some more rest here and take our chances with the sailor."

They sat down in the brothel to wait, and Rebecca turned to Stats. "And Max?" she asked.

"He's fine, in New York."

"Rosenthal?"

"Also fine."

"Really, tell me," she said. "Why come for me?" Her lip trembled.

"I couldn't leave you twice. When I found out you were still alive, I had no choice."

She cried softly, then quickly fell asleep while Stats watched her.

"Okay, it's time to go." Van der Stok stood up, and they left the brothel and headed to the docks. The Swede was there waiting for them.

"You're a man of your word," Van der Stok said.

"I'm a sailor," he said, tipping his cap. "Follow me."

He led them around to a small alley just off the dock. The ship was moored not fifty yards away.

"You'll need to hide in here," he said. "I must report to the Control office. After that, I board. Once all clear, I whistle for you to come aboard."

"Whistle?" Stats asked.

"*Ja,* whistle."

"What if we don't hear you?" Stats asked.

"Make sure you hear me," the sailor replied.

"How do we know you're going to do it?" said Stats.

"Do you have any other options?" the sailor asked.

The three of them looked at each other. They knew they had no one else to trust. So they waited.

And waited. They stared at the ship standing moored at the dock. No whistle.

"Damn it," Stats said. He could see how weak Rebecca was. "Look." Seamen were casting off the thick mooring lines. No signal. "I guess no whistle."

"He must have thought we were going to get caught," Van der stock said. "Now we have to get off these docks."

He stood up and looked around to make sure no one was walking by.

"It's clear," he said. "Let's move."

They walked back to the brothel, taking turns helping Rebecca. After an exchange of passwords, the door opened, and another group of sailors from Row's underground network greeted them.

"Another ship is putting in," said a sailor, also a Swede.

"We just tried that, and it didn't work," Stats said.

The sailor said, "Look, this is not a perfect science. You're not buying a ticket on a cruise ship. We'll get you aboard, but we won't risk everything if there's a chance you'll get caught." He walked away for a moment and let them alone.

"This is where we say good-bye," Van der Stok said.

Stats frowned. "What?"

"As I told you, better to travel alone. Three together is just reducing our odds."

"What are you saying?"

"You two go with them." He nodded toward the sailors. "I'll catch the midnight train to Bentheim, and we'll meet on the other side of tomorrow."

The sailor came back and said, "Well, what'll it be?"

"Okay, we go with you." Stats put his arm around Rebecca. "Just us two."

"Okay, let's go. A tram is waiting outside." He walked out, and the other sailor followed behind Stats and Rebecca. Stats turned to give his friend a last wave, but Van der Stok had already vanished.

The tram picked them up outside the brothel, and a few minutes later they were dropped off at a different dock entrance from before.

"Wait," the sailor said, and walked away. A few minutes later, he returned with three more sailors.

"Okay, now we go." They approached the German soldier on guard for the dock they needed.

"All part of the crew?" the soldier asked. The Swedish sailors were loud and boisterous. They enveloped Stats and Rebecca.

"Yes, except her," a sailor said, nodding at Rebecca and giving the soldier a wink as he handed him their papers.

The soldier smiled, and without bothering to inspect their papers, he waved them on.

Once on board, one of the sailors said to Stats, "You two need to hide. The ship doesn't leave for forty-five minutes. There's a final search before we sail. Follow me . . ."

He led them to a cargo hold. Once inside the room, he walked over to a loft area that held more cargo, and dropped a ladder attached above it. "Climb up here," he said.

The sailors helped Rebecca up the ladder and then followed behind them and pushed away some large crates. They pointed to a cleared-out area in the center of the loft.

"Will this do?" Rebecca asked, sidling through the crates to the open space.

A sailor gave her a friendly smile and said, "Perfect," and they moved the cargo back to cover the stowaways.

Before going back down the ladder, the sailor said, "You may as well catch a few minutes' sleep. Just don't snore," he added. "The Germans will be here in a half hour. They'll have dogs with them, but the dogs won't climb, and so they probably won't bother to look up here. Just don't make any noise."

They closed the cargo room door behind them and left, and Rebecca fell asleep in Stats's arms.

CHAPTER ONE HUNDRED TWENTY FIVE

The window shade was drawn and blocked most of the light coming through the only window in Wyckoff's office. "You can't let this slide," Rosenthal said. He reached across Wyckoff's desk and switched on the lamp. "The man is a fraud."

Wyckoff was unshaven, wearing yesterday's clothes. "Look," he said, "I can't tell from the lab journal which entries are his and which are hers. It's just not enough for me to act on." He rubbed his eyes. "Please shut that off." He looked as if hadn't slept in days.

"You're kidding, right? This guy sends bogus data to NIH. He manipulates things so his student takes the fall, and you're just going to sit on your ass?"

"Curt, I can't. My hands are tied. It's his word against Miss Wright's. If I dismiss him without proof, I'll be looking at a lawsuit for unlawful termination. He's tenured. You know that."

"If you don't fire him, I quit." Rosenthal turned and stopped at the door.

"What are you saying?"

"I'm saying it's him or me. Do the right thing." Rosenthal opened the door and left the office.

"Shit," Wyckoff muttered. He picked up his phone.

"Mary, get Dr. Kossman on the phone for me, please."

CHAPTER ONE HUNDRED TWENTY SIX

Van der Stok boarded the train for Bentheim and handed his papers to the post guard.

"Everything all right?" he asked in perfect Dutch.

"Everything's in order," the guard replied, and handed him back his papers.

He found a comfortable seat and pretended to sleep all the way to Oldenzaal and then on to Utrecht. At Utrecht, he left the train station and walked two miles out of town, along a country road that led to a farmhouse.

The farm appeared abandoned, as if no one had been there for years. There were no animals, and the fields were choked with dead weeds. The only implements in sight were a rusted harrow and a tractor with cracked, flat tires that surely hadn't moved in a decade or more. Behind the house, a dilapidated barn looked ready to collapse in the next stiff breeze. He double-checked the address on the crumpled note in his pocket, then walked past a sagging rail fence to the front door.

At the top of the door, Van der Stok noticed a small piece of white cloth firmly jammed in between the door and the frame. He pulled it out and knocked.

The door opened, and a large bearded man wearing a holstered pistol looked out at him. "We've been waiting for you," he said.

Van der Stok tossed him the piece of cloth. "Next time I'll request a private chauffeur," he replied, walking inside.

"This is from Row," the resistance fighter said. He handed Van der Stok identity papers and ration cards. "No time for niceties. You must move now."

"Not to worry, young man," Van der Stok said. "I've been at this a while."

"Look, ever since Germany invaded Holland, there are more spies and informers than you can shake a stick at. Our site is at risk of being compromised. We won't be here much longer." The resistance fighter led him behind the house to the barn and slid the door open. "This is for you." He pointed to the bicycle.

"Your next stop is Belgium. Row knows you're on your way. Here's the address."

Van der Stok took the address and wheeled the bicycle out of the barn.

"Good luck to you," the resistance fighter said as Van der Stok pedaled down the road.

CHAPTER ONE HUNDRED TWENTY SEVEN

Stats and Rebecca woke up to the sound of boots clomping on the deck below them.

Stats put his finger up to his mouth. A dog barked as the voices grew louder.

One of the soldiers lowered the ladder and called out to the soldier who held the leashed dog.

The two stowaways didn't move. The dog barked louder. The soldier with the dog stood beneath the ladder.

A few moments passed, and they heard the cargo room door close. The barking and the soldiers' voices grew fainter. The sailors were right: the soldiers had no interest in hoisting a hound up to the loft.

A few minutes later, the engines started, and the hull began to vibrate.

The stowaways had just started to breathe easier when the cargo door flew back open. Rebecca gave a little gasp of fear, but it was only the sailors, bearing ham and bread and pears and a bottle of red wine.

One of them yelled, "Time for the bon voyage party."

CHAPTER ONE HUNDRED TWENTY EIGHT

"What is it, Jack?" Dr. Charles Kossman asked. Dr. Kossman was one of the few practicing cardiologists whom Wyckoff respected above himself.

"Take a look at these and tell me what you see." Wyckoff laid two electrocardiogram reports in front of him.

Kossman held them momentarily, scanned them briefly, and tossed them back onto Wyckoff's desk. "This a test?"

"Just tell me what you see," Wyckoff said.

"There are abnormal T waves on both. Probably infarction or digitalis effect, or both."

"Thanks, Charles."

"That's it?" Kossman asked.

"That's it," Wyckoff said. "Sorry, Charles, just dealing with politics. It's killing me." He stared down at his desk.

Kossman stood up and waited for Wyckoff to tell him more, but Wyckoff went back to work at his desk.

"Okay . . . Well, let me know if you need anything else," Kossman said, and quietly left.

Wyckoff took out a pen and began to write.

Dear Ms. Wright,

I am sorry for the treatment you received while working at Dr. Cooper's lab. I have investigated the situation. If you're willing to accept, I would like to offer your position back to start at NYU medical school. I am truly regretful that you had to endure what you did.

Sincerely,
John Henry Wyckoff, Dean, NYU Medical School.

He drafted another letter, this one addressed to his wife:

Dear Elizabeth,

You're better off with integrity and a little insurance money than with a man who, through carelessness, has let his profession down.

All my love,
Jack.

He folded the letters, sealed them in their envelopes, and placed them on Mary's desk.

The next day, the *Times* headline read, "JOHN WYCKOFF, PROMINENT DEAN, FOUND DEAD IN ANATOMY LAB OF NYU MEDICAL SCHOOL."

EPILOGUE

Twelve months later

Walking through the campus, Max watched the fallen leaves scoot down the sidewalk as if before an invisible broom. He caught a whiff of cinnamon and hot apple cider.

Cooper, true to his word, had blackballed him from the medical school, but he didn't care. He was at peace, no longer fighting for his life or for his dream of being a doctor.

The Yankees had just clinched the pennant and led Hank Greenberg's Tigers by thirteen games. Max hadn't seen Stats in weeks—it was playoff time, and Stats covered the Yankees for the *Post.*

Stats had told him it wasn't the *Times,* but it was work, and he got to see Rebecca every day.

Rebecca, like her father, was a journalist, and like Stats, she worked at the *New York Post.*

Max looked up at the sky and took Virginia's hand as he walked her to class.

"Did you hear about Cooper?" Virginia said.

"Who cares?"

"He's chief of neurology at Columbia Presbyterian."

"Figures," Max said.

"Why?" she asked.

"Columbia has two neurology services: East and West. East has no Jews, and West has only a few tokens. He'll fit in perfectly."

"Did you see Rebecca's article in the *Post* today?" she asked him.

"No. Why?"

"Cooper's brought a lot of research money to Columbia."

"So?"

"So he wields a lot of influence there."

"And?"

"And Rebecca broke the story today."

"What story?" Max asked.

"Cooper wrote a letter to Dr. Putnam, a Columbia neurosurgeon and chairman of the National Committee for Resettlement of Foreign Physicians, and ordered him to get rid of all non-Aryan neurologists."

"What a thoroughgoing schmuck."

"Wait, that's not even the good part. They posted a portion of his letter, in his own handwriting, in today's paper, telling Putnam he should 'get rid of all Jews in the department or resign.'"

"They actually *published* that?"

"Yes. Putnam resigned and gave Rebecca the letter."

Virginia said, "The bastard is finally finished. No one will keep him on their staff no matter how much money he brings in."

"Hey, you never know." Max opened the door to the lecture hall, and they walked in and took a seat. "No one turns away money—not even doctors."

Rosenthal stepped up to the lectern, dropped a book on the floor with a loud bang, and stepped on it. He pressed it down and said, "It's not what you learn in books . . ."

CREDITS & REFERENCE

The Death of Medicine in Nazi Germany, by Wolfgang Meyers, published in 1998 by Madison Books, served as an inspiration as well as a reference book to provide accurate historical context.

This book is loosely based on actual people, places, and events. The rest, including dates, dialogue, story lines, and action, is pure fiction.

The following real people, places, and occurrences were used in this book:

Abwehr
American Bund
Brenner Pass
Bridge of Witches
Brown Shirts, Hitler's Sturmabteilung (SA)
Camp Nordland
Canaris, Wilhelm
Columbia Neurology Services, East and West
Cooper, Charles
Dachau
Detroit Free Press
Fry, Varian
Gisevius, Hans Bernd
Goebbels, Joseph
Greenberg, Hank
Heydrich, Reinhard
Himmler, Heinrich
Hirschfeld, Magnus
Hitlerjugend
Hofbrau House
Jadassohn, Josef
Jessner, Max

Klein, Jerome
Kossman, Charles
Kuhn, Fritz
League of Human Rights
Lion of Münster
Martin-Gropius-Bau
Mercedes-Benz 290-C
Museum of Decorative Arts
Neuner Violin Factory
Olde Grande Palace
Oster, Hans
Paragraph 175
Potthast, Hedwig
President Butler (Columbia)
Reed-Johnson Act
Reichsführer's Physicians Ordinance
Röhm, Ernst
Rosenthal, Curt
Rowecki, Stefan
Schellenberg, Walter
Seth Low Community College
Social Justice
Spanknoble
SS *Rex*
St. Elizabeth's Church, Breslau
St. Maria Magdalena
Stadelheim
University of Breslau Medical School

53269341R00258

Made in the USA
Lexington, KY
29 June 2016